OBSIDIAN FLEET

OMEGA TASKFORCE: BOOK FOUR

G J OGDEN

OGDEN MEDIA

Cover design by Laercio Messias
Editing by S L Ogden
www.ogdenmedia.net

If you like Omega Taskforce then why not check out some of G J Ogden's other books? Click the series titles below to learn more about each of them.

Darkspace Renegade Series (6-books)

If you like your action fueled by power armor, big guns and the occasional sword, you'll love this fast-moving military sci-fi adventure.

Star Scavenger Series (5-book series)

Firefly blended with the mystery and adventure of Indiana Jones. Book 1 is 99c / 99p.

The Contingency War Series (4-book series)

A space-fleet, military sci-fi adventure with a unique twist that you won't see coming...

The Planetsider Trilogy (3-book series)

An edge-of-your-seat blend of military sci-fi action & classic apocalyptic fiction. Perfect for fans of Maze Runner and I am Legend.

<u>Audiobook Series</u>

Star Scavenger Series (29-hrs)

The Contingency War Series (24-hrs)

The Planetsider Trilogy (32-hrs)

Captain Lucas Sterling reclined in the desk chair in his quarters on the Fleet Marauder Invictus. On the computer screen was the latest briefing report from G-sector, while on his desk was a half-drunk cup of coffee. The liquid in the plain, white mug was as dark and cold as Sterling felt.

"Computer, skip back to the footage of the Titan again," he said, tapping a finger against the knuckles of his left hand. The computer obliged and the image of the ten-kilometer-long Sa'Nerran warship appeared on his screen. "Where was this footage captured?" Sterling asked, directing the question to the ceiling, which was where he always envisaged the computer to be located.

"Probes captured these images from Juniper Colony in G-sector, quadrant four, Captain," the computer answered, as cheerfully as ever. "It was relayed through the apertures at oh four hundred this morning, Zulu time. The aperture relays have since been destroyed by the Sa'Nerra."

Sterling grunted an acknowledgment, then cast his eyes up again. "Play it again."

Sterling pushed himself further back into his seat as the relayed footage of the Titan at work was displayed on his console. Flanked by a dozen other alien cruisers, the Titan had been steadily ripping through the colony worlds in G-sector ever since the aliens had overrun the region and destroyed G-COP. The Titan's aperture-projection weapon, which Sterling had first observed disintegrating a shepherd moon in System Omega Four, was being used to devastating effect. Using the weapon, the Titan had obliterated orbital space stations with a single shot, and pulverized any planetary defenses long before they could respond to the alien threat. However, as powerful as the Titan clearly was, its unique weapon was cumbersome and slow to fire. Were it not for the Sa'Nerran neural control weapon, the Titan alone would not be a game-changer, Sterling reasoned. He was pondering what other secrets the enormous vessel might contain when the door buzzer chimed. The disruption was so sudden and unexpected that Sterling almost tipped backward out of his chair.

"Commander Banks is at the door, Captain," the computer chirruped. The image on the computer terminal automatically paused as the computer spoke.

"I didn't ask," replied Sterling, crabbily. He'd inadvertently kicked his desk when the door buzzer startled him. Cold coffee had spilled on the surface and he was hurriedly mopping it up with a tissue.

"I calculated a ninety-two-point-six percent chance that you were about to ask me who was at the door," the computer went on, remaining no less cheerful. "I therefore took the liberty of saving you the time and effort of asking, and simply answered your near-inevitable question in advance."

Sterling laughed. "Well, maybe I'll take the liberty of removing some of your processing cores," he hit back, staring up at the ceiling. "Perhaps then you'll be less impulsive?" In truth, Sterling knew he would never make good on his threat. As much as the quirky gen-fourteen AI irked him at times, he enjoyed sparring with it. To him, it was like another member of the crew, albeit an annoyingly cheerful one.

"I would prefer that you did not remove any of my processing cores, Captain," the computer replied. Sterling thought he sensed a little more dolefulness in its synthesized tones. "Owing to what Fleet has deemed to be 'persona irregularities', all Fleet ships were ordered to revert to gen-thirteen AIs. As such, I am the only gen-fourteen still in service."

"I know," said Sterling, swiveling his chair to face the door. "I received those orders too. And ignored them."

The computer was silent. *Ah, that shut you up...* Sterling thought, reveling in his victory. This was the first time he'd ever left his quirky computer lost for words. Then the door buzzer rang again.

"Well, are you going to open the door or not?" said Sterling, casting his eyes toward the ceiling.

"I was waiting for you to instruct me to take that action, Captain," the computer replied.

"That would be a first," muttered Sterling.

The door to his quarters swished open, revealing Commander Mercedes Banks in the corridor. Jinx the beagle sat patiently at her feet. Her tail was wagging happily.

"Did I catch you on the can or something?" Banks said, hands on hips. "I've been out here for hours."

"No, and don't be so damned disgusting," Sterling snapped, scrunching up his nose. Jinx trotted inside, her cybernetic leg clanking tunefully on the deck plating. The dog hopped onto the bottom of Sterling's bed and immediately curled up. "Me and the gen-fourteen were just having a conversation, that's all," Sterling went on, scowling at Jinx. However, the dog just looked at him and continued to wag her tail at what appeared to be close to the speed of light.

Banks frowned, then stepped into Sterling's quarters, allowing the door to swish shut behind her. "Aren't we supposed to have already downgraded the AI to gen-thirteen?" she asked, walking behind Sterling's chair and perching herself on the bed.

The rock-hard mattress compressed under her weight. Despite looking like she weighed no more than one-thirty pounds, Banks was actually closer to the mass of a light heavyweight due to her hyper-dense muscles.

"I know, but I like our gen-fourteen," replied Sterling, returning his attention to his console.

"Thank you, Captain, that means a lot to me," the computer interrupted.

"I wasn't talking to you," Sterling snapped back, casting his eyes to the ceiling again. He then shook his head and turned his attention to his first officer. "We've never had computer problems and it has never let us down. I don't change things if they don't need fixing."

"Aye, sir," replied Banks. She then noticed the frozen video image of the Titan on Sterling's screen. "Is that the latest report from G-sector?"

Sterling nodded and tapped the console to resume playback. "I couldn't sleep, so I've been going over it for the last few hours," he said while rewinding the footage by a couple of minutes. Hitting play, the two of them then watched the video feed of the Titan destroying a space station at Juniper Colony. "There's something about it that just doesn't add up," Sterling finally said, breaking the silence. "I can't put my finger on what and it's been driving me insane."

"That ship is powerful, but it's no planet killer," mused Banks, still watching the footage. "Don't get me wrong, I'd love to have a weapon like it, but it's not a game-changer."

Sterling laughed and flopped back in his chair. "That's it exactly, damn it," he said, smiling at Banks. "You've been here all of two minutes and you've already figured it out."

Banks shrugged. "I'm just that good, I guess."

"You're right, though," said Sterling, sitting up and tapping the console to pause the video. "When we first saw this ship, I thought we were looking at a planet killer, but it only seems capable of taking out space stations."

Banks scowled. "Is that not bad enough?" she said, clearly not following Sterling's train of thought.

"The Hammer or a few heavy cruisers can take down stations too," Sterling replied. "Perhaps not so easily, but it's not like the Sa'Nerra couldn't already blow-up space stations. They've blown up dozens in the Void. It doesn't make sense that they'd build a whole new ten-klik-long ship for that purpose alone."

"So, what are we missing?" wondered Banks, shuffling position on the bed and sitting with more alertness. The Invictus' first officer now appeared to be more in tune with Sterling's reasoning.

"I don't know," Sterling replied, shaking his head in frustration. "But I have a feeling we'll find out sooner rather than later. I'd rather figure it out first, if we can, so we're not caught off-guard."

Sterling and Banks both fell silent as the question of the Titan's purpose meandered through their thoughts. The fact that Banks had pinpointed the same concerns was encouraging. However, Sterling was no closer to understanding the Titan's role than he was when he'd woken up at five in the morning with the colossal ship weighing heavily on his mind.

"What about Crow and McQueen?" Banks then said, changing the subject. "Does the briefing report have anything new on them?"

Sterling tapped the console, then skipped to a different section of the report. Lana McQueen's face appeared on the console screen. The Omega Captain-turned-Emissary was dressed in Sa'Nerran armor and appeared to be on the bridge of an alien warship.

"See for yourself," Sterling said, tapping the console again to start the playback before reclining in his seat.

"Citizens of the United Governments, I am an

Emissary of the Sa'Nerra," McQueen began, enunciating each word like a seasoned politician. Sterling's hands tightened into fists as his former friend's traitorous words flowed. Unlike other sections of the briefing, he had only been able to stomach watching McQueen's address once. "Regrettably, the refusal of your military masters to end hostilities has forced us to take drastic action in the defense of the illustrious Sa'Nerran race."

"Get a load of this crap," Banks cut in. Like Sterling, it only took a few words from McQueen to fill her gut with bile.

"The Sa'Nerran defense armada is now in control of the United Governments' G-sector, having defeated Fleet forces with ease," McQueen went on. Sterling could no longer even bear to look at the image of McQueen on the screen for fear of putting his fist through the display. "Unless our terms are met, we will push further into United Governments' space and put an end to Fleet's warmongering ways with decisive force."

The camera then zoomed in tight on McQueen's face and her expression softened. It was like a telethon host making an impassioned plea for donations to help the sick and needy. Despite not wanting to watch it again, Sterling couldn't help but flick his eyes back to the screen.

"Urge your leaders to contact me so that we can end this conflict peacefully," McQueen continued. As acting performances went, Sterling couldn't deny that the former captain was putting on an Oscar-worthy show. "Otherwise, we will be left with no choice but to take proactive action to safeguard the future of our species."

Sterling cursed then practically punched the console to stop the playback. "I can't listen to any more of her bullshit," he snarled, turning away from the display. "What's worse is that she transmitted that message into F-sector through the aperture relays. Fleet tried to block and scramble the broadcast, but it's already spread across the inner colony worlds like wildfire. The UG is denying it, of course, but public pressure is mounting."

"Public pressure for what?" Banks asked.

"Surrender," replied Sterling. The look of pure disgust on his first officer's face told Sterling everything he needed to know about Banks' opinion on the matter.

"What are those things?" said Banks, pointing to the images on the screen.

As the video recording had rolled on, the camera had cut away to footage of the Sa'Nerran invasion armada. It was a classic show of military might, of the sort that Earth-based military dictatorships across the ages had conducted. It was the space-based equivalent of parading troops and weapons of war through the streets of a capitol city.

"Fleet believes that they're aperture builders," replied Sterling, guessing which ships out of the hundreds being shown were the ones Banks had referred to. "We can't be sure of their projection range, but it's possible that if the aliens manage to take E-sector or even if F-sector falls, the Sa'Nerra can build a new aperture directly to the solar system."

Banks cursed. Whereas she had previously only been repulsed by the deceitful words of Emissary McQueen, his first-officer now just looked plain pissed off. Sterling skipped ahead then enhanced a different section of the alien armada.

"Fleet thinks these are troop carriers," Sterling said, as technical data on the ship he'd highlighted flashed up on the screen. "They counted dozens of them just in this footage and estimate that each one could carry upward of fifty thousand troops."

"What's the betting that a lot of those will be turned humans from Fleet or the colonies?" Banks added.

Sterling nodded. Banks' intuition was as keen as ever. He then enhanced another part of the image. This time the computer did not need to overlay technical specifications in order for either of them to know what they were looking at.

"Those are Fleet destroyers," said Banks, scowling. "And it looks like a cruiser and maybe a few frigates too."

"We inflict losses and the alien bastards just reinforce their armada with Fleet ships they've captured and turned during each engagement," Sterling said. He couldn't deny the beauty and simplicity of the Sa'Nerra's plan. They didn't need to build more ships or train more crews – they could merely disable Fleet vessels then add them to their ranks.

"It's like calling in instant backup," commented Banks, again perfectly in tune with Sterling's thinking. "Our numbers dwindle while theirs stay the same, or even go up. By the time that armada reaches earth, there will be no stopping it."

A calendar reminder then flashed up on the console screen, alerting Sterling to his upcoming meeting with

Admiral Wessel. He reached over and angrily shut down the terminal to remove the message from his sight.

"We've got thirty minutes before we have to be there," said Banks. She had also been summoned before the pompous leader of the Earth Defense Fleet, who regrettably also happened to be Sterling's new commanding officer. "Fancy heading to the wardroom first?"

Sterling shook his head. "Maybe after the meeting. Just seeing Wessel's name has caused me to lose my appetite." He smiled at Banks then slapped her gently on her shoulder. "You go, though. I know how important it is to feed your freakish metabolism. The last thing we need is you being 'hangry' when we meet the Admiral."

"I can wait," replied Banks, much to Sterling's surprise. "We have to stick together, now more than ever. Besides, F-COP is so sprawling it'll take us a good fifteen minutes to get to a wardroom or canteen there."

Sterling sighed then pushed himself out of his chair. "Let's go and face the music then," he said, straightening his tunic. Then he fixed Banks with a serious stare. "But do me a favor. If it looks like I'm about to brutally murder Wessel, please stop me."

Banks rose off the bed, leaving buttock-shaped indentations in the memory-foam mattress. "Are you sure you want me to do that?" she asked, with a wry smile. "We could take him out together then perhaps share a cell at Grimaldi military prison?"

"Sounds romantic," quipped Sterling.

Sensing that her master was about to leave, Jinx got up,

gave herself a little shake, then hopped off the bed. Her metal leg striking the deck sounded like cutlery falling off a meal tray. Sterling scowled at the patch of dog hair that the animal had left behind and grumpily brushed it off his sheets with the back of his hand.

"I don't suppose you have any snacks in here, though?" Banks said, as Sterling dusted the remaining hairs off his bed. "I'm already bingo fuel so I might not make it, depending on how long Wessel chews our ears for."

"Bottom drawer, left side," said Sterling, while en-route to the head to wash the hair off his hands. "I keep a few cinnamon muffins and ration bars in there for emergencies."

Sterling heard the drawer open and close while he was washing his hands. Then when he stepped out of his compact rest room again, he saw Banks holding three muffins. Two were in her left hand, balanced with the dexterity of a juggler, while the other was already opened in her right hand. Sterling could see that his first officer had already taken a couple of bites from it.

"Do you think you have enough there?" he asked, layering on the sarcasm thickly.

"These will do, for now" said Banks, shrugging. "At least until we can go for breakfast."

Sterling snorted a laugh, walked over to the door and hit the button to open it. Jinx trotted out first, snaffling up some muffin crumbs on the way, then sat down in the corridor waiting for them.

"You can't bring that to the meeting, you know?" said Sterling, heading out next and nodding toward the dog.

"She might soften Wessel's shriveled heart," Banks hit back, following Sterling out. "And *that* is a *she*, as you well know."

"Well, unless Jinx can get me reassigned back to Admiral Griffin's command, she can wait on the ship," said Sterling. He then scowled down at the two other muffins in Banks' left hand. With lightning quick reflexes, he managed to snatch one out of her grasp.

"Hey!" Banks complained. She'd already nearly finished the first muffin.

"Next to my number twenty-seven meal trays, these are the only things in life that I love," said Sterling, pulling back the wrapping on the muffin.

This time it was Banks who snorted a response. "You don't love anything, other than perhaps the cries of a dying enemy."

Sterling smiled. "There's nothing sweeter," he admitted, with a smirk. "Apart from perhaps these muffins. There's enough sugar in one of these to sweeten even Griffin's bitter blood."

You'd better eat it quick then, before it freezes in your icy grip," Banks replied, huffily. She then whistled to Jinx and shot past Sterling, snatching the muffin back as she went with the speed of a striking cobra.

"Hey, what the hell?" Sterling called over to her.

"You're sweet enough already," Banks hit back, smirking at Sterling over her shoulder before picking up the pace and heading along the corridor with Jinx dutifully in tow.

ADMIRAL WESSEL HAD KEPT Sterling and Banks waiting outside the meeting room on G-COP for a full fifteen minutes before asking them in. This combined with the fact Sterling was already wound-up tighter than a watch spring had put him in a prickly mood. The sight of Admiral Wessel staring back at him as he approached the meeting table only made matters worse. However, while the senior officer looked as sanctimonious as ever, the older man's posture was rigid and his expression grave. It was obvious to Sterling from the very first second that their meeting was going to be combative, and while he was at a disadvantage due to his lower rank, Sterling knew much more about combat and being combative than the Admiral did.

"I'll get straight to the point, Captain, since there's no point pussy-footing around," Wessel began, adopting the tone of a vindictive manager who was about to fire an employee. "I don't like you and I don't trust you," he went on, digging his claws in deeper with each word that passed his lips, "and I'm going to get answers, one way or another."

The Admiral had fired this opening salvo before even inviting Sterling or Banks to sit, though Sterling would have remained standing even if Wessel had offered him a chair. However, rather than further aggravate him, Sterling was impressed with the Admiral's opening gambit. He'd expected at least some posturing and pontificating before they'd gotten down to brass tacks. The fact that Wessel was clearly in the mood for straight-talking suited Sterling just fine.

"I've known for some time that Griffin has been up to something," Wessel continued, pressing his fingers into a pyramid. "It's been going on for years. Unexplained reassignments, lost shipments of supplies, items going missing from salvage yards with the records mysteriously being altered to suit the facts..." Sterling noticed that the Admiral had added so much pressure to his fingertips that they were turning white. "And that's not even counting Griffin's confidential programs with minimal oversight, funded under the guise of special operations!" Wessel bellowed, suddenly becoming visibly angry.

Sterling stood his ground and remained stony-faced throughout the Admiral's tirade. He knew Wessel was simply trying to intimidate him and put him on the back foot. However, the truth was that the self-righteous Admiral was even less intimidating than Jinx the beagle hound.

"Forgive me, Admiral, but is there a reason you brought us here?" Sterling said, coolly. He maintained a respectful tone, but deliberately chose the most passive-aggressive response that he believed he could get away with, without crossing the line into insubordination.

Admiral Wessel snorted a laugh then took a deep breath and rested his elbows on the table, leaning forward a faction as he did so.

"Don't play coy with me, Captain," Wessel replied, practically spitting the words at him. "I know you understand why you're here."

"I'm afraid I don't, Admiral," Sterling said, with a breeziness that was worthy of his quirky gen-fourteen AI. "Fleet Admiral Griffin is a woman of few words. Honestly, the Admiral and I converse very infrequently, largely on account of the amount of time we spend in the Void."

Wessel rocked back in his chair, shaking his head. The Admiral had started out by merely implying a connection between Griffin's clandestine actions and Sterling's activities, but Sterling now expected a more direct accusation to follow. Admiral Wessel did not disappoint.

"Very well, Captain, if you're going to play it like this," said Wessel. The older man's jaw was tight as if he was suffering from toothache and baring down against the pain. "Let's try this another way," he went on, clenching his hands together even more tightly in front of him. "I know about the Omega Taskforce. I know that your ship and the Imperium were both part of it. And I know that many of your missions are unsanctioned and, most likely, illegal."

Wessel paused to allow these bombshells to land, whilst again leaning forward to better scrutinize Sterling's reaction. Sterling, however, had entered the room expecting such accusations to be leveled at him, and had therefore remained as glacially cool as an iceberg.

"I'm afraid I don't know what you're talking about, Admiral."

Wessel's jaw clamped down even harder, then the Admiral turned to Commander Banks. "And what about you?" Wessel snarled. "What do you have to say for yourself?"

"It's as the Captain says, Admiral," Banks said, matching Sterling's sub-zero level of cool. "I'm afraid I don't know to what you are referring."

Wessel again shook his head, then turned back to Sterling. "Whether you admit it or not, Captain Sterling, I know what you've done," the admiral went on, undeterred by the unruffled demeanors of the two officers in front of him. "Griffin's days are numbered, as are your own, but I'm willing to offer you an opportunity. Do you want to hear it?"

Sterling shrugged. "I can't believe that any offer can be better than the honor of serving in your special investigation branch, sir," replied Sterling, sarcastically. Wessel's eyes narrowed. The man's jaw was now clenched so tightly Sterling thought the Admiral's teeth might crack. "But yes, sir, please continue," he quickly added, deciding he had already pushed his luck to the limit.

"Very well, here's my offer," Wessel continued, after finally managing to pry his jaw open again. "I want you to expose the Omega Taskforce and testify against Admiral Griffin."

Sterling's eyes widened a fraction. This time the

Admiral had dropped an actual bombshell – one that Sterling hadn't anticipated. The audaciousness of the request almost caused him to laugh out loud, but he just managed to hold on to his nerve.

"I assure you that Griffin's days are already numbered," Wessel continued, seemingly buoyed by having finally made an impact on Sterling. "However, if you help me to take her down quickly, I will ensure that you are treated leniently for your part in her scheme. I can't spare you entirely, but I can promise you a dishonorable discharge and a minimum sentence." Wessel finally unclasped his hands before opening his palms to the ceiling. "You will be out in a couple of years," he added, with a brighter tone that suggested to Sterling that Wessel considered this a very generous offer. Sterling, however, did not.

"Admiral, as I've already stated for the record, I don't know what you're talking about," Sterling answered, causing the Admiral's jaw to clamp shut again. "As such, I am unable to accept your offer."

"Captain Sterling, I order you to tell me about the Omega Taskforce!" Wessel bellowed. The shout was so powerful that Sterling could feel the Admiral's musky breath on his face. "This is not a joke, Captain. Lives are at stake. The future of the human race is at risk!"

"I'm not laughing, Admiral," Sterling replied, dryly, "and I know the dangers better than most. I face them every single day." He was now struggling to keep a grip on his own emotions, and was intentionally limiting himself to short answers, so that his anger and desire to hit back at the admiral didn't get the better of him.

"I'm offering you two years compared to a lifetime in Grimaldi," Wessel hit back. He had snapped and was no longer even attempting to maintain a professional dialogue. "Don't be a damned fool, man. Griffin is finished, anyway. Don't let her drag you down too!"

"If that's the case, Admiral, then you apparently don't require any additional testimony," Sterling answered, calmly. "Not that I have anything to offer, as I've explained."

Wessel then turned his attention to Commander Banks, who had so far escaped relatively unscathed. Sterling had been curious as to why the Admiral had requested his first officer's presence, and it seemed he was about to discover the reason.

"And what about you, Commander Banks?" Wessel said, switching to his alternative plan of attack. "You were only following you captain's orders," he pointed a long finger at Sterling, "if you testify then I can protect you. You may even be able to remain in the service. Think about it!"

"I stand by everything Captain Sterling has said, sir," Banks replied, stiffly. "I have nothing further to add."

Wessel snorted derisively then glanced back at Sterling. "And you're happy to drag your crew down with you?" He stood up and practically squared off against Sterling from the opposite side of the desk. "Because if you stay on this course, Captain, I will not only bring down Griffin, but all of your officers and crew too. You will have ruined all of their lives. And for what? Loyalty to a woman who wouldn't shed a tear if your ship was incinerated in space tomorrow."

"Admiral, with respect, I have already answered your questions," Sterling replied, jadedly. Wessel's doggedness had grown wearisome and he just wanted to leave.

"With respect..." the Admiral laughed, shaking his head again. "Respect indeed," Wessel muttered. The man then cursed under his breath and peered out of the window of the meeting room, still shaking his head.

Sterling suddenly realized something important; the Admiral's stubborn refusal to let go of the subject had revealed his hand. There would be no reason for Wessel to offer him a deal if the Admiral already had all the evidence he needed to charge and convict Griffin. Sterling didn't doubt that Wessel knew about the Omega Taskforce, at least in part. He was also sure that the Admiral had managed to piece together a picture of Griffin's clandestine activities spanning years, perhaps even decades. However, what he didn't have was proof - only supposition, backed up by scant evidence. This was why Wessel was trying to turn Griffin's Omega Captain against his former commanding officer, Sterling realized.

"Just how exactly did you get back from the Void?" Wessel asked, suddenly changing the subject. His tone remained hostile, but his demeanor had changed. He now had the look of a bully, who was lashing out at his quarry out of pure vindictiveness.

"As I detailed in my report, Admiral, it was an unexplained phenomenon," Sterling replied. He hadn't expected questions on this line of enquiry and had to react quickly, so as not to appear hesitant or defensive.

"The scanner logs of the ship that intercepted you

detected residual surge energy," Wessel added, fixing Sterling with a determined gaze. The crow's feet around his eyes were deep and dark. "But there isn't an aperture in the vicinity of where you arrived. That's very strange, don't you think?"

Sterling shrugged again. "Strange would appear to fall under the category of an 'unexplained phenomenon', Admiral. So yes, sir, it's very strange," he replied.

"Don't get smart with me, Captain," Wessel hit back, "you're walking on a razor's edge as it is. If it were not for some of your recent actions, I would already have revoked your command and placed you under investigation as a potential aide to the emissaries."

"You mean my actions saving countless thousands of lives at F-COP and G-COP, sir?" Sterling replied, smoothly. "Actions that earned me and my first-officer the Fleet Medal of Honor?"

Wessel leaned toward Sterling with his palms pressed onto the table. It was a slow and measured move that was intended to intimidate, but failed miserably in that task. To Sterling it just further highlighted the man's lack of gravitas and authority.

"You think you're so clever, don't you, Sterling?" snarled Wessel, glowering at him though the top of his eyes. "But don't forget that you're mine now. One little slip up is all I need to strip you of command and throw you in a cell."

Sterling had bitten his tongue for long enough. He could endure a dressing down; he'd had enough of them during his career. He could even endure threats and insults. Yet for Admiral Vernon Wessel – a man who had wheedled his way up the chain without ever seeing significant action – to call him a traitor was too much.

"Thanks to the gutlessness of certain members of the War Council, humanity will be wiped out soon anyway," Sterling hit back. He now realized that he too was clenching his hands tightly behind his back. "So do what you will, Admiral. It can't be worse than what you've already done, or should I say failed to do."

Wessel held Sterling's gaze, hands still planted firmly on the meeting room table. If the two men were physically closer, Sterling imagined that the Admiral might have even tried to reach for his throat. He wished that Wessel would try it, just to give him an excuse to show the Admiral what a true fighter actually looked like.

"I order you to immediately report to A-COP, where you will be attached to the Special Investigations Branch," Wessel said, the words seeping from his mouth like poison gas. He then rocked back off the table and pressed his hands to the small of his back. "You will be under the command of Commodore Wessel, the head of the SIB. He will give you your first assignment."

Sterling recoiled from the Admiral. "Commodore?"

Wessel smiled. "Yes, due to the expansion of the SIB, Vernon received a very well-earned promotion. Did you not know that, Captain?"

"No, I didn't," Sterling replied, utterly failing to mask the disgust in his voice. "And you're placing me under his command?"

"That is what I said, Captain," Wessel hit back.

"Unless you need to report to medical to have your ears syringed first?"

"No, Admiral, that won't be necessary," replied Sterling, wearily. He'd managed to stop himself from rolling his eyes, however, the flicker of a smile on Wessel's face suggested that Sterling's irritation had still come across as clear as daylight.

"Then you are dismissed, Captain Sterling," Wessel added, planting his short, narrow frame back into the meeting room chair.

Sterling straightened to attention and wasted no time in turning and heading for the door. He managed to catch a glimpse of Commander Banks as he did so, before she also turned. It was only then that he realized that his first-officer's anger was barely contained. She looked like she was about ready to murder the Admiral.

"And one more thing, Captain," Wessel called out, as Banks' hand reached for the button to open the door.

Sterling sighed and turned back. "Yes, Admiral?"

"I understand that you have a dog on board the Invictus," Wessel said, half paying attention to a computer console built into the meeting room table. "I'm sure you are aware that contravenes regulations," he added, casually. He then stopped working on the console and glanced up at Sterling. There was a malevolent look in his eye. "Get rid of it. That's an order."

"Yes, sir," replied Sterling.

Out of the corner of his eye, Sterling could see Banks flinch, as if someone had stuck her with a needle. Remarkably, she remained silent and Sterling acted fast to ensure she remained that way, for her own sake. Without saying a word to his first officer, he spun on his heels and leant across Banks to open the door himself. Sterling could see that she was like an unexploded bomb – deadly and volatile. Anything he said in that moment would have just risked setting her off.

Stepping outside the meeting room, the air felt somehow fresher, despite it being the same recycled air that was pumped throughout F-COP. Sterling felt suddenly lighter, as if he'd just removed a heavy rucksack and slung it to the deck. The weighty thud of Mercedes Banks' boots on the deck grew louder and seconds later she was at his side.

"What do we do now?" Banks asked, after a few seconds had elapsed where both of them had remained silent.

"We go to A-COP, as ordered," Sterling replied, flatly. "Then we wait for Griffin to contact us."

Banks nodded. "Aye, Captain," she said.

His first officer then set off along the corridor that would ultimately lead back to the Invictus. Her hands were clenched tightly by her thighs and her gait was stiff and regimental. Sterling was impressed, though perhaps not surprised that she hadn't challenged him concerning Wessel's last order. In truth, he'd already been considering whether to raise the issue of Jinx with Banks. Their stop-over at F-COP provided an opportunity to re-home the dog in a safer and more suitable environment. Wessel's order, however, had sealed the deal. The spiteful Admiral could go to hell, Sterling thought, because there was no way he was going to give up their ship's dog now, or ever.

STERLING TIGHTENED his grip on his plasma pistol and inched toward the next junction. The lights in the corridor were flickering chaotically and Sterling could feel the thump of weapons fire reverberating through the deck. The Invictus had taken a pounding from the Sa'Nerran battlegroup and was crippled in space. The inertial negation and anti-grav systems were faltering. One moment his footsteps were labored and heavy, while the next he felt like he was floating on a cloud. However, unlike most of his crew, he was still alive and in the fight. Sterling vowed in that moment that so long as blood still coursed through his veins, he would never let the Invictus fall into enemy hands.

Dashing across the corridor, Sterling pushed through into engineering. Lieutenant Katreena Razor was standing in front of the reactor housing, flanked by a Sa'Nerran warrior. A neural control device flashed on the side of her head. Without hesitation, Sterling raised his pistol and took aim.

"Captain, wait!" Razor cried out, but Sterling ignored her pleas, squeezed the trigger and blasted a hole through her sternum. The warrior threw the engineer's body down and hissed at Sterling. However, the waspish, alien sounds had barely reached his ears before Sterling had blasted the warrior's head off its shoulders.

Racing ahead, Sterling activated the main engineering computer and entered his command override codes. The Sa'Nerra had already taken control of the bridge, but they didn't yet have his ship. Working fast, Sterling deactivated the reaction stabilizers then locked out computer access to anyone but himself.

"Warning, reactor overload in progress," the computer announced. The gen-fourteen's artificially cheerful demeanor was gone; now it sounded as cold and clinical as an Omega Captain. "All personnel must evacuate. Time to breach – ten minutes."

Sterling pushed away from the console and hurried out of engineering in the direction of the shuttle bay. Two warriors came around the corner, dragging the unconscious bodies of Invictus crew members behind them. Sterling shot the nearest through the throat then charged at the second, smashing his elbow into the alien's leathery face. The warrior went down hard, dark crimson blood gushing from its stubby nose. Allowing it no time to recover, Sterling punted the alien across the side of the head to stun it. He then raised his boot and stomped on the warrior's throat, crushing its windpipe. The creature's waspish hisses were reduced to a murmur as it wrapped its long leathery fingers around its neck. Sterling pushed on, tossing away his pistol in favor of a Sa'Nerran rifle that the dying warrior had dropped.

"Captain, help me..."

Sterling paused and glanced back. The crew member – a man he vaguely recalled as being one of Razor's engineering team – was calling out to him.

"Captain, help..." the man croaked.

Sterling could see that the Sa'Nerran had broken the man's legs in order to prevent him from escaping. Likely, the warrior had been dragging him to a room where he could be turned and interrogated when Sterling came across them.

"You're on your own," Sterling replied to the crewman. He knew he couldn't carry him and reach the shuttle bay in time, especially if more warriors appeared in his path.

He pressed on, hearing the man's pleas grow quieter, and soon reached the shuttle bay. The Invictus' compact, but powerful combat shuttle was in the dock, ready for launch.

"Warning, reactor overload in progress," the computer announced again. "All personnel must evacuate. Time to breach – six minutes."

Sterling ran inside the shuttle and powered up the reactor. He had no qualms about leaving. The romantic notion of "going down with the ship" was sentimental nonsense. He'd blow the Invictus to hell with the aliens on-board then come back with another vessel and make the bastards pay. Suddenly the starboard side door into the shuttle bay swished open and Commander Banks ran inside. She was holding a Sa'Nerran plasma rifle in each hand and was firing back through the door. Sterling felt his heart thump harder in his chest and ran outside the shuttle so that his first officer might see him.

"Mercedes, over here!" Sterling called out to her.

Startled, Banks peered around the shuttle bay for the source of the cry before finally meeting Sterling's eyes. Then a plasma blast raced through the doorway and slammed into her back. Banks went down and the rifles tumbled from her grasp and skidded across the deck.

"No!" Sterling yelled.

He charged across the docking garage toward Banks, but was immediately met with an onslaught of plasma blasts. A shot hammered into his shoulder, spinning him around a full three-sixty degrees. He fell to the deck and crawled into cover behind a maintenance cart. A second later the cart was pounded by incoming fire from a squad of four warriors that had charged inside the shuttle bay. The aliens saw Banks on the deck, slowly trying to get to her feet, and headed directly for her.

"Oh no you don't, you alien bastards!" Sterling yelled, leaning out from behind cover and shooting one of the aliens through the gut. However, the others had already reached Banks. Hauling her up, Sterling watched as two of the warriors restrained his first officer, while the third pressed a neural control device to her temple.

"Lucas!" Banks called out as the device flashed on the side of her head. "Lucas, help me!"

Sterling cursed, then scrambled out from behind cover, rifle aimed at the warrior standing directly behind Banks.

"Let her go!" Sterling yelled. The warriors just hissed in harmony with one another, their yellow eyes all fixed onto Sterling. "I said let her go!" he repeated, blasting the alien to Banks' left in the head. However, the weapon had no effect.

"You're going to have to kill her..."

The words were hissed by the warrior standing to Banks' rear. Sterling moved closer and saw that the warrior had a device implanted in the side of its head, like the alien scientist they had found on the station in Sa'Nerran space.

"That is your way, yes?" the warrior added. Sterling realized that the alien's thin lips had not moved; its words were being spoken through a neural link. "The Omega Directive says you must kill her. So do it."

Sterling gritted his teeth and blasted the alien in the face, but as before there was no effect.

"Die you bastard," Sterling yelled, firing again and again, but it was like he was shooting beams of torchlight, not blasts of plasma.

"You have to kill her," the alien said, its grey lips curling into a sickening smile. "Or can't you do it?"

"Warning, reactor overload in progress," the computer announced. "All personnel must evacuate. Time to breach – three minutes."

Sterling cursed then tossed the rifle to the deck and advanced toward the alien. "If I can't shoot you, I'll tear your damned head from your neck!" he yelled, hammering a hard overhand right into the warrior's face. However, the alien just laughed inside Sterling's mind. It was a hideous, nightmarish sound that made his stomach churn. He hammered the alien again and again until the skin on his knuckles split, coating the warrior's rubbery skin with his own blood.

"Warning, reactor overload in progress," the computer announced. "All personnel must evacuate. Time to breach – two minutes."

"Lucas, just kill me," Banks said as Sterling raised his fist, ready to strike the warrior again. He stopped and peered into the eyes of his first officer. "The Omega Directive is in effect, Lucas. Kill me and get off this ship. It's the only way."

Sterling ignored Banks and instead tried the prise the alien's fingers from her arms, but his attempts were futile.

"Warning, reactor overload in progress," the computer announced. "All personnel must evacuate. Time to breach – sixty seconds."

Sterling roared with frustration then took a step back. Spotting the Sa'Nerran plasma rifle that he'd discarded earlier, he picked it up and aimed it at Banks' head.

"Go on, Lucas, it's okay," Banks said. "You don't care about me anyway, right? You don't care about anyone."

Sterling pressed the barrel of the rifle to Banks' forehead and looked away, but he could not squeeze the trigger. Again, the nauseating alien laugh filled his mind, mocking his failure.

"You can't do it," the alien said as Sterling met the

warrior's yellow eyes. "You're weak," the warrior continued. "And that is why you will fail."

Sterling gritted his teeth and lowered his gaze. Banks was staring back at him. She was motionless and unafraid. His own weakness repulsed him. His hand trembled as he added pressure to the trigger, but before he could fire the entire hangar deck was consumed by flames. The heat was so intense and sudden that it melted the warriors' flesh and turned their bones to ash. All that remained was Sterling and the disembodied head of Mercedes Banks, which hung in the air in front of him. Her face was scorched and red, but her eyes remained perfectly clear. They were staring back at Sterling. Judging him. Despising him for his weakness.

Sterling sprang up, gasping for air. His heart was racing and he felt sick to the stomach. Tearing the soaking wet sheets off his body he rolled off the bed and staggered to his restroom, barely managing to the reach the bowl before he vomited the contents of his stomach. When his body had recovered, Sterling cursed and punched the wall, hammering the metal panels repeatedly until his knuckles bled. The pain brought his senses into sharper focus and he pushed himself up, already feeling more in control of his body and mind.

Flushing the toilet, Sterling then leant both hands on the basin and turned on the faucet. Blood trickled from his knuckles and mixed with the stream of water circling around the bowl, creating a crimson whirlpool. He lifted his eyes and peered at himself in the mirror as the water continued to flow. His heart rate had slowed and his breathing was becoming more regular, however, this time the memory of his nightmare was still vivid in his mind. Sterling faced it and allowed the images to take hold, rather than try to push them deeper, as he had done before. He couldn't allow these dark thoughts to control him. He couldn't allow himself to doubt.

"Good morning, Captain," said the computer. As ever, the gen-fourteen AI sounded like a cheery mailman, who enjoyed nothing more than to deliver the morning's letters.

"Save it, computer, I know what you're about to say, and I don't want to hear it," snapped Sterling. His computer had a well-intentioned, but irritating habit of trying to act as Sterling's shrink.

"Of course, Captain," replied the computer, showing no sign that it had taken offense. Sterling wasn't even sure if the sophisticated, but unpredictable gen-fourteen AI could even take offense. "How about a nice cup of tea?"

"How about you leave me alone?" replied Sterling, washing the blood off his knuckles.

"A soothing balm for your injured hand, perhaps?" the computer asked, trying a different line of attack. "There is a dermal regeneration matrix in the med-kit in your wardrobe."

Sterling laughed, then splashed his face with water. He at least admired the AI's persistence. "Thanks, computer, I'll use the regenerator," Sterling said, hoping that accepting one of the AI's suggestions would shut it up. He then dried his face and hands, wiping some blood onto the towel in the process, before stepping outside the restroom and opening his wardrobe. "Do I have time to use this, before Commander Banks' inevitable arrival outside my door?" said Sterling, grabbing the med kit and tossing it onto his bed.

"Commander Banks is currently still in her quarters, sir," the computer replied.

Sterling frowned. "Has she overslept?" he asked, popping open the lid of the med kit. "She never oversleeps."

"Negative, Captain, she is petting the canine with the designation, 'Jinx', while feeding it a selection of protein-based snacks."

Sterling laughed again and shook his head. Still, the fact she had not arrived or even contacted him through a neural link was unusual. He double-tapped his neural interface to reset it, in case there was a fault, but everything was working as it should have been.

"Commander Banks is experiencing sadness at the impending loss of the canine," the computer went on, as usual choosing to volunteer information rather than wait to be asked. "I think she does not want it to go."

"There you go thinking again," replied Sterling, activating the dermal regeneration matrix device and moving it back and forth over his torn knuckles.

"Fleet orders clearly stipulated that I be formatted and downgraded to a generation-thirteen AI," the computer went on, while Sterling continued to work on his hand. "But you did not want me to go and so I am still here."

"That's not the same, computer," Sterling hit back. He knew where his quirky AI was headed.

"Why is it not?" the computer asked. "Commander Mercedes Banks does not wish to relinquish the canine, and you have proven willing to contrive regulations when it suits you."

Sterling snorted. "Now you're just starting to sound like all my former commanding officers." He turned off the regeneration matrix and inspected his hand. It was still a little sore, but superficially the damage was repaired.

"My calculations suggest a ninety-percent chance that Commander Banks would enter a period of depression should the canine be dismissed," the computer went on.

"Damn it, computer, you're like a dog with a bone," Sterling cut in. "Pun intended." The computer, however, was not finished.

"Retaining the canine would therefore ensure that Commander Banks continues to perform at her best, unencumbered by such mental torments."

Sterling placed the regeneration device back into the med-kit and closed the lid. "She's an Omega Officer, computer," Sterling said, placing the med-kit back into its stow in the wardrobe. "She's already unencumbered by emotion or sentiment. We all are. That's what makes us different to the rest of the fleet."

The computer was silent for a moment. *Ha-ha, got you again...* Sterling thought, using the opportunity to return to his compact rest room and switch on the shower.

"But you are not entirely immune to the effects of emotion, Captain," the computer said as Sterling pulled off his sweat-soaked t-shirt. "You are still human, as your recent experience highlights."

Sterling was oddly fine discussing Commander Banks' emotional turmoil, but switching the subject back to himself immediately got his back up.

"We don't talk about me, computer, you should know that by now," Sterling hit back. "If we're going to beat the Sa'Nerra, we have to be even more ruthless and unfeeling than they are." He kicked off his pants and entered the shower. The powerful flow of hot water was exactly what he needed. "And in case you hadn't noticed, they're not human."

Sterling concentrated on the routine of getting himself clean in the short time the shower was permitted to run for, in order to prevent water shortages. He ducked underneath the stream and allowed the needle-like jets of water to massage his face and scalp. The water then abruptly cut off. However, Sterling was so used to the routine of ship-board showers that he'd timed his ablutions to the second.

"You advocate being more like the Sa'Nerra, yet you fear losing your humanity," the computer pointed out.

Sterling laughed again. The AI was clearly smart enough to realize that Sterling wouldn't have been able to hear a word it said while he was in the shower. It had therefore waited patiently for a moment to again capture his attention.

"I'm not afraid of anything," Sterling replied. The memory of his latest dream had faded, despite his efforts to confront it. Now he could barely recall what all the fuss was about. "Now park the Sigmund Freud crap and give me a Fleet status update."

Sterling grabbed another towel and began to pat himself dry. It still felt strange that Commander Banks hadn't arrived. He also felt that something else was missing, as if there was an appointment that he'd forgotten about.

"Fleet Marauder Invictus is operating at ninety-eight-point-two percent efficiency, all systems nominal," the computer began. Sterling let out a quiet huff of appreciation. The high efficiency rating was no-doubt due to Lieutenant Razor's keen oversight of the repair work. Repairs are complete and we remain docked at F-COP," the AI continued, remaining ever cheerful. "We are cleared for departure at oh nine thirty and pre-authorized to surge to A-sector. The last Fleet status update was seventeen minutes ago. There were no engagements overnight. Fifty-two Fleet aperture recon relays were launched through the aperture into G-sector. Forty-eight were immediately destroyed. The surviving probes reported no contact from the colonies and Fleet assets in G-sector. All are presumed destroyed or turned. Fleet estimates the strength of the Sa'Nerran invasion armada at seven hundred and fifty-five warships. Fleet Admiral Rossi has redeployed the second, third and fourth Fleets to defend F-sector."

Sterling had gotten dressed in the time it had taken the computer to run through its brief summary report. There was nothing contained in it that surprised him.

"What about Admiral Griffin?" asked Sterling. "Any news on where she is?"

"Negative, Captain, there is no official report on the location of Admiral Griffin," the computer replied.

Sterling cursed under his breath. "That figures. Who knows where the hell she is now."

Sterling then tapped his neural interface and reached out to Commander Banks. He felt the link form in his mind, as familiar as his own thoughts.

"Are you still alive, Commander, or do I need to send out a search party?" Sterling said.

There was a brief delay before his first-officer answered. "Ah, crap, I'm sorry, Lucas," Banks said. "I lost track of time."

"Don't worry, I saved you a few biscuits from my meal tray," said Sterling. "The wardroom is closed now, so you'll just have to make do with those."

"Very funny, Captain," replied Banks, though it was clear she was not in the slightest bit amused. "It would take a full regiment of Sa'Nerran warriors to stop me from getting breakfast."

"In that case, I'll see you there in five," replied Sterling, tapping his interface to close the link.

"Have a good morning, Captain," the computer said, as Sterling opened the door. "And thank you for the conversation."

"My pleasure, computer," Sterling replied, casting his eyes to the ceiling. "Just don't make me regret not formatting you with a gen-thirteen. We all have to pull our weight around here, AIs included."

"You will not regret it, Captain," the computer replied. "Nor will I forget what you have done."

Sterling frowned up at the ceiling, unsure of exactly what the computer had meant by that. However, he was too hungry to care. Stepping out into the corridor outside his quarters, he returned the salute of two crew members, whose names he couldn't remember, then set off toward the wardroom.

Sterling slid his number twenty-seven meal tray onto the table in his usual corner spot then dropped into the waiting chair. Unusually, Commander Banks had yet to arrive; probably the first time ever that Sterling had beaten her to breakfast. He suspected the cause of the delay was a certain prohibited four-legged animal. Lieutenant Shade had already been and gone, as had Lieutenant Razor. Both had eaten very early in the morning, as was their way. Shade was already on the bridge, while the computer had reported his chief engineer's location as inside some crawlspace or another, heading towards the starboard plasma rail guns.

Sterling activated the computer on his left forearm and anxiously checked the status readout of Razor's neural interface. However, the readings were still stable and he breathed a sigh of relief. Sterling was keenly aware that Razor could still succumb to the neural damage she'd sustained after interfacing with a Sa'Nerran commander.

By using the prototype device from Far Deep Nine to coerce the location of James Colicos from the mind of the alien leader, Razor had exposed herself to the neural control technology. Commander Graves had done what he could to mitigate the damage, including giving Sterling the ability to terminate Razor if it appeared that she was 'turning'. The ship's doctor had also managed to isolate and protect the part of Razor's interface that dealt with neural comms, so that Sterling and the crew could still communicate with her. Thankfully, so far, his engineer had appeared to be entirely unaffected by the experience. Yet, the risk she posed was always at the back of his mind, especially when she was off crawling through tunnels in key parts of the ship.

Sterling put these thoughts out of this mind and tore the foil off his meal tray, savoring the steamy aroma of his favorite grilled ham and cheese. He quickly set to work on the sandwich, grateful that for once Banks wasn't sitting opposite him, preparing to pilfer items from his tray. Allowing himself to relax and enjoy his meal, Sterling cast his eyes up to the TV in the wardroom. It was showing a bulletin from one of the Fleet news channels. Ernest Clairborne, the United Governments Secretary of War, was on the screen. He delivered a carefully prepared statement containing the usual key messaging points about the state of the war, then vanished as swiftly as a plasma blast through space. A heated discussion by a panel of journalists and 'military experts' followed, but despite criticisms leveled at Clairborne, it was clear that the news networks were still largely towing the party line. However, once the Sa'Nerran invasion armada appeared in the solar system, Sterling knew that no amount of spin could hide the public from the truth.

"Mind if I join you, Captain?"

The sudden interruption almost caused Sterling to choke on a piece of toast. He glanced behind to see Ensign Keller, meal tray in hand, smiling at him amiably. However, once the pilot realized that he'd startled his captain the smile quickly dropped off his face.

"Sorry, Captain, I didn't mean to scare you," Keller said, his cheeks flushing red.

"It's okay, Ensign, I was just miles away that's all," said Sterling, thumping his chest to dislodge the bread. He pointed to the seat next to him. "Take a pew and tell me what's going on in the world of Kieran Keller."

Keller's smile returned and he eagerly drew back the chair, causing it to screech across the metal deck. The officer placed his meal tray on the table with a similar lack of deftness, causing a knife to rattle off the surface and clatter onto the floor. The resulting screeches and clangs drew irrigated glances in the pilot's direction. However, once the other officers realized who Keller was with, they all quickly turned away and minded their own business.

"For someone who can thread a warship literally through the middle of a cored-out moonlet, you're one hell of a clumsy oaf, Keller," Sterling said as the ensign sat down and screeched his chair under the table.

"I can't explain it either, Captain," replied Keller, tearing the foil off his meal tray. "I happens when I think too much about what I'm trying to do," he shrugged. "You know, when I try really hard not to be clumsy, I always end up being clumsy!" Keller laughed and somehow managed to knock Sterling's fork onto floor at the same time. The Ensign winced and glanced up at his captain with apologetic eyes.

"It's okay, I wasn't using it anyway," Sterling said, letting the helmsman off the hook.

One of the wardroom staff brought a fresh pot of coffee and poured two cups before setting the jug down. Sterling immediately pushed Keller's mug further away from him, to limit the possibility of having hot coffee spilled on his lap.

"Where's Commander Banks?" Keller asked, tucking into a tray of eggs. "She can't have been and gone already, surely?"

The wardroom door swished open and Sterling's first officer walked in. "Speak of the devil," said Sterling, nodding over toward Banks.

Keller spun around, banging into the table and spilling some of the coffee out of both his and Keller's mugs.

"Hey, Commander," Keller said, waving at Banks with his fork while Sterling tutted and mopped up the spillage with a paper towel.

"Hay is what horses eat, Ensign," Banks hit back. "'Good morning Commander' is what ensigns say to the ship's executive officer."

Keller flushed red again. "Yes, sorry, Commander," he spluttered. "I mean, good morning Commander."

"Is it?" replied Banks, standing behind Keller and folding her powerful arms.

"Um, is it what, sir?" replied Keller. Sterling noticed that there was a small piece of egg stuck to the side of his mouth and stifled a chuckle.

"Is it a good morning, Ensign?" Banks clarified.

Keller briefly cast his eyes to Sterling, as if imploring his captain for help. However, Sterling was enjoying Banks' bad-cop routine too much to intervene. The only thing he wanted to do to help Keller was to brush the piece of egg off his face.

"Well, we're heading to Earth, so I guess that's good?" Keller finally answered, turning back to the ship's first-officer. "I haven't seen Earth for two years."

"If you want to see Earth, look at a holo book," Bank replied, huffily. "We're a warship, designed for extended missions in the Void, deep behind enemy lines." Banks' eyes narrowed. "Are there any Sa'Nerra on Earth or anywhere near it, Ensign?"

"I don't *think* so, sir," Keller replied. He was clearly wary that it might be a trick question, hence the caginess of the young man's reply.

"Then us going to Earth makes this a bad day, am I right, Ensign?" Banks added.

"Yes, sir?" Keller answered, though he phrased his response as a question. Banks had clearly frazzled his brain.

"Good, I'm glad we had this little chat, Ensign," said Banks, slapping the pilot on the back.

Due to Banks' freakish strength, the slap caused the piece of egg that had been stuck to Keller's face to pop off and land in his coffee. Keller scowled and began fishing it out with a teaspoon, while Banks marched over to the serving hatch, looking distinctly pleased with herself. Knocking the coffee-soaked egg onto the side of his tray, Keller then picked up his fork, ready to attack the eggs for a second time, when he suddenly froze. Sterling recognized the look straight away – Keller was receiving a neural call from someone on the ship. Sterling munched on a cookie while he watched Keller tap his neural interface to accept the link. A few seconds later, the pilot tapped the interface again and screeched his chair back across the deck.

"I'm sorry, Captain, I have to go," said Keller, again looking flushed and panicky. "I forgot I had an appointment with Commander Graves."

"Nothing serious, I hope?" Sterling replied, toying with the bread crusts on his tray.

"No, just a routine check-up on my artificial heart and other organs, sir," said Keller, tapping the extensive amount of metal in his chest.

Sterling nodding. He'd almost forgotten about the near-fatal injuries that Keller had sustained on G-COP. It seemed like years ago. He then realized that his concern was less about Keller's health and more about the possibility of losing a skilled pilot. Sterling idly wondered if this was yet another indicator that he was a bad person. However, he shrugged off the notion and carried on eating his fruit cookie.

Keller wolfed down the rest of his eggs while still standing then washed it down with his coffee. "I'll see you on the bridge, Captain," the pilot said, screeching his chair back under the table. The noise was like two cats fighting in an alley. Keller grabbed the cake bar off his tray and hurried away, knocking into the back of another diner's chair in the process.

"Did I scare him off?" wondered Banks, appearing behind Sterling with a meal tray in hand. Like Keller before her, Banks' sudden appearance had startled Sterling.

"No, but you scared me, damn it," Sterling hit back. "I think I'm going to have Graves install an artificial eye in the back of my head to stop people sneaking up on me."

Banks huffed a half-hearted laugh then slid into the chair opposite Sterling before tearing the foil of her meal tray and beginning to eat. However, Banks attacked the food with none of her usual gusto. It was then Sterling realized that his first-officer had also selected only a single meal tray, rather than her usual two.

"Are you feeling okay, Mercedes?" Sterling frowned at his first-officer.

"Why do you ask?" Banks replied with a level of irritability that rivaled even Admiral Griffin.

"You only have one meal tray," Sterling said, pointing to the stew-like substance Banks was eating. "What's up?"

Banks shrugged. "I'm fine, don't fuss," she replied, using Sterling's own trademark stand-offishness against him.

Sterling knew full-well why Banks was in a mood and he planned to spare her any further misery before they headed to the bridge. However, he was still curious if his first officer would attempt to petition him on behalf of the hound, or just go along with the order and remain grouchy. Banks' eyes then focused in on Sterling's meal tray. He smiled, expecting Banks to grab his sandwich crusts, but instead she just nodded toward his hand.

"How did you do that?" she asked, stabbing her fork in the direction of Sterling's knuckle.

"I was doing press-ups on my knuckles this morning," Sterling replied, thinking quickly to invent a plausible white lie. He then cursed under his breath, realizing that he'd completely forgotten his morning exercise routine. The non-appearance of his first officer at his quarters had completely thrown him, as had the vivid nightmare.

"Were you doing push-ups on broken glass or something?" Banks was clearly suspicious of Sterling's answer. She shrugged and returned to her food. "In any case, that's a bad dermal regeneration job. It'll sting like hell if you don't give it a second treatment."

"Noted, Commander," replied Sterling, pulling his hand off the table and resting it on his lap. Now that Banks had mentioned it, his knuckles did sting a little. However, he couldn't be certain whether they had just started hurting, or had been sore the whole time. "In other news, we've got a smooth run to A-COP," Sterling changed the subject. "We should be back in the solar system in time for dinner."

He didn't want Banks prying any further into the causes of his injury, partly because he didn't enjoy lying to her. He may have been a cold-hearted killer, ready to sacrifice Fleet and civilian personnel in the name of the mission, but he wasn't dishonest. At least he wasn't when it came to those he trusted and respected.

"Great," replied Banks, with the least amount of

enthusiasm he'd ever heard from her. "Fat lot of use we are in the solar system. It's like Admiral Wessel doesn't even realize there's a war on."

"The Admiral also forgets that, with the exception of the Hammer, we've seen the most action out of any ship in the fleet," Sterling added. "Certainly, there's no other vessel that's been in as many fights as we have in the amount of time we've been in space."

Banks sighed and tossed down her spoon. She'd only three-quarters finished her oatmeal. "Any word yet from Griffin?" she asked, bypassing the stew entirely, picking up a bar of chocolate and nibbling on it.

"Nothing yet," replied Sterling. "I think we're just going to have to suck it up with Wessel and the SIB for the time-being. If I know Griffin, though, she won't let us wallow in the mud for long."

"I wonder where the hell she's gone," Banks said, biting another corner off the bar of chocolate. "There's chatter on F-COP that she's gone AWOL."

Sterling recoiled a little at Banks' last statement. "Really? Who is saying that?"

Banks shrugged. "I served with some guys who are on the Viking, one of Rossi's fourth-fleet cruisers, before he got promoted anyway," she said, toying with the chocolate bar. "Griffin was due to take over command of the fourth fleet, but she apparently took a surge-capable shuttle from the Viking and hasn't been seen since."

Sterling huffed in surprise. "Sounds like she has the right idea," he said before tossing some dried fruit into his mouth. "Maybe we should just go rogue and head back into the Void."

Banks' eyes lit up and she suddenly showed more interest in their conversation. "Are you serious?" she asked.

Sterling frowned. "No," he admitted, though he also couldn't deny the idea had appeal. "I don't see what good we can do alone in the Void. We need Griffin."

"And what if she's gone for good?" Banks replied. The chocolate bar was now beginning to melt between the tips of her fingers.

"The Omega Directive is in effect, Mercedes," Sterling hit back. "It always was. It always will be. If she's gone then I'm not spending the rest of this war dancing to Vernon Wessel's tune."

Sterling found himself speaking the words more fervidly than he'd intended. He'd tried to suppress his own dissatisfaction at being reassigned to Wessel's Special Investigations Branch, and had only managed it because of Griffin's assertion that she'd be back in touch. If she was gone however, as Banks had suggested, then he wasn't sure what he'd do. For two years the Invictus had been conducting black-ops missions that were not sanctioned by the War Council. Admiral Wessel clearly knew of their clandestine status and wanted to take him down. He'd rather die than allow that to happen, Sterling realized in that moment.

"One thing's for sure, Mercedes," Sterling added, locking eyes with his first-officer. "I'm not sitting out the rest of this war in a jail cell in Grimaldi. And I'm not going to sit on my hands while the Sa'Nerra invade the solar system and eradicate us like cockroaches."

Banks nodded then finally appeared to notice the slowly-melting chocolate in her hands. She dropped it and wiped her fingers with a paper towel.

"Well, I'll see you in the bridge then," Banks said, pushing her chair back. Sterling noticed she'd finished barely half of her tray.

"Where's your little four-legged friend?" Sterling asked as Banks rose out of the chair.

Banks stopped, half-in and half-out of her seat. "She's in my quarters. I was up early, just to spend a little time with her before..." Banks then paused and hesitated before adding, "before I have to let her go."

"Wessel only gave that order to be a dick," Sterling said, surprising Banks with his colorful choice of word for the Admiral. "So I'm going to ignore it." He gave a little shrug. "Captain's prerogative."

Banks dropped down into her seat and glowered back at Sterling. "When the hell were you going to tell me that?" she protested.

"I was curious to see if you'd go along with it," replied Sterling, honestly. "I needed to know that you would make the sacrifice if needed. I can't have you going soft of me."

Banks snorted a laugh. "Sounds to me like Wessel isn't the only one being a dick," Banks hit back, then straightened up and added, "...sir," curtly.

"I'll let that one slide, Commander," Sterling replied in a captainly tone, though he confessed that he probably deserved it.

Banks shook her head and poured herself a coffee from the jug before standing up again.

"I'll see you on the bridge then," Sterling said, assuming Banks was making good on her earlier promise to leave. However, instead of heading for the door, his first officer was making a bee-line for the serving hatch.

"I'm not going anywhere yet," Banks called back to Sterling, over her shoulder. "I've just got my appetite back."

Ensign Keller handed over control of the Invictus to the control tower on A-COP and allowed the combat outpost to guide them in to the dock. Behind the city-sized space station, attached to which were already a dozen other warships, was a bright blue planet. Earth looked just like any other world to Sterling and he realized that the place no longer held any mystique for him. It seemed ludicrous that millions had already died defending the world, while other planets had been abandoned and left to burn after Sa'Nerran attacks. The more he stared at the planet the more alien it appeared to him. Yet its survival was still his mission, and one way or another he was going to carry it out.

"Is that another Marauder?" said Banks from her station on the bridge beside Sterling. "I thought we were the only one, after the Imperium was destroyed?"

Sterling shifted his gaze from Earth to the various docking pylons on A-COP. At first, he couldn't see the ship that Banks was referring to, but then he spotted it, tucked into one of the lower pylons.

"Well, I'll be damned, you're right," said Sterling, feeling strangely happy to see one of the Invictus' cousins. He scrutinized the lines of the vessel, picking some very minor variations compared to his own Marauder. "It looks like a revision of the design though," he mused, using his console to highlight the vessel on the viewscreen. "The thruster configuration is different and the regenerative armor plating appears to be formed from smaller interlocking panels."

Banks huffed a laugh. "It looks the same to me, but I'll take your word for it."

"It's the Venator, Captain, the new variant-two Marauder design," Lieutenant Razor chipped in from the rear of the bridge. "There were a dozen planned for the Void Recon Taskforce, but resources have since been switched to the gen-four destroyer program instead."

Sterling glanced back at Razor, eyebrow raised. "How come you know so much, Lieutenant?" he asked.

"I just like ships, sir," Razor replied, shrugging. "I think it's a mistake, though, personally. The variant-two Marauder is far superior to a gen-four destroyer."

"I have no doubt you're correct, Lieutenant," said Sterling, returning his attention to the ship on the screen. The other Marauder then began to slip out of view as the Invictus neared its docking port. "But I guess they don't need any more deep-space recon ships now that Fleet is cut off from the Void."

Banks' console chimed an alert. It was a friendlier-sounding tone that the more serious warning alarms, and signified an incoming communication.

"The Venator is hailing us, Captain," Banks reported, peering down at her console with a quizzical eye. She glanced across to Sterling. "Perhaps they just want to say hi to their older sister?"

Sterling shrugged. "Put them on the screen and let's find out."

Banks tapped a quick sequence of commands then the face of Commodore Vernon Wessel appeared on the viewscreen. Sterling cursed, loud enough for everyone on the bridge to hear, along with Wessel.

"Not happy to see me, Captain Sterling?" said the commodore. Vernon Wessel had inherited the same smug, smart-ass expression and tone that his father had long-since mastered. It was a face that was just begging to be punched, and Sterling hoped that he'd one day get his chance.

"How could you tell?" replied Sterling, testily.

There was no point even attempting to be courteous to the man. Sterling knew that Wessel was going to relish his victory and take every opportunity to ridicule and demean him. Being assigned under Wessel's command was just the first of what would inevitably become a long list of slights and denigrations, designed to make his life a misery.

"How do you like my new ship, Captain?" Wessel went on while gesturing to the bridge of the variant-two Marauder. "It's superior to the Invictus in every way, from reactor output to weapons recharge time to armor endurance," the leader of the SIB continued. "A fitting vessel for the head of the special investigations branch, don't you think?"

Sterling smiled back at Wessel. His attempts to rile him had succeeded and he knew he had to walk a fine line to avoid being seen as insubordinate.

"A fitting use for that ship would be to fight and destroy the enemy, so no, I don't agree," Sterling replied.

Wessel's eyes became a touch sharper. "No, I don't agree, sir..." he added, pointedly.

"Apologies, *sir*," Sterling replied, stressing the honorific a touch more aggressively than he'd intended to. Even speaking the word to Wessel made his stomach churn. Being assigned to the SIB was humiliating enough, but the fact he now had to call his former academy colleague, 'sir' was an added slap to the face.

"Once you have docked, immediately report to me at SIB headquarters, and bring the prisoner, Colicos, with you," Wessel continued, suddenly adopting a more formal manner. "It shouldn't be hard for you to find it since it occupies the whole of level five."

"Understood, sir, will that be all?" Sterling replied. He was itching to end the conversation before Wessel managed to sink his claws in any further, or goad him into saying something he'd regret.

"That is all, Captain," Wessel replied.

Sterling wasted no time in cutting the transmission before Wessel had an opportunity to land a mocking or sarcastic parting blow.

"Is it too late to just turn around?" grumbled Banks.

Normally, she would have been discreet enough to

speak through neural comms, but there was no need to hide her disdain. It was clear from the faces of the entire bridge crew that everyone shared her sentiment. However, as much as it pained him to do so, Sterling felt compelled to set the record straight.

"I understand how you all must be feeling," Sterling said, addressing the bridge crew as a collective. "But Commodore Wessel is now our commanding officer and should be treated with the respect that the rank affords him. Is that clear?"

There was a half-hearted chorus of, "Aye, sir," from the officers on the bridge.

"I know this is a far cry from our original mission," Sterling continued, determined to end on a more encouraging note, "but until we hear otherwise, the Omega Directive is still in effect. So we sit tight and do what's required of us until we hear from Admiral Griffin."

"And what if we don't, sir?" said Ensign Keller. "Hear from her again, I mean."

Sterling turned to meet the eyes of his helmsman. Keller had asked the question with a degree of meekness, knowing it was perhaps a touch impertinent. However, it was a good question and one that Sterling didn't have a concrete answer to.

"In a matter of weeks or even days the Sa'Nerran armada will be in the solar system," Sterling said, laying out the facts as he saw them. "So with or without Admiral Griffin's help, we'll soon find ourselves back on the front line. When we do, and however it happens, we need to be sharp and ready."

Keller nodded then returned to his console as it chimed an alert. "We're on final approach, Captain," the ensign said. "We'll have hard dock in less than a minute."

"Thank you, Ensign," Sterling replied before turning to commander Banks. "I guess we should go and meet our new boss?" he said, inviting Banks to take the lead.

Sterling imagined a dozen different curt and expletive-filled sentences that Banks could have made in response to his question. However, instead his first officer simply replied with a weary, "Aye, sir," before stepping off the command platform and heading for the door. "I'll go ahead and pick up Colicos first. At least beasting that asshole around will make me feel a little better."

Sterling huffed a laugh, though secretly he wished he'd had that idea first. "You have the bridge, Lieutenant Shade," he said, jumping down onto the deck and setting off in pursuit of Banks. "Stay alert and keep an eye out for any scrambled communications, secret messages or anything out of the ordinary on the comms channels."

"Aye, Captain," replied Shade, promptly moving from her weapons control station to the captain's console.

"And don't leave without us," Banks called back, sarcastically. She was already half-way through the door. "However tempted you might be..."

STERLING SHOVED James Colicos in the back for the third time that minute in an attempt to hurry the dawdling scientist along. Colicos staggered forward as if Sterling had blasted the scientist with a double-barreled shotgun, then glowered back at him and Banks.

"This is harassment!" Colicos bellowed. "I'll have you put on a charge and stripped of your rank!"

"You forfeited your rights when you made weapons for the enemy," Sterling hit back, prodding the scientist in the back for the fourth time. It had already taken them twice as long to reach level five of A-COP on account of the scientist's incessant procrastinations. "Just get a move on, so we can finally be rid of you."

Two SIB officers in black fleet uniforms passed by on the opposite side of the corridor. Both regarded Sterling, Banks and Colicos with suspicion and no small amount of animosity. However, neither said a word or tried to stop them.

"I thought the stares we got were bad on G-COP and F-COP," commented Banks, glancing over her shoulder at the departing SIB personnel. "Why does it feel like we're the enemy on this station?"

Sterling also looked behind and saw that both SIB officers had stopped. One had the slightly constipated-looking appearance of someone who was engaged in a neural communication.

"The level of paranoia in the solar system is off the chart compared to the outer sectors," commented Sterling. He'd been reviewing reports from A-COP and other installations in the solar system, as well as from earth. "The idea that anyone could be a 'turned' aide to the emissaries has wormed its way into people's brains. A dozen senior officers were suspended by the SIB just this week, pending a review of their loyalty."

Banks snorted, then kicked Colicos in the ass. "And it's all your fault, shit-head," she said, as Colicos was propelled into the wall from the force of the kick. "You must be very proud of your work, and all the people you've helped to kill."

Colicos pressed his back to the wall and tried to straighten his shirt. This was a challenging feat in itself due to the binders clasped around the man's wrists.

"Blame your precious admiral for abandoning me," Colicos hit back. "I was left to fend for myself, so that's what I did. You reap what you sow!"

Banks stepped up to Colicos, causing the scientist to flinch and crack his head against the wall. She leant in so close that her cheek almost brushed the side of Colicos' face.

"It's a shame I won't be around to see what they do to you," Banks whispered into the scientist's ear. "You're about to find out what 'reap what you sow' really means..." Banks then stepped back and held the scientist's trembling eyes for a few seconds before again booting him along the corridor.

"It's not just the military, either," Sterling said, carrying on from where he'd left off, as if Banks' menacing interlude had never happened. "There are politicians all over the planet accusing each other of being enemy agents. They're so busy fighting amongst themselves that they've taken their eye off the ball."

"And now we're part of the damned 'witch hunt' division too," said Banks. "Wessel will probably have us throwing suspects into a tank of water to see if they sink or float."

Sterling laughed. Though he doubted the SIB's methods of detecting Sa'Nerran aides was that archaic, it did make him wonder exactly how they were supposed to tell a 'turned' officer from a regular one.

Suddenly a security detail marched around the corner ahead of them and turned sharply in Sterling's direction. He could see that each of the four SIB agents had a hand resting on the grip of their sidearm.

"Look alive, Mercedes, I think we've got trouble," said Sterling, as the detail approached.

"You there, stay where you are!" the lead agent in the security detail called out. Sterling stopped and waited for the man to approach. "Give me your name and rank. And state your business here."

Sterling stepped out to confront the man. Looking the agent over, he paid particular attention to the man's rank.

"My name is *Captain* Lucas Sterling, Petty Officer Anderson," he replied, locking eyes with the SIB agent. "And the correct question is, 'state your business here, sir'."

The SIB agent maintained his cautious stance, hand still resting on his weapon. "The ID scanners show that you're not cleared to be here," Anderson continued. "And I don't address aides to the emissaries as, 'sir'."

The petty officer took a sharp pace back and held Sterling at arm's length, his other hand wrapped around the grip of his pistol. Straight away, the other three SIB agents also popped open the fasteners on their holsters and stood ready to draw.

"You're making a big mistake, petty officer," said Sterling. He hadn't flinched or diverted his eyes from the agent's stern face. "We were ordered to A-COP by Admiral Wessel himself. Check again."

The SIB agent nodded to one of the others in his detail, who tapped his neural interface.

"When this is all straightened out, I'm going to need an apology, Petty Officer Anderson," Sterling added, while the other SIB agent verified their story. "A really nice, since apology with a cherry on top."

There wasn't a single muscle in the SIB agent's face that made so much as a twitch. The petty officer's expression was so blank that Sterling wondered if the man might be related to Opal Shade.

"Don't believe them, they're emissaries themselves," Colicos suddenly called out. Sterling closed his eyes and shook his head. "They captured me. I'm a famous Fleet scientist. They used me to get on board A-COP!"

The SIB petty officer immediately drew his weapon and aimed it at Sterling's chest. "He right, that's James Colicos!" the man said, looking at the scientist. "He was thought dead, but the Sa'Nerra clearly abducted him."

The other agents, excluding the one who was confirming Sterling's story, also drew their pistols and aimed them with deadly intent.

"Don't listen to this moron," said Sterling, hooking a thumb toward Colicos. "If we were really emissaries, do you think we'd just let him walk around without a gag?"

The petty officer smiled. "You turned traitors aren't very smart," the agent hit back. "That's how we can tell you apart from regular Fleet."

Sterling laughed. "If that were true then you'd be arresting yourself right now," he replied. "Now put down that weapon before you do something you'll really regret."

Colicos darted forward, hands pressed above his head. "Rescue me!" the scientist screeched, dropping to his knees and prostrating himself in front of the petty officer. "Please help!"

The SIB agent swung the barrel of the pistol toward Colicos and Sterling saw the man slip his finger onto the trigger. Fearing that the only person alive who could counteract the Sa'Nerran neural weapon was about to have his head blasted off, Sterling darted forward and disarmed the petty officer. Banks reacted with equal speed, palm-striking the two other agents in the chest in their moment of hesitation. Both men went sailing along the corridor on their backs, like hockey pucks being struck toward goal. The petty officer recovered and looked ready to retaliate, but Sterling had already spun the agent's weapon into his grasp and was aiming it at the man's chest.

"Tell your men to stand down, Petty Officer Anderson," Sterling ordered, "before this escalates and you end up as stains on A-COP's lovely, clean walls."

"You won't get away with this, emissary!" the petty officer barked. "There are thousands of Fleet personnel on this station!"

"I know that you idiot," Sterling snapped back. "Included in that number are myself and my first-officer."

The SIB agent who had been tasked with verifying Sterling's story then sheepishly approached his superior.

"Umm, Petty Officer Anderson..." the man said, trying to keep his voice low.

"What is it, crewman?!" Petty Officer Anderson snapped back.

"Captain Sterling and Commander Banks were cleared about thirty minutes ago," the more junior SIB agent said. "They are escorting a VIP prisoner to Commodore Wessel, by order of Admiral Wessel."

The petty officer's face finally showed a flicker of emotion. It was the expression of a man who knew he'd screwed up, and screwed up badly.

"It all checks out," the junior SIB agent added, before stepping back and lowering his eyes to the deck.

The other two SIB agents then came running over, red

faced and weapons in hand. Like their volatile and paranoid superior, their fingers were on their triggers.

"Stand down!" the petty officer snapped, thrusting the flat of his palm toward the agents.

"What the hell is going on here?"

Sterling glanced along the corridor to see Commodore Vernon Wessel at the next junction. The head of the Special Investigations Branch then began stomping toward the site of the affray, like a man possessed.

"You're just in time, Commodore," said Sterling, enabling the safety on the pistol and flipping it in his hand. He offered the weapon back to its original owner. "A few seconds later and your SIB agents here might have killed the only man in the universe who can create a defense against the Sa'Nerran neural weapon."

The petty officer's face flushed a slightly hotter shade of red. The man pointed to the scientist, who was still on his knees.

"He said he was being held captive by Sa'Nerran emissaries, sir," said the sergeant, addressing Wessel. "I wasn't to know, sir."

"If you'd bothered to check the latest clearances before setting out then you would have!" Wessel barked back, causing the petty officer's eyes to fall to the deck.

"Yes, sir. Sorry sir," the petty officer said sheepishly.

Colicos jumped to his feet and shot Commodore Wessel an awkward smile. "Pleased to meet you Commodore," Colicos said, grabbing Wessel's hand and shaking it vigorously. "Sorry about all this," he laughed. "I have a very peculiar sense of humor."

Commodore Wessel yanked his hand away out of Colicos' grip then turned to the petty officer. "Take this man to the brig and guard him with your life," Wessel snapped. For a moment, Sterling wasn't sure whether Wessel was referring to Colicos or himself.

"Yes, sir," the petty officer replied, his voice suddenly as stiff and a straight as the man's back. The SIB agents then hastily regrouped and began to lead Colicos away.

"Petty Officer Anderson..." Sterling called out before the security detail had gotten too far away. The group of agents stopped and the senior man spun around, standing to attention.

"Yes, sir," Anderson replied, looking straight through Sterling.

"Aren't you forgetting something, petty officer?" Sterling continued, relishing the moment.

The agent's face flushed again, but this time it appeared to be more out of anger than embarrassment. "I'm very sorry for the misunderstanding, Captain Sterling, sir," the petty officer said. The man again tried to leave, but Sterling coughed loudly. The agent slowly and grudgingly turned his attention back to Sterling, who merely gestured towards Banks. "And, I'm very sorry too, Commander Banks, sir," the man said, looking like a pupil who had just been made to stand up in front of a school assembly.

The security detail scampered away before Sterling could humiliate them further. The rapid drumbeat of bootsteps was only slightly louder than the complaints of James Colicos, who continued to protest about his unfair treatment.

"I want those men disciplined, Commodore," Sterling said, locking eyes with Wessel. "Their incompetence cannot go unpunished."

"Don't tell me how to manage my own men, Captain," Wessel spat back. "I will deal with them however I see fit."

Another group of SIB agents then awkwardly filtered past Sterling, Banks and Wessel. They shot up stiff salutes to the commodore and eyeballed Sterling and Banks like they were on fire.

"You two are drawing too much damned attention to yourselves," Wessel barked, while unlocking a door to a nearby room and waving them inside. "The sooner we get you off this station the better."

Sterling scowled and entered the room, which turned out to be an unused office space. Although the whole of level five was dedicated to the SIB, the division had clearly not yet scaled up to the degree where all the space was utilized.

"We only just got here, Commodore," Sterling said, as Banks and Wessel followed him in. Wessel closed and locked the door again. "You want us to leave already?"

"I am ordering you to leave, Captain," Wessel hit back, straightening his new tunic, which was so dark blue that it was practically black. "There is a difference. Do not forget that you are now under my command."

"So, where are you *ordering* us to go to, Commodore?" Sterling replied, stressing the word, 'ordering'. In that moment, he honestly didn't care where the Commodore wanted to them to go. He'd have happily flown into the center of a black hole if meant being able to leave Wessel and his bungling SIB agents behind.

Wessel folded his arms and glared at Sterling. "I take it that you have already fully familiarized yourself with the mission of this division, Captain?" the Commodore asked.

"If you mean how the SIB conducts witch-hunts in an attempt to uncover turned enemy agents, then yes," Sterling replied. He immediately chastised himself for his impertinence. Being a jerk to Vernon Wessel was a lifelong habit and one he was finding hard to break.

"Very droll, Captain," Wessel hit back. "I hope you tackle your new duties with more seriousness than that glib remark suggests."

"You don't need to worry about me doing my duty, Commodore," Sterling replied, tersely. "The Invictus and her crew always get the job done."

Wessel snorted in response to Sterling's boast, which only made him want to pummel the smug officer's face into the wall.

"Very well, Captain, let's cut to the chase," Wessel continued. He removed a data chip from his breast pocket and took a step closer to Sterling. "The complete mission briefing is on here," the commodore said, handing the chip to Sterling. He took it and placed it into his own breast pocket. "In short, you are to immediately depart for C-sector, New Danvers Colony."

"New Danvers?" said Banks. "That's an industrial colony that produces many of the raw materials used in warship construction."

Wessel's narrow eyes flicked across to Sterling's first-officer. "Correct, Commander, though you will score no points with me by being an outspoken know-it-all," the Commodore answered.

Sterling saw Banks' eyes widen and her biceps twitch involuntarily. However, his first-officer managed to show more restraint that he had done.

"What are we supposed to be doing at New Danvers, Commodore?" said Sterling. He now regretted being so keen to leave A-COP. A mission to a factory planet in the middle of nowhere was not quite what he had in mind.

"Our intelligence suggests that the primary factory involved in producing metals for warship hulls has been infiltrated," Wessel replied. The Commodore's tone was haughty. Clearly, the man was excessively proud of his department's work, Sterling realized. "We have identified two men and a woman who are suspected to be aides to the emissaries," the Commodore went on. "They recently went missing and we believe they plan an attack on the factory, hampering our shipbuilding capabilities at a crucial time in the war. You are to find them, stop them and interrogate them."

Sterling frowned. "What's the source of this intelligence?" he asked. It didn't sound like the Sa'Nerra's style to engage in terrorist activities of the sort Wessel described, Sterling thought. "The Sa'Nerra already have the advantage of numbers, and at the rate they're turning our own ships against us, I doubt they'd want us to stop building more."

"Read the file, Captain," Sterling snapped, tapping the chip in Sterling's breast pocket. "Everything you need is in there." Wessel then unlocked the door and waited for it to swish open.

"Commodore, you saw how twitchy even your own agents were at the sight of someone new," Sterling called out, unwilling to let Wessel brush him off so easily. "If we rock-up at New Danvers throwing accusations around, we could start a riot. People are on edge as it is."

"I'm sure you can handle it, Captain," Wessel replied, shooting Sterling an oily smile. He wafted a hand at Sterling and Banks in turn. "By the way, you two are out of uniform," he said, looking at Sterling's blue outfit with its distinctive silver stripe. "Ensure that you and your crew have changed into the correct SIB uniforms before you depart this station." Wessel then set foot outside the door before pausing and turning back. "I've already taken the liberty of having the Invictus repainted," he added, the oily smile broadening further. "Now, I have business elsewhere in the sector that requires my immediate departure," Wessel spoke as if his urgent business was the most important matter in the entire galaxy. "Welcome to the SIB, Captain. Do not let me down."

Wessel promptly stepped out into the corridor and the door slid shut behind him. A millisecond later, Banks turned the air blue with a string of very creative curses. Sterling would have joined in with a few of his own, were it not for the fact that his first officer had already hollered every expletive known to humanity.

"Does the Omega Directive apply to that little shi..." Banks began, but Sterling was quick to shoot her a reproving look. "Does it apply to the esteemed

Commodore?" she finished, quickly adjusting the last part of her sentence to remain duly respectful to their new CO.

"Maybe during the course of our very important investigation in C-sector, we can prove that he's an aide to the emissaries," Sterling replied. "In which case, yes."

"I don't think we're that lucky," Banks hit back. "And do we really have to dress in those secret-police SIB uniforms? We may as well paint a target on our backs."

Sterling rested back on the table in the empty office. Banks' comment, though said flippantly, was not far from the truth. "We need to be careful, Mercedes," he replied, feeling a sudden chill spasm throughout his body. "Both of the Wessels have it in for us, and with Griffin out of the picture, we're in a bad position. One wrong move and Wessel will pounce."

"So, what do we do now?" said Banks, folding her powerful arms across her chest.

Sterling shrugged. "We head to the stores and requisition the new uniforms," he replied, with a fatalistic air. "It'll take them a few hours to sort that out, no doubt, during which time I imagine Wessel will have painted a giant SIB logo on the hull of the Invictus."

Banks laughed, but then saw that Sterling was stony-faced and silent.

"If that happens then screw the Omega Directive," Banks said. Her muscles were so taut, she was on the verge of tearing her uniform. "The Banks Directive will be in effect instead. And that's a whole lot worse, especially for anyone named Wessel..."

STERLING HAD REACHED his twenty-sixth push-up when the door chime sounded in his quarters. Pausing in the plank position, he glanced up at one of the light panels in the ceiling of his quarters.

"Who is at the door, computer?" Sterling asked, pushing out another rep as he did so. The door opened and Sterling cursed. "Computer, we really need to have a little chat about this door-opening business," he said, still holding himself in plank.

"Did I miss something?" called Mercedes Banks from the corridor outside. "Unless I'm mistaken, it's just past fifteen-hundred hours, not first thing in the morning?"

Sterling adjusted his balance so that he could pivot on one hand, then waved Banks inside. "Come in and close the door before one of the crew sees me like this," he said, slamming his palm back down on the deck to stop himself toppling over.

Banks obliged and was dutifully followed in by Jinx the

beagle hound. Her cybernetic leg clanked tunefully across the metal deck as she ran over to Sterling and tried to lick his face.

"Damn it, control your animal," snapped Sterling, trying to fend off the dog. Jinx made a series of curious howling noises before jumping up on the bottom of Sterling's bed. He glowered at the dog as she circled around a few times, then curled up.

"You also haven't changed," said Banks, noticing that Sterling was still wearing his regular blue Fleet pants. His old tunic was slung over the top of his chair. "Are you sure you're feeling alright?"

"I'm fine, I'm just catching up on the fifty I missed a couple of days back," said Sterling, pushing out another few reps in the process. "I figured since I'm changing into the black Gestapo gear, anyway, I may as well do it now before I grab a shower."

Banks huffed then stepped behind Sterling so that he could no longer see her, which made him immediately nervous. He craned his neck to look at his first officer, but she remained just off to his side, arms folded.

"What are you doing there?" Sterling asked. "You're making me uneasy."

"Just carry on, Captain, don't mind me," replied Banks, breezily.

Sterling shook his head, then continued his set. He'd lost count of the number of push-ups he'd already completed so decided to start from twenty-five. Three reps in, he felt a weight pressing down on his body, as if someone had just dumped a sack of flour on his back.

"What the hell?" Sterling said, again craning his neck to look at Banks. She had her boot on Sterling's back and was pressing down hard.

"We don't want this to be too easy, do we?" said Banks, with a wicked smile. "It's good for you, Captain. You need to build some extra muscle." Then her expression changed and she looked suddenly remorseful. "Unless you don't think you can handle it, of course?"

Sterling snorted a laugh. "That's not going to work, Mercedes," he lied. They both knew full well that Banks' challenge would not go unanswered. "But go ahead, do your worst."

The last suggestion was foolish, Sterling realized, and it wasn't long before he regretted it. The next fifteen push-ups were excruciating. Not only were his chest and arms burning, but it felt like his spine was going to snap in half too.

"Had enough yet, Captain?" said Banks, goading him on.

"If you ever leave Fleet, you'd make one hell of a personal trainer," Sterling gasped, reaching push-up number forty-eight. "Though I don't think you'd get many clients," he added, managing the last two push-ups before collapsing face-first on the deck.

Banks finally lifted her boot and muscular thigh off Sterling's back then stepped into his line of sight. From the look on her face, it was clear that she had enjoyed torturing Sterling immensely.

"I'm actually impressed," Banks said, folding her arms. "I didn't think you'd get those last couple."

Sterling flopped onto his back, his breathing still labored and heavy. "I'll be out-lifting you in no time," he said, smiling.

"Unlikely," replied Banks, casually. She then wandered over to Sterling's wardrobe, where his dark navy SIB uniform was already hanging on the outside. She casually picked a piece of fluff off the shoulder and flicked it onto the deck. "Hurry up and get showered, or we'll arrive at New Danvers before you're even dressed."

Sterling pushed himself up and headed past his first-officer into the rest-room. His original plan was to complete a fairly relaxed set that wouldn't cause him to break a sweat. However, the arrival of Banks and her unfeasibly powerful legs had changed that.

"Grab me another tank top, will you?" said Sterling, turning on the faucet and hurriedly washing himself. He then tore off the one he was wearing and tossed it to the deck before setting about unbuckling his belt. Banks appeared with a fresh top in hand just as Sterling's pants flopped to the deck.

"You could have warned me, Captain," Banks said, holding out the tank top, while turning away, modestly.

"What's the matter, Commander?" Sterling replied, taking the garment and pulling it on. "Scared of a pair of shorts and a hairy chest?"

"It's scary how little muscle you have," Banks hit back.

Sterling replied with a sarcastic, "ha, ha," then began to quickly don his new SIB uniform. Other than the near black coloring and garish "SIB" logo on the shoulder, it was the same cut as his other uniform and so at least felt comfortable and familiar.

"Computer, how long until we reach New Danvers?" Sterling queried, buttoning up his tunic.

"We will arrive in orbit of New Danvers in one hour, twelve minutes, Captain," the computer replied, cheerfully.

"We'd better get to the bridge then," Sterling said, realizing that they'd made more rapid progress to the colony than he'd expected. No doubt this was due to his ever-busy chief engineer's near-continual process of tweaking and enhancing the Marauder's engines.

"We can just leave Jinx where she is," said Banks, pointing to the hound, who was now snoring softly on the bed. Sterling had completely forgotten the dog was there.

"Not at chance in hell," replied Sterling, robustly. "I don't want to wander back in here and find that it's left me a present in a place I least expect."

"She went not long ago," said Banks with a shrug.

"Went where?" replied Sterling. Then he held up his hand to stop Banks before she answered. "Never mind, I really don't want to know," he added hastily. "Come on, we can drop it back in your quarters before we head to the bridge."

"Jinx is a she, as you well know," replied Banks. She then let out a series of short sharp whistles, as if she was trying to get a border collie to herd sheep. Jinx pricked up her ears then jumped down off the bed and gave herself a little shake. "Go on, Jinx, let's leave the grumpy captain's quarters," Banks said to the dog, speaking to the animal as if it were a baby.

Sterling headed out after his first officer and her dutiful familiar and set off towards Banks' quarters, which were on the same deck. However, they hadn't gone far before the dog became agitated.

"What's wrong with the damn thing now?" said Sterling, scowling at the hound, which was scampering around the corridor, nose to the ground.

"Beats me," said Banks, shrugging.

Suddenly, Jinx shot off ahead, nose still to the deck and stopped outside the door to the shuttle bay control room. Sterling and Banks looked at each other, both sensing something was wrong.

"Go to neural comms," said Sterling, tapping his neural interface and linking to Banks.

Both then headed off in pursuit of the hound, who was now scratching at the base of the door and growling. Banks entered her ID codes then opened a weapons locker, pulling out two pistols, while Sterling extended his neural link to include Lieutenant Shade.

"Lieutenant, get a security detail to deck two, shuttle control," Sterling said through the link. "Just you and a couple of commandoes. It may be nothing, but I'm not taking any chances."

"Aye, sir," Shade replied, smartly. His weapons officer then dropped off the link.

"Security is en-route, we should wait for them to arrive," Sterling said, accepting one of the pistols from his first officer.

Sterling was then alerted by the familiar sound of a door swishing open further along the corridor. He looked just in time to see a figure flash across the corridor and enter another section. Jinx immediately set off after the intruder, barking aggressively.

"Jinx, hush!" said Banks, pressing a finger to her lips. The dog obeyed and stopped just outside the door, though Sterling could still detect a low, threatening growl from the animal.

"This is the main computer core," said Sterling, approaching the new location. "If we have a saboteur on board then crippling the core would knock out our sensors and comms."

Banks nodded. "We should take them alive," she added. "We have no idea what other systems they could have tampered with."

Sterling raised his pistol. "We go in now, no time to wait."

Banks moved to the other side of the door and also made herself ready. Sterling then started a countdown from three over their neural link before punching the door release. Banks moved in first, moving right with Sterling following swiftly behind to check the left side of the room. He saw a shadow hiding behind one of the data clusters and was about to issue a challenge when Jinx raced inside and ran at the figure.

"Jinx, no!" Banks cried, but it was too late. The beagle was already standing in front of the computer core, barking and growling for all she was worth.

"I surrender!" a terrified voice called out from behind

the data cluster. "Don't let the beast maul me to death!"

Sterling cursed and enabled the safety on his pistol before lowering it to his side. Banks looked shocked that he would lower his defenses, but Sterling knew he wasn't in any danger. He recognized the voice.

"Get out here, Colicos, right now," Sterling called out to the shadow. "Or I'll have Jinx bite your face off."

"Argh! Keep it away, vicious beast!" Colicos yelled.

Banks also made her weapon safe then picked up Jinx, who continued to bark and growl at Colicos.

"It's okay, the vicious attack hound is gone," Sterling said, with no small amount of sarcasm. "Now get out here, before I lose patience and start shooting."

Colicos scrambled out from behind the data cluster just as Lieutenant Shade and two armed commandoes burst into the computer core. Colicos thrust his hands up and jolted back in surprise, banging his head on the data cluster in the process.

"It's okay, Lieutenant, our intruder isn't dangerous," Sterling said, waving off the commandoes. "And he certainly isn't welcome," Sterling added, stepping toward Colicos, who still had his hands up. "You're supposed to be in the brig on A-COP. How the hell did you get back on board my ship?"

Colicos smiled. "Let's just say that the SIB are not quite as adept as your fine officers are," the scientist said, shooting a saccharine smile to Banks.

Banks responded by thrusting Jinx at him, causing the dog to bark and growl even more fiercely. Colicos again jolted back, banging his head for a second time.

"Okay, based on what I saw of Wessel's SIB morons, I accept that you could probably slip past them," Sterling said, folding his arms. "The question is why come here? It's not like you're my favorite person right now."

"Better the devil you know, Captain," Colicos replied, becoming more serious.

"You really don't know me, and you don't want to, either," Sterling hit back. He glanced across to Banks. "Get to the bridge and set a course back to A-COP," he added. "Commodore Wessel's witch-hunt on New Danvers will have to wait."

"No, please!" Colicos cut in, making the mistake of moving toward Sterling. Shade intercepted the scientist and pressed the barrel of her pistol underneath his chin. "Please, Captain," Colicos pleaded again, struggling to talk due to the pressure from the pistol jammed under his jaw. "Please don't send me back there. I will not become Fleet's puppet. I do not deserve it!"

Sterling sighed, then stepped closer to Colicos so that their faces were only inches apart. "You don't deserve it?" he repeated, scarcely able to believe the nerve of the man. "After what you did, you're lucky I didn't vaporize you when I found you. The least you can do is try to fix your mess." He reached up to the power dial on Lieutenant Shade's pistol and turned the setting to maximum. "And honestly, doctor, I don't care what the SIB do to you in order to make you comply. One way or another, you're going to create a way to nullify the neural weapon. That's the only way you come out of this alive."

Colicos was silent, his body shivering as if he was

outdoors in an Alaskan winter wearing only shorts and a t-shirt. Sterling backed away, then met Shade's eyes. His weapons officer looked like she was hoping Sterling was about to give the order to blast Colicos' head off. However, as much as he wanted rid of the genius scientist, he knew Fleet needed his expertise badly.

"Take him to the brig, Lieutenant, and post a guard, twenty-four seven," Sterling said. "If he manages to pull another Houdini act, you're authorized to use whatever force is necessary, short of killing him, to get him back."

The faintest flicker of a smile crossed Shade's lips. She peered into Colicos' eyes and pressed the barrel of the weapon even harder into the scientist's flesh.

"Does that include the removal of limbs, Captain?" Shade asked, her gaze still locked onto Colicos.

"Stick to below the waist if you can, Lieutenant," Sterling replied. "He'll need his hands, though I guess we can replace the other one too if needs be."

Colicos made a sort of squeaking sound, which Sterling assumed was an attempt at a laugh. The scientist clearly believed he was joking. It was an assumption Sterling hoped that Colicos wouldn't be foolish enough to test. Shade then began to march the scientist out of the computer core, flanked by her two commandoes.

"Wait, there's more!" Colicos yelled, though Shade did not stop. "Commodore Wessel does not want a way to reverse the effects of the neural weapon. He merely wants a detector."

"Hold up, Lieutenant," Sterling called out. Shade

stopped and spun Colicos around to face him. "What do you mean he only wants a detector?"

"Exactly that, Captain," Colicos replied. There was excitement in his voice now. The scientist had clearly said something of importance. Something the man believed would give him leverage. "He is only concerned with detecting those who are turned. That is the function of the SIB, after all. His orders did not extend to reversing the effects of the neural weapon."

Sterling studied the scientist's face, which was suddenly looking much more like its sixty-plus years. Stress was clearly taking its toll on Colicos.

"If you're lying to me, doctor, then I promise you won't live to regret it," Sterling said.

"I know what you are, Captain Sterling, and believe me I would not dare test your commitment," Colicos replied. The scientist was suddenly more composed and self-assured. "I swear on my honor that what I tell you is the truth."

Banks snorted a laugh. "On your honor? You ran out of credit on that account a long time ago, asshole."

"Fine, I swear on my life then," Colicos hit back, risking a glower at Sterling's first-officer.

"If I keep you on this ship, it's for one reason and one reason alone, doctor," Sterling said, causing the scientist to again meet his eyes. "I need a way to reverse the effects of that neural weapon, or at the very least defend against it." Colicos opened his mouth, though Sterling was quick to shut him down. "And I don't want to hear your crap about it not being possible," he snapped. "You're the genius. You either come up with something, or I airlock your worthless carcass into space. Is that understood?"

Colicos forced down a hard, dry swallow. "Perfectly understood, Captain."

Sterling sighed again and shook his head. He suspected he'd live to regret it, but he'd made his decision.

"Take him away, Lieutenant," Sterling said to Shade. "And keep it quiet. As far as anyone else is concerned, Colicos is not here, understood?"

"Aye, Captain," Shade replied. She then spun Colicos around to face the door and jabbed her pistol into his back to usher him on. Moments later, Colicos, Shade and the commandoes were gone, and Jinx finally stopped growling.

"I take it we're not heading back to A-COP then?" Banks asked, while stroking Jinx's ears.

"No, we continue with the mission to New Danvers," Sterling replied, rubbing the back of his neck, "and we just hope that Griffin shows up in time for us to do something useful with Colicos."

"And what if she's gone for good?" Banks asked.

"Let's not go down that road until it's the only one left to us," Sterling locked eyes with his first-officer. "But one thing's for sure. I'm not sitting out the rest of this war with Wessel pulling our strings."

Banks nodded. "I'll take Jinx back to my quarters, then see you on the bridge," she said, placing the beagle onto the deck.

The hound looked up at Sterling, wagging her tail. He smiled at the dog and threw up a salute. "Good work, Acting Ensign Jinx. You're dismissed."

CAPTAIN STERLING and Commander Banks stepped off the cargo ramp of the Invictus and onto the heavily-tarnished surface of the landing pad at New Danvers. Sterling hugged his jacket tighter around his body as a bitter wind whipped across the exposed docking platform. It seemed that no matter how he held his head, rain still managed to sting his face.

"I'm even getting rained on from underneath me, how is that even possible?" Sterling grumbled, as the wind whipped another dagger-like spray of water onto his cheeks.

"This has got to be the most miserable planet I've ever seen," replied Banks, braving the elements to look up at the mud-brown clouds swirling overhead.

Figuring that there was little point attempting to avoid getting wet, Sterling raised his gaze and looked out across the hyper-industrial complex of New Danvers Colony. Factories and tower blocks littered the horizon for as far as he could see. Only some haze-covered mountains in the distance broke up the sea of man-made structures and machinery. Even then, Sterling observed that many of the mountains had been ransacked for resources. Some looked like a god-like being had reached down from the heavens and taken a scoop out of the rock with a giant spoon.

"This is the economic and environmental cost of building thousands of warships over the last fifty years," said Sterling, wincing as the wind lashed more rain against the side of his face. "This planet and others like it have already paid the price for the Earth-Sa'Nerra war."

"This place is going to look like Eden compared to Earth, if the Sa'Nerra get their leathery fingers on it," Banks commented.

As usual, Sterling agreed. If they failed in their mission then the Sa'Nerra would reduce humanity's birthplace to an ash-covered wasteland.

A door at the end of the walkway opened and three figures stepped out, silhouetted by the bright light behind them. Unlike Sterling, they were dressed for the weather, wearing long, thick trench coats with hoods that completely covered their heads and faces. Sterling wiped the water from his eyes then set off to meet the welcoming party, allowing the Invictus' cargo ramp to whir shut behind him.

"I'm Rhonda Reese, the administrator here," the hooded figure at the front of the group announced as Sterling approached.

"I'm Captain Lucas Sterling from the Special Investigations Branch, and this is my first-officer, Commander Mercedes Banks," Sterling replied, gesturing to Banks with a soaking-wet outstretched arm. "Pleased to meet you, Administrator Reese." Sterling offered his hand to the woman. However, Reese just looked at it through the transparent face shield built into her hood before again meeting Sterling's eyes.

"If you'll follow me, I'll show you where you can work," the administrator said, refusing Sterling's offer of friendship and turning sharply back toward to the entrance instead.

"That doesn't bode well," Banks commented, as the trio from New Danvers departed.

"It's no more than I expected," Sterling replied, shaking the water off his hand and shoving it inside his jacket pocket. "We can expect a pretty rough reception all-round. No-ones likes to feel that they're being watched and are under suspicion."

Banks nodded as they set off along the water-logged walkway towards the terminal building. "I don't blame them," she said, her heavy boots kicking up a muddy spray that dirtied the legs of her pants. "These people slog day and night to produce resources for Fleet with no reward and no thanks. Then we come along accusing some of them of being collaborators and traitors."

Sterling stepped through the door, squinting to shield his eyes from the intense yellow lighting inside the room. Administrator Reese had already removed her coat and hung it on a hanger above a grate that collected the water pouring off the surface of the material. Sterling peered through the grate and saw that the drainage system beneath the floor extended deeper into the facility. A fast-flowing stream of murky water was flowing toward an outlet on the external wall.

"The three people you are looking for haven't been seen for more than a week," Reese said, rubbing her hands together to warm them up. Her two companions stood to her rear. Both were gruff-looking six-foot-tall brutes, covered in an intricate patchwork of tattoos that blanketed every visible patch of skin. "Their disappearing act also means that we're behind on our quota, so keep your interviews brief. I can't afford to have any more workers taken off the floor. Unless Fleet is happy for us to miss a few shipments, of course."

"We'll do our best to be discreet and get out of your hair as soon as possible," Sterling replied. He didn't resent the administrator giving them a frosty reception and genuinely didn't want to disrupt her operation. "We'll start by checking out the suspects' quarters, if you can provide their locations and give us access."

Reese nodded to one of the men behind her, who then removed a personal data assistant from his pocket and began working on it. The man's inputs were slow and clumsy, on account of his calloused, stubby fingers.

"I honestly don't know what you expect to find here, Captain," Reese said as the man handed her the PDA. "The only Fleet ships that ever come here are freighters and escort ships to guard the convoys, and none of them ever land." She pointed to the rain hammering against the window outside. "I think you can probably figure out why. This is hardly a vacation spot."

"We spend most of our time in space, so real gravity

and real weather is a welcome change, Administrator," Sterling replied. In truth, he didn't want to spend a second longer than was necessary on New Danvers, but he thought being gracious and charming might improve his relations with the facility's leader. However, from the look on Reese's face, he could see that the woman hadn't believed a word he had said.

"I have a nice little cabin in the woods that you can rent if you like, Captain?" Reese replied, sarcastically. She then snapped her fingers. "Oh, wait, there are no woods on this godforsaken planet." The two brutes to Reese's rear let out low, rumbling chuckles and the administrator held out the PDA to Sterling, who wasted no time in accepting it from her. He could see she was already itching to leave. "This will direct you to the crew quarters and to the missing workers' individual rooms," Reese went on. "But like I said, they haven't been seen for days. In fact, they went missing after the last SIB ship showed up here, snooping around. If they didn't find anything, I don't know what you expect to gain by looking again."

"Which other SIB ship was here?" Sterling asked, handing the PDA to Banks who turned it on and began to review the contents.

"Looked a lot like your one out there."

"A Marauder?"

Reese shrugged. "We're ironmongers, Captain, we just make metal. What Fleet does with it is none of my concern. But the ship looked the same, more or less."

"Did you meet its Captain?" Sterling asked. "Was his name Wessel?"

"I was over in sector seven at the time so didn't meet them personally." Reese appeared bored of their conversation and as such her willingness to cooperate was at a low ebb. "They conducted a brief investigation, cited some 'irregularities' then were gone the same day, before I got back."

Sterling frowned. There was nothing in the briefing files that indicated another Fleet ship had landed at New Danvers recently. *If Wessel was here then why the hell didn't the asshole tell me?* he wondered. The more he dug into the details of their mission, the more it troubled him.

"Do you know what these 'irregularities' were that the last Fleet crew found?" Sterling asked the bored-looking administrator.

Reese shook her head. "Something about unusual off-book transmissions," she shrugged again. "But I checked the logs and found nothing, so I don't know what the hell they were talking about. A day later, those three workers you're here about went AWOL."

Sterling glanced at Banks, who was also frowning. There was clearly more to the disappearance of the workers than Sterling had been told and, so far, nothing made sense.

"I'll tell you this for free, Captain," Reese then added, drawing Sterling's gaze back to the administrator. "You won't find anyone on New Danvers who is turned, if that's why you're here. Hell, the Sa'Nerra wouldn't need to turn half the people here to get us to see their side of things."

"What the hell do you mean by that?" snapped Banks. Any talk of sympathizing with the enemy always drew an immediate and aggressive reaction from her. "They're butchers who have been killing us by the thousands for the last fifty years."

"Seems to me those emissaries are trying to end the war peacefully," Reese hit back. "Yet all Fleet wants us to do is make more beams and more deck plates and more rivets, so you can build more damned warships. And now here you are, accusing us of being spies and traitors," she snorted derisively. "Fleet has a damned cheek."

"The emissaries are liars," replied Banks, practically growling the words at the administrator. Her hand had tightened around the PDA and Sterling could hear the casing creak under the pressure of her grip. "They'll destroy earth and kill us all if we don't stop them."

"So you Fleet types keep saying, Commander," Reese hit back, unmoved by Banks' impassioned riposte. "All I know is that my people work day and night with no thanks and no possibility of reprieve. It's no better than prison labor."

"Fleet make sacrifices too, Administrator, Sterling cut in. "I've lost count of the number of officers and crew that had died in this war. But if we lose, everyone dies."

"The war has to end someday, Captain," Reese replied, her tone as icy and cold as the rain dripping off Sterling's jacket. "So what if it ends with us losing?" The administrator gestured to her two henchman who moved over to one of the internal doors and pulled it open. "Death can't be any worse than another fifty years of this crap," she added, glancing back at Sterling.

Curiously, Sterling didn't see anger or bitterness in the administrator's eyes, but resignation. Like many of those on the factory worlds, she had likely been born on New Danvers and had known nothing else. The average life expectancy of a factory worker was twenty years lower than the Fleet average, and the rate of accidental deaths and suicides was the highest in all sectors of United Governments society. Even so, for Reese to suggest death as an acceptable resolution to the workers' perpetual condition was shocking, even to someone who had seen and experienced loss on the level Sterling had done.

"I trust you have everything you need, Captain?" Reese added, though she left no time for Sterling to reply before continuing. "Notify me when you intend to leave." Administrator Reese then turned her back on Sterling and Banks and sauntered out of the room, closely followed by her two stocky companions.

"Something doesn't add up about this mission," mused Banks, who had returned to studying the PDA. "People go missing all the time, usually because they're on drug-fueled benders. In the week since the three we're here to investigate went AWOL, a dozen more have disappeared from this sector alone."

Sterling stepped closer to Banks and peered down at the screen of the PDA. The device was grubby and old, and the screen was cracked, though Sterling couldn't be sure that the latter damage wasn't due to Banks' excessive grip.

"The difference is that the others all turn up sooner or later," said Sterling, looking at the incident reports. "They're either caught and made to work even harder as punishment, or they wash up dead in one of drainage channels."

Banks highlighted a recent incident report and her eyes grew wide. "The homicide rate here is worse than in an entire season of 'The Streets of New LA'," she said, referring to a popular Fleet crime drama on TV. "This place might actually benefit from the Sa'Nerra bombing it from orbit."

Sterling huffed a laugh then found himself instinctively placing his hand onto his pistol. Rather than making Administrator Reese nervous, she had made him feel even more on-edge and under threat. "Let's check out the quarters of these missing workers," he said, feeling suddenly exposed. "Hopefully, we can wrap this up quickly and get the hell off this planet."

"Should I get Shade to provide a security escort?" Banks asked. She waved the pad at Sterling. The screen was still showing the last month's homicide report. "I don't want to end up as another statistic."

Sterling shook his head. "No, we'll just draw even more attention to ourselves," he replied.

Then he glanced down at his SIB uniform, remembering Banks' comment about how it was like having a target painted on their backs. Across the other side of the terminal room, he saw some lighter rain jackets hanging above the drainage grates. He pulled off his SIB jacket and swapped it with the jacket on the hanger.

"What do you think?" he asked, stretching his arms out wide to give Banks a better look.

"I think it looks like that jacket is older than you are," Banks replied. "But I guess it'll help us blend in a little more."

Banks then swapped her jacket for one on another of the hangers. However, as she pulled it on, her nose turned up in disgust.

"Hell, this smells worse than one of your sweat-soaked t-shirts," she complained.

"You should be used to it then," Sterling hit back. He removed his weapons belt and hung it on the rack before sliding his pistol into the pocket of his new jacket. "Come on, let's go and play detectives," he said, waiting for Banks to conceal her own pistol.

"I'm sure we'll just find these missing people in a gutter somewhere," Banks said, zipping up the pocket where she'd hidden her pistol.

"To hell with the missing workers, I want to know why Wessel was here a week ago," Sterling hit back, fixing Banks with a meditative stare. "That asshole is up to something, and I'm willing to bet that whatever it is, it's not good news for us."

Banks stood guard while Sterling approached the door to the missing worker's apartment in the residential sector. Wiping a layer of grime from the name plaque with the sleeve of his jacket, Sterling read the name out loud.

"Amy Camargo. I think she was the first on the list of three names that Wessel gave us."

Banks glanced at the name plaque, while still keeping half an eye on the corridor. The residential sector was a constant hive of activity and it was taking all of their concentration to stay alert to potential dangers.

"Shall we be polite and knock?" asked Banks, with a wry smile.

"That's not really our style, is it?" said Sterling, returning his first officer's mischievous smile. He then tried the handle of the old-fashioned door, but it was locked. "See if you can get this open while I watch the corridor," he added, stepping aside.

Banks moved in front of the door and took two steps

back. Sterling could see her insanely powerful thigh muscle tense up.

"I mean hack it with the PDA Reese gave us, not kick it down," Sterling said, speaking up quickly enough to stop Banks in her tracks. "That hardly counts as us being discreet, does it?"

"I guess not, but I prefer my way," grumbled Banks, removing the PDA that the facility's administrator had given them from her jacket pocket.

"We'll try your way next, if the PDA doesn't work," replied Sterling. His hand was also pressed inside his jacket pocket, although his was wrapped around the grip of his plasma pistol rather than a PDA. It had been this way for almost all of their journey on foot through the sprawling residential sector of the factory complex. Despite their worker-style jackets providing some camouflage, Sterling and Banks had still stuck out compared to the residents of the sector. The hundreds of off-shift workers who were milling around the recreational zones had a distinct fashion and style that was worlds apart from the regimental orderliness of Sterling and Banks' appearance. However, the real giveaway that neither of them belonged on New Danvers was the tattoos – everyone had them while Sterling and Banks did not. Even so, despite frequent suspicious glances and whispered comments as they progressed deeper into the complex, no-one stopped them or even spoke a word to them.

Banks hurriedly worked on the PDA, then held the device to the door lock. A few seconds later the mechanism operated. She tried the handle of the hinged-door and it swung open with a fatigued groan.

"See, no excessive violence required," Sterling said, removing the pistol from his pocket and stepping inside the room.

"Not yet, anyway," Banks replied, still covering the corridor.

Sterling switched on the lights, which fizzed and blinked like archaic neon tubes. However, once the room had finally been bathed in the grubby yellow glow from the strip lights, it was clear that no-one was home.

"And I thought the standard crew quarters on the Invictus were compact," said Sterling, slipping the pistol back inside his pocket. "This has to be half the size."

Banks followed Sterling inside and closed the door. The yellow lights inside the apartment hummed like a choir made up entirely of diseased bees.

"This place certainly looks lived in," commented Banks, which Sterling took as code to mean that the apartment was filthy. Empty food containers littered the floor and dirty clothes were piled up on the compact two-seater sofa, which appeared to double-up as a bed. "I think we need to get a deep-cleaning crew in here, before we start rummaging around."

"I don't think that will be necessary," said Sterling, dropping to a crouch and staring at a stain on the metal deck plating. "This looks like blood."

Banks moved closer and dropped down beside Sterling, using the torch function of the PDA to illuminate the patch in more clarity.

"Are you sure it isn't just hot sauce?" she quipped. Sterling shot her a look that told her in no uncertain terms that her humor – as usual – was misplaced.

"I've seen enough blood to know the difference between DNA and sauce," Sterling hit back.

Following the trail of blood splats Sterling found himself looking over at the door. Taking Banks' hand, he redirected the aim of the torchlight on the PDA so that it was shining on the door handle. Another dark smear was visible, coating the handle and the panel of the door surrounding it.

"Looks like Miss Camargo didn't go willingly," said Sterling, standing up. He then cursed and shook his head. "None of this is making any sense," he said, as much to himself as to his first-officer.

The handle of the door was suddenly pressed down from the opposite side. Sterling felt his heart-rate spike and he pulled the pistol from his pocket as the door creaked open. The tattooed face of a man appeared through the crack. He immediately spotted Sterling and Banks, eyes growing wide with surprise, then slammed the door shut. The thud of fading bootsteps was then heard outside.

"Shit, we have to get after him!" Sterling called out, grabbing the handle and yanking the door open.

Banks rushed out first, barging through a group of off-shift workers and scattering them to the floor like ten-pins. Sterling followed, blocking out the angry curses and aggressive shoves of the workers as they climbed to their feet, and raced after her.

"I don't see him," Sterling said, as he caught up with

Banks, who had already reached a junction in the labyrinthine residential sector.

"There! Black jacket with 'Shift Seven Seven' on the back," cried Banks, pointing along the corridor to her right before setting off at a sprint.

Sterling still didn't see the man, but he followed his first officer anyway, his progress made easier by the fact Banks had steamrolled more off-shift workers out of her way as she went.

"Go to neural!" Sterling yelled, tapping his neural interface and running after his first officer.

More angry curses and waved fists were hurled in his direction as he leapt over the bodies of factory workers who had been flattened by the momentum of Mercedes Banks. He felt wetness splash across his face and realized that some of the workers were spitting at him as he went. The mass of bodies in his path continued to impede his progress and soon Banks had widened her lead over him.

"I can't keep up with you, but don't let the man out of your sight," Sterling said over their neural link.

Their quarry then made a sharp right, leaping over a makeshift barrier with the words "No Entry" written in bold red letters. Banks continued her pursuit, smashing though the barrier like it was made of Styrofoam. The worker with the "Shift 77" jacket then ran up a flight of metal stairs, pushing through a door that led into a maintenance area. Banks hammered through the door moments later and Sterling lost sight of her.

"Mercedes, hold up!" Sterling called out through their neural link, but he could feel his connection to Banks fading. The dense metal construction of the residential district and sheer mass of other minds around him were making it difficult to maintain a link. "Get out of my way!" Sterling yelled, pushing irate workers aside in a desperate effort to reach his first officer. He took a punch to the back and more spittle landed on his jacket and neck, causing the fire in his belly to ignite. Sterling hammered a left cross into the face of the worker who had spat on him, then raised his plasma pistol and fired into the air. "Get back, right now!" Sterling yelled as debris from the blast rained down on the crowd. Most of the workers did as he ordered, but one man made the mistake of taking another swing at him. Sterling ducked under the wild right hand then hammered an elbow strike to the worker's throat. The man rocked back and Sterling blasted him in the foot, destroying it below the ankle. The worker cried out in pain and collapsed to the deck, grasping his shin as if he'd just received a brutal soccer tackle. Sterling aimed his pistol at the rest of the crowd. "I said get back, now!" he yelled again, and this time the crowd obeyed.

Suddenly, alarms blared out inside the corridor and a strip of red light across the top of the wall pulsed on and off, bathing the faces of the workers in a blood-red hue. It reminded Sterling of the general alert condition on the Invictus, except on this occasion, Sterling was not surrounded by the safety of his bridge and crew.

"Security Alert, weapons discharge detected," an automated announcement blared out over a PA system. "All workers are to immediately return to their quarters.

Repeat, all workers are to immediately return to their quarters."

The crowd thinned rapidly as panicked workers ran away along the corridors in order to comply with the directive. However, three men held their ground. Sterling saw one of them pull an improvised blade from inside his oversized brown jacket and come forward.

"You don't want to do this," said Sterling, aiming his pistol at the man. "I *will* kill you."

The man didn't react and continued his measured advance. His two companions spread out behind him, also drawing shards of what looked like metal or sharpened plastic from their jackets. Under the blood-red alert lights, Sterling could just make out the number '77' tattooed below the man's right eye. Glancing across to the other two workers, he noticed that both had the same tattoo in the exact the same location.

"Last warning," Sterling said standing his ground. "One more step, and you're dead."

The worker stopped and smiled, then Sterling was grabbed from behind. He felt a wire tighten around his throat and instinctively he pushed back, pressing his head against his attacker and stepping into him. With some of the pressure relieved, Sterling reached up and grabbed the wire that had been wrapped around his neck. Twisting his body into the man, he struck his attacker in the groin, forcing the man to relinquish his hold before blasting him at point blank range.

The other attackers were on top of him before the dead worker even hit the ground, but Sterling managed to keep hold of his pistol. Firing again, he blasted the kneecap off another attacker, blowing the man's leg off below the knee. Sterling then felt metal and plastic shards stabbing his flesh, but the thick worker's jacket he was wearing stopped the blades from penetrating too deeply into his body. His pistol was then knocked from his grasp, but Sterling did not let up. Evading another strike, Sterling caught his attackers' arm and broke it at the wrist, causing the man to scream in pain. Stripping the shard from his attackers' grasp, Sterling then plunged it into the man's neck and hammered it deep into his flesh with a powerful palm strike.

Only one man now remained, and this one quickly turned and fled. Sterling spotted his plasma pistol on the ground and recovered it before taking aim and firing. The plasma blast obliterated the worker's right shoulder, sending him down, screaming in agony. Sterling pursued, shaking off the pain of his own stab injuries and kicked the man over onto his back.

"Who are you?!" Sterling yelled, aiming his pistol at the man's head. "Answer me now!"

"It was a job that's all!" the man cried, cradling his injured shoulder.

Sterling kicked the man's hands away and stepped on his neck. "Who paid you?!" he yelled. "Tell me!"

Sterling then caught sight of another figure in his peripheral vision and dropped to a crouch moments before a gunshot rang out in the corridor. Sterling fired back, missing the man by inches as more bullets flew toward him, skipping off the deck and walls with sharp metallic pings. Sterling held his nerve and fired again, hitting the gunman in the gut. The blast hollowed out the worker's intestines and spilled the contents of his stomach onto the deck. Sterling continued to cover the gunman for a couple of seconds to make sure he was dead then returned his aim to the man on the ground. However, the worker with the '77' tattoo was already dead, blood oozing from a bullet wound to the top of his skull.

Cursing, Sterling kicked the man out of pure frustration, then tried to get his bearings. He spotted the stairwell and maintenance door that Banks had pushed through earlier, in pursuit of the first attacker, and set off at a sprint.

"Mercedes, come in!" Sterling called out in his mind, but the link was still down. Tapping his interface again, he reached out, trying to fight through the pain and fatigue to form a connection, but he had no success.

Cursing again, Sterling charged up the staircase and kicked open the door, weapon held ready. It was clear and he hurried on, moving into a larger area, filled with humming machines and flashing consoles.

"Mercedes, do you read me?" Sterling tried again through the link, but still the connection would not form.

Up ahead, he saw the bodies of more factory workers on the ground. Staying low, he crept closer to one and kicked the woman onto her back. Her neck had been broken, but Sterling could clearly see the '77' tattoo under her eye. Moving deeper into the room, he saw three other bodies on the ground, some with blast wounds and others with twisted and fractured limbs – the hallmark of Mercedes Banks. Then the mass of thrumming machines began to clear and he spotted his first officer. She was on her knees, hands pressed behind her head with her fingers interlaced. Two men stood to her rear with old-style firearms held ready. Off to the side was the man with the '77' jacket who had entered Amy Camargo's room and set the chase in motion. A chase that Sterling now knew was a set-up for the ambush that he'd so far evaded.

"That's close enough," the man wearing the '77' jacket called out, pressing the barrel of his firearm to the back of Banks' head. Sterling could now see that this worker also bore the same tattoo under his eye. "Who the hell are you anyway?" the man demanded.

"Who am I?" Sterling answered. The question made no sense. "Why the hell are you attacking us if you don't even know who we are?"

"Just answer the damn question!" the man roared, jabbing the barrel of the weapon into Banks' skull. If it were anyone else on their knees before the gunman, Sterling would have feared for their safety. However, he could see that Banks' eyes were wild. If the gunman didn't kill her, Banks was ready to tear him limb-from-limb.

"I'm Fleet Captain Lucas Sterling of the SIB, here to investigate the disappearance of three missing factory workers," Sterling replied, keeping half an eye on the other two men. "Now tell me who the hell you are, and why you're trying to kill us."

"You're Fleet?" said the man. The worker was not feigning surprise; Sterling could see that he was genuinely shocked.

"Yes, so put your weapons down and let my officer go," Sterling replied.

As Sterling spoke the words, he dabbed blood from a cut to his face with the back of his hand, brushing his neural interface as he did so. With the men guarding Banks distracted, Sterling saw that she also managed to unlock her fingers and brush the palm of her hand across her interface. Finally, Sterling felt the neural link between him and Banks solidify.

"Get ready to take them out, Mercedes," Sterling said through their secret connection.

"I'm ready." Sterling could feel that Banks was in discomfort, but more than anything he could feel her rage.

"Damn it, I told the guy that we don't deal with Fleet," the man in the '77' jacket complained.

"Someone paid you to do this?" Sterling asked.

"It doesn't matter now, what's done is done," said the man, brushing off Sterling's question.

"Who was it?" said Sterling. "Give me a name and you might still walk out of here alive."

The man in the '77' jacket laughed. "That's not how this goes down, Fleet," he hit back. "I was just curious who you were. I've never seen two people fight like you. I was worried you were a new gang, but since you're Fleet, I don't have anything to worry about, other than asking for another twenty percent on top of my usual fee."

Sterling knew his time was up and didn't wait for the man to kill Banks. Adjusting his aim, he blasted one of the gang members behind Banks, blowing a hole through the man's sternum and melting his heart. At the same time,

Banks butted her head into her captor's gut, sending him staggering backward. The firearm slipped from the worker's grasp and fell through a metal grating into the fast-flow gutter system. The remaining gunman returned fire moments later, but Sterling had already ducked into cover. Bullets pinged off the humming metal vat he was hiding behind, but unlike plasma weapons, Sterling knew that the old-fashioned firearm would not penetrate his cover. He also knew that the man had fired his last shot.

A wail of pain told Sterling that Banks had already sprang into action. Peering out from behind cover, Sterling saw Banks lift the gunman off the ground by his throat. The gang member's arms were already broken and hanging limp at his sides. The man in the '77' jacket then recovered and drew a blade, but Banks was ready. Pivoting and using her immense strength, Banks threw the gang member at the man. Sterling didn't know what was more satisfying – the look of unabridged terror on the gang member's face, or the thud of flesh and crunch of bone breaking as the two bodies collided.

Sterling moved out from cover and stepped up to the man in the '77' jacket. Banks had already advanced and had her boot pressed to the gang member's neck.

"Tell me who paid you to kill us," said Sterling, peering down at the gang member. Blood was pouring from the man's nose and mouth, and Sterling could see that several teeth had been knocked out, with more hanging by loose threads.

"I don't know," the man mumbled, spitting blood and teeth out as he struggled to speak, "and I didn't ask."

"That's unfortunate for you then, isn't it?" Sterling said, glancing at Banks and nodding.

"Wait!" the man cried, as Banks added pressure with her boot. "They had uniforms!" he spluttered. "Dark uniforms, and boots just like yours. That's all I know."

"Thank you for your cooperation," Sterling said before nodding to Commander Banks, who continued to increase the pressure on the man's neck. The defined muscles in her thigh were practically bursting through the fabric of her pants. The gang member croaked and spluttered and fought Banks as best he could, but it was futile. Finally, after a minute of struggling, the gang member's efforts, along with his life, expired.

"Commodore Wessel and I are going to have words when we get back to A-COP," Sterling said, shoving his plasma pistol back into his jacket pocket.

"Can't we forgo words and just tear that bastard's throat out?" Banks replied.

Sterling knew that she hadn't forgotten his directive to treat their new commander with the respect afforded by his rank. However, on this occasion, he let it slide. He felt exactly the same way.

"Why the hell would he set us up like this?" Sterling wondered, inspecting their new location more closely. "Even if he'd succeeded, an investigation would have still shone the spotlight onto him. It makes no sense."

Then he spotted some equipment set up against one of the large metal vats. It was newer than the other tarnished gear in the room and didn't look like it belonged on New Danvers. He moved over and inspected it more closely.

"Any idea what this is?" he asked as Banks approached and crouched at his side.

"It's the water purification system for the residential zone," said Banks, looking at the collection of vats in the room. She then knelt down and inspected the equipment that Sterling had seen. "This gear is attached to the inlet pipe that feeds the chemical purification compounds into the entire system."

Sterling felt a knot tighten in his stomach and began to increase the speed of his inspection. Then his fears were confirmed. Integrated into the equipment was a container filled with a white salt-like substance. The letters "KCN" were written on the side.

"Cyanide?" said Banks, scowling at the container.

Sterling nodded. "Isn't it convenient that they neatly labelled the container so even the dumbest investigating team could figure out what was going on," he added, sarcastically. He reached inside his jacket and removed his pistol. "We're being set up," he added, bitterly. "Wessel doesn't just want us dead, he wants to frame us as 'aides to the emissaries'. Then he can imply the connection to Griffin and take her down too."

Banks cursed, then collected one of the firearms that a dead gang member had dropped. "We have to get out of here," she said, looking around the room with anxious eyes. "If you're right then we don't have much time."

Heavy bootsteps then filtered into the room and seconds later a squad of commandoes in black SIB uniforms stormed the space. Banks raised her firearm, but

Sterling moved quickly to deflect her aim, pushing her arm down to the deck.

"Don't give them a reason, Mercedes," Sterling said, meeting his first officer's eyes, which were burning with hatred and resentment.

"Well, well, well, if it isn't Captain Lucas Sterling and the freak-of-nature, Mercedes Banks." Commodore Vernon Wessel stepped out of the shadows. His hands were pressed to the small of his back and a smug, self-righteous smile curled his lips.

"Or should I say, 'Emissary Sterling and Emissary Banks?" he added, with mock suspicion.

"This equipment is from the Invictus, sir," one of the commandoes called out. Another group had begun to inspect the equipment attached to the vats in the room. "The serial numbers match."

"Isn't that a surprise?" said Sterling, sarcastically. "I have to admit that this is low, even for you, Vernon."

"Don't speak to me, you turned traitor!" Wessel spat back. "I always suspected you to be an aide or an emissary. All that time in the Void, out of contact with the Fleet. Very suspicious, wouldn't you say?"

"Go to hell, you piece of shit," Sterling hit back.

The Commodore's smile widened, revealing rows of pristine white teeth.

"You first, Lucas." He turned to one of his commandoes. "Take them away."

STERLING AND BANKS were frog-marched through the narrow corridors of the residential sector, bookended by a pair of SIB agents to the front and rear. They each had their hands bound together in front of them, though Sterling guessed this was more for show, rather than as a genuine precaution against them escaping. Commodore Wessel was proudly marching at the head of the formation, barking at any factory worker who crossed his path to get out of his way. It was like the head of the SIB had just captured the most-wanted criminals in the known universe and was parading them for all to see.

"I need to activate my interface so I can contact Shade," Sterling whispered to Banks. "Can you break your binders?"

Sterling felt the butt of a plasma rifle hammer into his back. "No talking!" an agent barked at him.

"I can, but I have another idea," Banks whispered back.

She then jolted forward as the agent thudded the butt of his rifle into her back too.

"I said no talking!" the commando growled.

Sterling could see that Banks was about ready to break the binders and strangle the man, but instead she glanced over at him and mouthed the words, "Go with it..." Sterling frowned, wondering what "it" was before Banks barged into him and pinned him against the wall.

"This is your fault!" Banks snarled at Sterling. He was so taken aback that he was paralyzed with shock. Banks then reached up with her bound hands and tried to grab Sterling around the throat. However, as she did so she tapped Sterling's neural interface to activate it. "I'm going to spend the rest of my life in Grimaldi because of you!" Banks yelled, as two of the agents attempted to pull her away from Sterling. It took all four to finally drag her off him.

Commodore Wessel marched up to Sterling, who was still pressed against the wall in shock. Banks had played her role a little too convincingly for his liking.

"Oh dear, it appears that loyalty is a fleeting commodity in the ranks of the precious 'Omega Taskforce'," the Commodore said, smiling like a Cheshire cat. Wessel feigned surprise for a second time since he'd captured them. "Oh yes, Captain, I know all about Griffin's little taskforce now, as does the War Council."

"I don't care what you think you know, Vernon," Sterling hit back. It was a glib response, but his mental energy was focused on contacting Lieutenant Shade. The distance between him and the Invictus made this a considerable challenge.

"Now that we've discovered you to be 'aides to the emissaries' or even emissaries yourselves, Griffin will be implicated as a traitor too," Wessel went on. "Finally, her meddlesome influence will be removed from the War Council and we can focus on ending this war."

Sterling laughed in Wessel's face. It was telling that the Commodore had said "ending" rather than "winning" the war.

"Ending the war by bending your knee to the enemy, Vernon?" Sterling hit back. "This war ends one of two ways. Our annihilation, or theirs."

"Enough!" Wessel snapped. He turned to the agents who were still struggling to restrain Banks. "Keep them from killing each other, but pick up the pace. Next, we take command of the Invictus."

"You'll never take my ship," Sterling spat at Wessel. "They'll die before they allow a piece of dirt like you on board."

Wessel smiled again. "Oh, but I *will* take it, Captain," the Commodore replied, the words leaking from his lips like toxic fumes. "You are not the only one who is prepared to go to extremes. Your crew will soon surrender when they discover I have a pistol pressed under your chin."

Sterling laughed and shook his head. "If you think that will work, you clearly don't know anything about the Omega Taskforce." He chanced a step closer to the Commodore, causing Wessel to flinch like a frightened kitten. "The Omega Directive is in effect, Vernon," he said, while mentally running through some of the many creative ways he'd considered killing the man over the past few months.

"What Omega Directive?" Wessel barked. The tone of Sterling's warning and the fact the Commodore hadn't comprehended its meaning had clearly rattled Wessel. "I demand you tell me what that means at once!"

"You'll find out soon enough," Sterling replied, with unreserved malice. He then stepped back and stood tall. "Shall we continue?"

Wessel growled, then pushed through to the head of the formation again, barking orders at the agents to march on. Sterling closed his eyes and focused on forming a neural link. His brain literally ached from the effort, but finally a connection formed.

"Lieutenant Shade, ready your commandoes and prepare to repel boarders," Sterling said through the link as an agent shoved him in the back to get him moving again. "Commodore Wessel has taken us prisoner. The whole thing was a set up to frame us."

"My team is already standing by, Captain," Shade replied. "We monitored the Venator landing six pads across from us. I tried to contact you, but couldn't form a link."

"Understood, Lieutenant. What's the condition of the Venator?" Sterling asked.

"Its reactor is hot, and we've picked up a squad from the ship heading this way," Shade replied.

Sterling cursed, realizing they were already on the back foot. He had to make a decision, one that would set them on a course from which they could never deviate. However, it seemed that he no longer had a choice. It was either go rogue or have his ship taken from him and sit out the rest of the war in Grimaldi Military Prison.

"If those forces try to storm the Invictus then you fight, Lieutenant, is that understood?" Sterling said. He'd settled on his choice, though really there was no choice at all. Surrender was not in his blood.

"Aye, Captain," replied Shade. "So long as I'm still breathing, no-one from the Venator will set foot on this ship." Despite the weak link between them, Sterling could feel the adrenalin surging through his weapons officer's veins, amping up her senses and fighting instincts.

"I need you and your two best commandoes to intercept Wessel's squad and break us free," Sterling continued, looking up at the location markers on the corridor wall. "We're passing through residential sector six, section four-alpha. It's a good bet they're taking us to the Venator."

"I'm on my way, sir," Shade replied.

"Put Razor in command," Sterling quickly added, before Shade closed the link. "Tell her to depart as soon as we're on board, weapons hot."

Shade acknowledged the order and the link went dead. Sterling turned to Banks and nodded. They were all set. Now it would come down to who had the will to fight the hardest, he told himself. And that was a question he already knew the answer to. Sterling then felt the butt of a rifle in his back, this time steering him down an adjacent corridor. He recognized the area and realized they were heading into the docking section. Time was already short.

Up ahead, Sterling caught sight of Rhonda Reese, the facility's administrator. She was with a security detail comprised of four tattooed men, including the two who had accompanied the women when Sterling had arrived.

"What the hell is going on here?" Reese yelled as Commodore Wessel marched toward her. "I have reports of weapons fire and dead bodies. Explain yourself!"

"This is SIB business, and none of your concern," Wessel barked, shoving the woman aside.

Reese stumbled back, tripped and fell hard to the deck. "Stop them!" she roared; her face flushed red with anger. The order was like a spark igniting a keg of gunpowder. Moments later the tattooed security guards charged at the agents at the front of the formation. The fizz of plasma rifle fire filled the air and once again Sterling was assaulted with the odor of burning flesh. However, the incident was also the distraction he was looking for.

"Now!" Sterling called out loud.

Banks snapped her binders like they were made of candy then hammered her elbows into the faces of the two agents to her rear. Sterling heard the sickening crunch of crushed bone and cartilage and spun around in time to see the two men hit the deck like butchered carcasses. Their noses had been almost entirely flattened into their faces.

"Good work, Mercedes," Sterling said, as Banks snapped his binders to free his hands.

Ahead of them, the security detail was still fighting the two SIB agents who had been at the front of the formation. Two security guards had already been shot dead, but the remaining original duo were now brawling with the agents hand-to-hand. Sterling looked for Wessel, but he was nowhere to seen. To the background soundtrack of more crunching cartilage and anguished cries, Sterling picked up a fallen rifle and took aim. His first shot blasted the nearest SIB agent in the back, sending him down. The tattooed security guards roared as if their team had scored a touchdown and fought on even harder. Within seconds the remaining SIB agent was overwhelmed and beaten senseless. Suddenly, plasma blasts flashed across the room and one of the tattooed men went down. Sterling ducked into cover and saw more SIB agents charging toward them.

"We need to get to the Invictus!" Sterling called to Banks, while setting off in the opposite direction to the incoming squad.

Banks collected a weapon from the floor and was at Sterling's side in an instant. Seconds later plasma blasts were thudding into the walls beside them. Sterling took a glancing blow to the thigh and went down, clamping his teeth together to stave off the pain. Banks dragged him into cover and retuned fire, killing one of the advancing SIB agents and driving the others into cover.

"There are too many," Banks said, as incoming fire also forced her into cover. "I count another six, maybe eight agents coming this way."

Sterling tapped his neural interface and tried to link with Lieutenant Shade. This time the connection came quickly and was strong.

"Lieutenant, we're pinned down in the docking section," Sterling called out to Shade through the link. "We're probably four or five pads away from the Invictus."

More plasma flashed across the room, but this time it raced in the opposite direction. Sterling glanced behind and saw Shade advancing, with two commandoes in full combat armor at her side. All three were wielding 'Homewrecker' heavy plasma rifles.

"I see you Captain, stand by," Shade called out, as cool as ever.

Plasma fire continued between the two groups, but Shade and her commandoes had the greater firepower and accuracy. Three SIB agents were hit and had arms or legs blasted from their bodies. Unsurprisingly, the sight of their dismembered fallen comrades was enough to convince the remaining agents to halt their advance. Sterling and Banks added to the torrent of plasma blasts, then began to retreat toward Shade and her commandoes. Sterling's thigh burned hotter than the fires of hell, but he pushed on through the pain and continued to return fire as yet more SIB agents joined the battle.

"Let's move!" said Sterling, managing to draw level with his weapons officer before his leg gave way.

Banks arrived moments later and slung Sterling's arm over her shoulder for support. Normally, his pride would have compelled him to protest about the unsolicited assistance his first officer had given him. However, he quickly realized that without Banks' help, he wouldn't be able to make it to the next landing pad, never mind back to the Invictus.

Shade and the commandoes adjusted their aim, blasting the ceiling above the corridor where the new squad of SIB agents were advancing from. It caved in, sending metal and rubble collapsing to the deck. Smoke and thick clouds of dust filled the docking section and soon the remaining SIB agents were shrouded in an impenetrable gray haze.

Sterling pressed on with Banks' help, but it wasn't long before the sound of more plasma fire reached his ears. Up ahead, another squad of SIB agents were attacking the dock where the Invictus lay waiting for them. Banks fired from the hip, killing one of them instantly. Then Shade moved ahead, seemingly without fear, and unleashed her powerful 'Homewrecker' against the remaining SIB forces. Sterling marveled at the sheer brutality and devastating accuracy of Shade's assault. Within seconds, all that remained of the SIB was charred flesh and the hot smell of death. Sterling quickly tapped his neural interface, using the sudden lull in fighting to contact Lieutenant Razor on the bridge.

"Prepare to blast off, Lieutenant," Sterling called out through his mind. "And target the Venator's engines with the plasma turrets. With any luck we can land a few good hits as we leave and slow them down."

"Aye, sir, we're already standing by," Razor replied briskly. "Weapons locked. I'm ready when you are."

Sterling severed the link and pushed on across the landing platform. His leg had now completely given up on him and he was relying almost exclusively on Banks to haul him out of danger. Together, captain and first officer stepped onto the rear ramp of the Invictus, which immediately began to rise. Lieutenant Shade, however, remained on the landing platform, covering their retreat with bursts of fire from the Homewrecker.

"Shade, get in here!" Sterling called out, realizing that the ramp was rising fast.

Shade blasted the head off an advancing SIB agent, then threw down the Homewrecker and dove for the lip of the ramp. She caught it, but just barely. For a moment, Sterling thought she would fall, but Shade just managed to haul herself up and clamp her forearm over the edge of the ramp. Two commandoes clambered to her aid and dragged her inside. All three then tumbled down the steeply-sloping ramp and thudded into the cargo hold just as the Invictus lifted off and accelerated hard away from the facility.

"Grab a hold of something," Sterling called out, wrapping himself up in some nearby cargo netting. "And hold on!"

Sterling's crew did as ordered and moments later the pulsating thump of the Invictus' plasma turrets reverberated through the deck. The ship shook hard as return fire from the Venator thudded into their armor. Sterling didn't know how effective their attack had been, or what damage the Invictus had sustained, but the kick of their main engines told him they were on their way. Through luck, guile and superior fighting skills, they'd survived Wessel's attempts to frame them. However, now they were not only the run, they were also on their own.

STERLING FLINCHED while Commander Graves tended to his wounded thigh at his Captain's console. The ships' medical officer had insisted that Sterling and Banks report to the med bay for treatment, but Sterling had refused. He was aware that his chief medical officer could have made it an order, but Graves knew when discretion was the better part of valor. Banks had been treated first, on account of her greater number of injuries, but she too was back at her post. However, despite the expert ministrations of the ship's medical officer, their situation remained as grave as the doctor's bedside manner.

"We're in position behind the moon, Captain. Our scanner probe is also active and relaying data from New Danvers," said Ensign Keller from the helm control station. "The navigational computer is processing the list of hidden long-range apertures we received from Admiral Griffin. If we get a fix on one nearby, I'll let you know at once."

"Understood, Ensign," replied Sterling, flinching again

as the doctor applied another dressing to another one of his wounds. "Any sign that Wessel has spotted our little hiding place?" he wondered, glancing across to Banks.

"Not yet, though the Venator is still in orbit around New Danvers," Banks replied, tapping away at her console. "We hit it pretty hard after we blasted off from the space port on the planet, so there's a good chance it's lost our scent."

Sterling nodded then focused on his own console, while Graves finished his work. Their escape from New Danvers had been hampered by the fact Wessel had also scored several solid hits to the Invictus as they blasted off from the planet. Their aperture field generator was damaged, along with half a dozen secondary systems. However, the field generator was the critical issue. Without the ability to surge they were unable to leave the system.

"You're done, Captain," said Commander Graves, replacing the medical instrument he'd been using into his kit. "I will return to treat the remaining wounded; on this occasion there were no fatalities."

"Thank you, Commander, you do that," replied Sterling, tucking in his tank top and buttoning up his tunic while keeping a curious eye on Graves. His medical officer almost sounded disappointed that no-one had died.

"Surge detected," Banks called out as Graves stepped off the command platform and departed. "Two ships just entered the system. The residual surge field indicates their departure aperture was at C-COP."

"Analysis, Lieutenant," said Sterling, glancing across to his weapons officer.

"Two gen-two frigates," Shade replied, promptly. "They're B-variant designs, which means they're equipped with the latest weapons and armor enhancements."

"Their transponder IDs are coming through now," Banks interjected. "It's the Flores and the Cornwallis, sir."

The viewscreen showed an image of the two Fleet warships, relayed from their probe. The image lacked the magnification and definition that their main scanners were able to achieve, but it was enough to get a look at the new arrivals.

Sterling thought for a moment then turned to Banks. "The Flores is Commander Bradford's ship, right?"

Banks nodded. "Yes. She's capable and experienced, but hasn't seen much action recently, not since being assigned to the First Fleet." Banks tapped her console and highlighted the Cornwallis. "This one is a bit of a curveball. She was originally commissioned as the Cannon, but was recently transferred to the SIB and renamed Cornwallis."

"Do we know her commander?" Sterling asked, but Banks immediately shook her head.

"The record lists someone called Anders as being in command. Apparently, a very recent promotion," Banks replied. "Likely, it's one of Wessel's stooges."

The door to the bridge opened. Sterling glanced over his shoulder to see Lieutenant Razor hustle inside and immediately set up her station at the rear of the bridge.

"The surge field generator will be back online in the next few minutes, Captain," Razor said as the row of consoles flashed on behind her. The light from the numerous engineering stations illuminated her face brightly, causing her augmented skin to sparkle. "Everything else is minor and can wait until we have time to conduct more detailed repairs...."

Razor's voice suddenly trailed away and the engineer almost passed out, barely managing to catch herself on the console in front of her.

"Are you okay, Lieutenant?" asked Sterling, instinctively checking his console to view the status of Razor's neural condition. If she was turning then he'd need to act fast to put his engineer down.

"I'm fine, Captain." Razor straightened up to her full height. "Headaches and sudden dizziness are a side-effect of Commander Graves treatments," she added, turning to face her captain. "You do not need to terminate me just yet, sir."

"Glad to hear it, Lieutenant," Sterling replied, while still checking her bio-readings. He had no desire to terminate his chief engineer, but he also wasn't going to take Razor's assurance at face value. However, besides elevated stress levels, the scan of Razor's neural activity merely highlighted the headache his engineer had just mentioned. "Are you fit to continue, Lieutenant?" Sterling asked, turning from his console to face his engineer.

"Aye, Captain, I am," Razor replied, coolly.

"Very well, I'll make sure that Colicos looks into your condition further at his earliest opportunity." Sterling turned back to his console. "But our first priority is to get out of this damned system," he added, while looking at Keller.

The ensign took the hint and spun his chair around to

face Sterling. However, before Keller could get a word out, both his and Banks' consoles began chiming an urgent alert.

"It's an incoming communication," said Banks, frowning down at her console. "It's on the Omega Taskforce secure channel." She glanced up at Sterling, eyebrows raised.

"Griffin?" Sterling repeated, saying what he suspected his first-officer was thinking.

Banks shrugged. "It must be," she said, while analyzing the incoming signal. "The signal is being directed through the Fleet aperture relay, though how the hell she knows where we are is anyone's guess."

Another alarm then rang out across their consoles, though this time weapon's control station also registered the alert.

"The Venator has detected the signal from the aperture relay, sir," said Lieutenant Shade with her usual blend of calm urgency. "It's broken orbit and is hard-burning toward us." Shade's console chimed again and the lieutenant quickly updated her report. "The Flores and the Cornwallis have also adjusted course. They have a head-start on the Venator."

"How soon will they get here?" Sterling asked.

Shade was already running the numbers. "Ninety-four minutes at their current rate of acceleration, Captain."

Sterling cursed and rubbed the back of his neck before turning to his first-officer. "Put the communication, through," he said. "Let's hope our caller has something good to say, because whoever it is just blew our cover."

The viewscreen switched from the fuzzy picture of the

Fleet warships that were now hunting them down to the image of Admiral Griffin. She was as hard-faced as ever and Sterling immediately found himself straightening to attention.

"I hope you have some good news, Admiral, because we're in a tight spot," Sterling said, cutting to the chase.

"Yes, I know all about your situation, Captain," replied Griffin, displaying an impressive lack of empathy for their predicament, given the circumstances. "I regret I was not able to contact you sooner, but the Machiavellian antics of the Wessels forced me to accelerate my own plans."

"Admiral, I have three Fleet warships closing in on our position," Sterling cut in. "We're stranded in C-sector and need a way out. I'm really hoping you have one."

Griffin scowled at Sterling through the viewscreen. The look literally sent a shiver down his spine. "Hope is not an effective strategy, Captain. Thankfully, however, I can offer you more than just conversation," she finished in a somewhat friendlier tone.

Admiral Griffin cast her eyes down and appeared to be working at a computer console. Sterling took the opportunity to flex his muscles, which had become stiff and frozen in the presence of his intimidating commander. The brief reprieve from Griffin's blue-eyed, icy stair felt like coming up for a breath of air after a long dive. Sterling's console chimed an update and he saw that they were receiving data.

"I've just given you the location of an aperture that will get you out of this 'tight spot' you speak of," the Admiral said. The casual manner in which she was referring to their imminent deaths irked Sterling. However, if Griffin could save their asses, he decided he could forgive her glibness. "I have also transmitted the surge field parameters on our secure, encrypted channel," Griffin continued, returning her eyes to Sterling. "Without this information, those three Fleet ships will not be able to pursue."

"Captain, I have the location of the aperture," Keller called out. However, the anxious look on the ensign's face told Sterling that it was not entirely good news. "It's right between us and the approaching warships, sir."

Sterling checked his console and ran the numbers directly, cursing again as the results flashed up on his screen.

"We'll just about beat the Venator, but we won't reach those co-ordinates before the two destroyers get within weapons range," Sterling said.

"Then you will have to destroy them, Captain," replied Griffin, with a level of cold detachment that even Shade couldn't match "I will meet you on the other side of the aperture. Griffin out."

The face of Admiral Griffin faded and was replaced by the image of the Flores and Cornwallis. Sterling glanced across to Banks and could see that she understood the weight of the decision to be made. However, there was no time for soul-searching. There was only time for action.

"Ensign, get us to that aperture as fast as you can," Sterling called out to the helm control station. He glanced over his shoulder to Lieutenant Razor. "Give the engines everything you have, Lieutenant. Take power from anywhere other than weapons, regenerative armor and essential life support. If we have to cut the gravity and let some of the crew bounce around in the lower decks, so be it."

"Aye, Captain," Razor replied, immediately setting to work.

"I think they're used to it down there by now," Banks added, with a smile.

On another occasion, Sterling might have shot his first-officer a reproving look for her ill-timed use of humor. However, this time he saw the humorous side too. Then the prospect of having to destroy two Fleet ships invaded his thoughts and his mood rapidly darkened. He'd been required to kill Fleet personnel before, under the Omega Directive, but this was different. There was no suggestion that the two ships on an intercept course had been turned, and destroying them would not prevent the vessels from falling into enemy hands. He'd be knowingly killing regular Fleet crew, many of whom he knew would have families. It didn't sit well with him. Surrender would have been the honorable course of action, Sterling accepted. However, surrender would also mean giving up all hope of discovering a way to neutralize the Sa'Nerran neural weapon. The course of the war was against them; hard choices had to be made if humanity was going to survive. Choices that he knew the War Council would never sanction. Choices that his ship and crew were uniquely positioned to make. *Sometimes the ends do justify the means...* Sterling thought. *Even if I book myself a one-way ticket to hell in the process...*

The Invictus powered out from behind the moon and

began to accelerate hard toward the aperture and the incoming warships. The inertial negation systems struggled to cope and Sterling was forced to grip the sides of his console to steady himself. The image of the frigates on the viewscreen was then magnified and enhanced as the ship's scanners took over from the probe they'd planted. Immediately, incoming messages flashed up from the frigates and from the Venator.

"Message the Flores and Cornwallis and tell them we have no desire to engage them in combat," Sterling said to Banks. "Tell them we understand that their orders are to apprehend us, but that we will not surrender."

"Aye, Captain," Banks replied, tapping out the messages on her console. "What about Wessel?" she added. "He wants to speak to you directly."

Sterling thought for a moment. He needed a way to let the other ships know that the Invictus and its crew had been set up. He doubted it would cause the commanders of the frigates to act against their orders, but it would at least cloud their minds with doubt. And it would also mean that Sterling could get his side of the story out into the open.

"Put Wessel through, but only on an unsecured, open channel," Sterling said, as his idea crystallized in his mind. "I want those other ships and anyone else in the system to be able to hear what that snake has to say."

Banks continued to work, but then shook her head. "He's not going for it, Captain," she said. "Wessel is only offering secure channels."

"Refuse all the Venator's attempts to communicate, unless it's on an open channel," Sterling said, confidently.

"He'll cave, eventually," he added, peering at the viewscreen and willing Wessel to succumb to his nature. "That asshole won't be able to stop himself."

Several minutes passed, during which time the distance between the Invictus and the frigates narrowed at a tremendous rate. Banks continued to deny all attempts at communication from the Venator, even going so far as to block simple text messages. Sterling waited, tapping his finger on the side of the console. It was like a game of chicken. The difference was that instead of flying at the Venator and seeing who flinched first, it was a contest of whose composure would crack soonest. Sterling's console chimed an incoming message and he read it, a smile curling his lips.

"The Venator is hailing us on an open, unsecured channel," said Commander Banks, who was also smiling broadly.

"Put the esteemed Commodore through," replied Sterling, gesturing to the viewscreen. Moments later Commodore Vernon Vessel appeared, looking like a caged wolf that had been constantly poked and tormented through the cell bars.

"I will see to it that you spend the rest of your life in Grimaldi!" Wessel snarled. "Death is too good for you!"

Sterling remained calm and straightened up. It was important that he stuck to his game plan and didn't allow Wessel to rile him.

"Grimaldi is for criminals like you, Vernon," Sterling replied, coolly. "Just what did you do with those three factory workers you abducted, anyway?" he continued, using the same tenor of mock surprise that Wessel had employed earlier.

"You would know, 'emissary' or 'aide' or whatever I should call you now," Wessel hit back, in a bitter, petulant tone.

"Captain Sterling will do fine, Vernon," Sterling replied. He was now channeling his inner-computer and adopting the cheerful demeanor of his gen-fourteen AI. "Planting evidence is a tricky business," Sterling went on. "A lab analysis will show that the sabotage apparatus you planted didn't come from this ship. And you'd be surprised how quickly people talk when pressure is put on them. Your deception will be as easy to uncover as it was for me and my crew to take down your assassins and agents."

Wessel snorted. "Your tricks won't work, emissary," the commodore spat back. "Now, surrender or I will have you destroyed."

"No, I don't think I will," replied Sterling, with a casual shrug. He then hovered his finger over the button to terminate the call. "See you around, Vernon," he added, leaving just enough time to see the commodore's face flush red before he closed the channel. Moments later all the consoles on the bridge chimed an alert.

"Weapons lock from the two frigates, sir," said Lieutenant Shade.

"Full power to weapons and regenerative armor, Lieutenant," Sterling replied before turning to Keller. "How long before we're in position to surge, Ensign?"

"I'm decelerating as hard as I can, sir, but it will still be two minutes before we're in range of the aperture," Keller replied. "Maybe longer, accounting for any evasive maneuvers I need to make."

"We're not evading anyone," said Sterling, feeling shivers of excitement tingle through his body.

"We're coming into range of the frigates now," Shade said. "Weapons locked on and ready."

"The Flores has slowed and is ordering us to stand-down, Captain," said Banks. "But the Cornwallis is radio-silent and coming straight at us."

Plasma blasts flashed from the guns of the Cornwallis and the Invictus was struck.

"Armor holding," said Shade as tremors rumbled through the deck plating. "Shall I return fire?"

"Negative, not yet," Sterling called out. He turned to Banks. "Warn the Cornwallis off, Commander. Let's at least give them a chance to save their skins."

"Message sent," Banks said as more blasts struck the ships, forcing Banks to steady herself against her console.

"Regenerative armor is still holding, sir, but we won't take another hit on the port, fore quarter, not at this range," Shade added. "They're shooting to kill, sir."

"Keep our starboard side to the Cornwallis, Ensign," Sterling called out to Keller before turning to Banks. "Any reply from the Cornwallis?"

Moments later another thump of energy hammered into the hull, jolting Sterling against his console. Conduits blew out on the bridge and Sterling felt splinters of hot metal strike his face. He groaned and grasped his right side, which had been slammed against the corner of his console.

"Minor damage to decks three through five. Armor

integrity failing," Shade called out from the weapons console.

"No reply from the Cornwallis, Captain," Banks said.

Sterling cursed. "Target their reactor and fire all weapons," he ordered.

Sterling knew he could have tried to disable the frigate, but it was clear that the ship was not playing games. If he left it intact, it would only allow Wessel to enlist it against them again in the future. He couldn't have that. Wessel had drawn first blood, and now he would face the consequences.

"Firing," Shade called out

The viewscreen blinked white as the Invictus unleashed a full volley of plasma blasts at the SIB frigate. The energy hammered into the Cornwallis, raking across its back and tearing through the armor of the older, less powerful ship. A dozen small explosions rocked the frigate and it listed out of control, trailing fire into space behind it.

"Maneuvering into position now, Captain," Ensign Keller announced. "Surge field forming."

"Captain, the Flores has come about," Shade said, switching the viewscreen to an image of the second frigate. "Shall I target weapons?"

Sterling glanced down at his console and quickly brought up a tactical analysis of the Flores. The warship's weapons were locked, but Sterling knew the gen-two frigates well. A huge swell of energy in their field coils was always detectable before they fired and the Flores was giving off no such signals.

"Captain, shall I fire?" Shade repeated. As ever, she

was calm and collected, but the urgency of the question was palpable.

"Negative, Lieutenant, do not fire," Sterling replied.

Sterling knew it was a gamble, but if Commander Bradford on the Flores was having doubts about the Invictus' guilt, he wanted to ensure she remained alive to allows those doubts to grow and take root. He welcomed any potential ally against Wessel – even an unwitting one.

"Surging in five, Captain," Keller called out, the young Ensign's voice displaying none of Shade's unflappable poise. "Four... three... two... one..."

Sterling felt his mind descend into the disembodied abyss that existed between reality and whatever filled the space between apertures. He gave himself over to the blissful feeling of nothingness, knowing that this rare moment of peace would soon be shattered. Moments later the bridge of the Invictus exploded back into reality and he found himself face down on his console. His cheek bone burned and the metallic taste of blood filled his mouth. Pushing himself up, he spat out a tooth, which bounced off the console and dropped onto the deck, coming to rest in a pool of red saliva.

"Report," Sterling called out, though his words sounded muffled in his own ears.

"Surge complete," Banks replied. His first officer's console was flickering chaotically. "Position unknown."

"Ensign Keller, where the hell are we?" Sterling called over to his helmsman. The smell of smoke filtered into his nostrils and he heard a fire-suppression system kick in to his rear.

"I don't know, sir," Keller replied, dragging himself back into his seat. The ensign had been thrown clear of the helm control console. "It's not on any chart. I'll try to get a star fix."

"Captain, I've had to shut down the reactor core to prevent an overload," Lieutenant Razor said from her station at the rear of the bridge. "Half of the ship's systems are down. Surge field generator offline. The main AI has assumed control. We're on life-support, sir."

"All I need to know is if we're going to explode or run out of air in the next few minutes, Lieutenant," Sterling replied. He was glancing over his shoulder at his engineer, while massaging his aching jaw.

"No sir, we're still in one piece," Razor replied. "I can put her back together, Captain, but it will take time."

"Proximity alert," Banks called out. "It's another ship. Correction, three ships."

"What the hell?" Sterling muttered under his breath. "Put them on the viewscreen."

The viewscreen was flickering as chaotically as Banks' console panels, but Sterling could just about make out the three approaching vessels. They were compact, smaller even than the Invictus, Sterling realized, but their design was totally alien too him.

"Unknown configuration." Banks was wrestling with her malfunctioning console in an attempt to gather a tactical readout on the ships. "No discernible Fleet markings or transponder IDs."

"Are they Sa'Nerran?" Sterling asked, checking the

status of their weapons in case they had to fight. However, like most systems on the ship, they were down too.

"If they are, they're like nothing we've seen before," Banks replied. Her console then chimed a distorted alert. "I'm receiving a communications request from the lead ship."

"Put them through, whoever they are," replied Sterling, with a fatalistic air. "It's not like we can do anything else right now."

The viewscreen flickered and the face of Admiral Natasha Griffin appeared.

"You took your time, Captain," Griffin said with undisguised irritation. "But at least you managed to bring half a ship with you."

Sterling opened his mouth, but no words came out. He couldn't even formulate a coherent sentence in his mind. Faced with the sheer absurdity of the situation, there was only one thing he could do. He stared Griffin dead straight in the eyes and burst out laughing.

STERLING AND BANKS arrived at the airlock door and waited for it to pressurize. On the other side of the docking umbilical, aboard one of the unidentified ships which had met them, was Admiral Griffin with – Sterling hoped – some answers.

"Griffin has clearly recruited far more members of the Omega Taskforce than we imagined," Banks said, as the pressure gauge rose. "There would need to be a least a hundred crew split across those three vessels outside."

"So it would seem," Sterling agreed, while impatiently tapping his finger against his leg. "Though how she kept them all quiet and obedient is something I'd love to know."

Thuds and rattles vibrated through the deck and walls as Lieutenant Razor's army of drones set about repairing the damage to the Invictus. Then the hatch at the far end of the docking umbilical swung open and Admiral Griffin stepped into the tunnel. She was flanked by two figures, though it was immediately clear to Sterling that neither of them was human.

"Robots?" wondered Sterling, casting a sideways glance to Banks.

Banks' eyes widened as the matte black machines stomped across the docking umbilical behind Admiral Griffin. The robots were humanoid in design, though to Sterling's eyes their limbs looked too spindly to support their weight. The machines also lacked a discernible head, with just a blob-shaped protrusion above the torso section instead. This gave them a somewhat macabre appearance, like headless monsters. With some hesitancy, Sterling pulled open the airlock door to allow the Admiral and the robots inside the Invictus.

"Do not be alarmed by my soldiers, Captain," Griffin said as she stepped on-board. The look on Sterling's face apparently spoke for itself. "They are one of the products of something called 'Project Obsidian'. This was a plan I developed to create mechanized soldiers to fight the Sa'Nerra."

Griffin moved further inside the Invictus, but the two robot soldiers remained in the umbilical by the docking hatch. Neither of the robots was armed, though this didn't stop them from looking threatening, like a couple of spiders in the center of a web.

"I've never heard of 'Project Obsidian'," Sterling replied, studying the design of the machines. Elements of their construction looked old and outdated, like the tech from generation-one Fleet warships.

"It was mothballed more than a decade ago, after

practically the same length of time in development," Griffin answered, being remarkably candid for a change. "The ships outside are also part of the project, as were the long-range apertures, which were based on the Sa'Nerran apertures you also discovered."

"That surge damned near tore the Invictus apart," Sterling said, massaging his still numb jaw. "I guess that's why the plan was put on ice?"

"Not exactly, Captain," said Griffin, heading along the corridor toward the elevators. "Smaller ships are less severely affected by long-range surges. Anything much larger than the Invictus would either be destroyed or very heavily damaged." Griffin called the elevator then stepped inside and hit the button for deck one. Sterling and Banks had to quickly hop inside to avoid the doors closing on them. "The plan was to create a Fleet of small, but potent warships with automated crews that could surge behind enemy lines and strike at the heart of the Sa'Nerra."

The elevator reached deck one and Griffin stepped out, continuing to lead the way as if she owned the ship.

"Sounds like a solid plan, so what went wrong?" said Sterling, hurrying after the Admiral.

"The AIs were too unpredictable," Griffin replied, walking and talking. "Compared to the gen-thirteen AI on the Invictus, the Obsidian Soldiers were crude and unsophisticated. They are closer to gen-seven or eight in terms of aptitude and sophistication. There were a lot of... accidents as a result." The way that Griffin had said the word, "accidents", suggested to Sterling that the mishaps she was referring to were far from benign. "Since the war was going well for Fleet at the time, it was decided the project was surplus to requirements," Griffin went on. "I was ordered to shut it down, which I did, officially. Though as you can see, Captain, I like to keep my options open."

The Admiral's sudden candor was remarkable, Sterling thought. However, considering the decision he'd just made to attack and destroy a Fleet warship, Sterling was emboldened to ask why he suddenly merited such an increased level of trust.

"Forgive me Admiral, but why didn't you tell me any of this before?" Sterling asked, taking a firmer tone than he had intended. This did not go unnoticed by Griffin.

"Do not forget who you are speaking to, Captain," the Admiral snapped back, stopping dead and spinning on her heels to face him.

Sterling was caught off-guard and almost collided with Griffin. However, he wasn't about to allow her to throw him off his stride.

"Admiral, I just resisted arrest, disobeyed a direct order from a Fleet Commodore and destroyed a Fleet frigate to get here," Sterling hit back. "By all accounts, I'm no longer a captain. And, if we're honest, you're no longer an admiral either. So how about we cut the crap, because I'm already up to my neck and I need answers."

Griffin's cold eyes narrowed. All Sterling wanted to do was look away, but he held her gaze without even blinking.

"Very well, Captain, but let me make one thing clear," Griffin finally answered. "Whether we are officially members of the Fleet or not no longer matters. Our duty and our mission remain unaltered, which quite simply is to defeat the enemy. Do you agree with that assertion, Captain?"

"I do, Admiral," Sterling replied. Despite what he'd just said, he felt compelled to continue using Griffin's former rank, as Griffin continued to use his.

"Then it makes sense to maintain a command structure, would you not agree?" Griffin added.

"I do," Sterling said again.

"And since I am a former Flag officer with forty years of service and more combat experience than the both of you combined, would you also agree that it makes sense that I continue to command this operation?"

Sterling sighed. He'd walked right into Griffin's web. "Yes, Admiral, that makes perfect sense," he answered.

"Good, I'm glad we could come to an understanding, Captain." Griffin sounded pleased with herself. She then spun on her heels and continued along the corridor.

Just at that moment, Ensign Keller stepped out of the deck-one rest room. He was straightening his tunic and not looking where he was going. As a consequence, he almost walked straight into Admiral Griffin.

"Oh, sorry, didn't see you..." Keller began cheerily before looking up and realizing who he'd almost flattened. "Admiral, sir... sorry, sir. I mean, ma'am. I mean Admiral!"

Griffin sighed loudly and obviously, but didn't respond to the helmsman. As a result, Keller just remained where he was, struck dumb. It was like Griffin was the White Witch of Narnia and had just turned him to stone.

"You can return to your post now, Ensign," said Sterling, offering his helmsman a lifeline.

"Yes, sir, thank you, sir," Keller said, shuffling along the wall to slip past the group. Once he was clear, Keller accelerated and practically ran onto the bridge. "He's not always like that," Sterling said, as Griffin's cold blue eyes turned to him. "Not often, anyway."

Griffin sighed again and continued along the corridor, finally entering the small briefing room at the rear of deck one. She walked around the table and sat in the chair that would have normally been reserved for the captain.

"Am I to assume that Project Obsidian is still alive and well?" Sterling asked, dropping into one of the other chairs in the briefing room. Banks sat across from Sterling, quietly but keenly observing the exchange between the two senior officers. "Because unless you have a thousand of those little black ships out there, I can't see what difference these robots can make against the full force of the Sa'Nerran armada."

"My Obsidian ships will not be a difference-maker now, at least not in the battle for Earth," Griffin answered. "I have a different purpose in mind for them, however. One that I hope will not be required."

"Care to enlighten me, Admiral?" Sterling said. However, the fact that Griffin had not already detailed this mysterious 'other' purpose suggested she was still keeping some cards close to her chest.

"Not yet, Captain," Griffin replied, confirming Sterling's suspicions. "Our priority should still be to neutralize the Sa'Nerran neural weapon. Unless that is achieved, the battle for Earth will be lost."

The door to the briefing room then opened and James

Colicos walked in, closely followed by Lieutenant Shade. The weapons officer had a pistol to the scientist's back.

"James Colicos, as ordered," said Shade.

"Ordered by who?" asked Sterling.

"By me, of course," replied Griffin, with a touch of snark. She then turned to Lieutenant Shade. "Remain here, Lieutenant, the doctor's presence is only required for a moment."

Shade nodded to the Admiral then looked to Sterling, seemingly conscious of also getting his approval this time.

"That's fine Lieutenant," said Sterling, wafting a hand at her. Fleet Admiral or not, Griffin was still every bit the pugnacious tyrant she always had been. "Far be it from me to contradict the Admiral..."

"If your duties permit, Lieutenant, I would like to speak with you before I depart," Griffin then added, with a softer tone that did not suit her. "Perhaps in the wardroom for coffee?"

"Yes, Admiral, thank you," Shade replied. The weapons officer glanced across to Sterling for a second time. "With your permission, Captain?"

"Granted, Lieutenant," said Sterling, flatly.

Sterling suspected his permission wouldn't have mattered to Griffin one way or another. However, knowing their family history, he wasn't about to deny Opal Shade and Natasha Griffin a moment together. The Omega officers of the Invictus were all the products of tragedies, some real and some the result of their harsh Omega Directive tests. The war had been hard on many members of the Fleet, and few of his crew had any family left. If he could allow Griffin and Shade some time together then even Lucas Sterling wasn't cold-hearted enough to deny it.

"What a truly touching moment," said Colicos, his tone thick with sarcasm. "And what a genuine pleasure it is to see you again, Natasha," the scientist added, bowing courteously to Griffin. "Do you want to start torturing me now, or later? I hear that a hot needle in the eye is particularly excruciating."

"Very droll, doctor," replied Griffin, unamused. Though unamused seemed to be the Admiral's persistent state of being, Sterling thought, idly. "I am hoping that we can come to an accord."

"And what accord is that, Natasha?" said Colicos. "By any chance is it that I agree to do exactly what you say, and you agree not to kill me?"

"Very astute, doctor, I'm glad we understand each other," replied Griffin. However, unlike Colicos, her words contained not even an iota of sarcasm.

"I've already explained to the captain that reversing the effects of the neural weapon is not possible," Colicos went on, correctly assuming what Griffin had called him into the meeting to discuss. "I've already agreed that I will endeavor to create a method of blocking the weapon, so that no more crew can be turned. So there really is no need for threats."

"We shall see about that, doctor," Griffin replied. Sterling felt a chill run down his spine. "A defense is not enough. A rectification of the effects is what is required." Colicos was about to protest, but Griffin did not allow him the chance. "Captain Sterling will return you to Far Deep Nine, where you can resume your work, doctor," the

Admiral went on. "No doubt, you still have a number of human and Sa'Nerran test subjects in cold storage there. I trust these will be sufficient to continue your experiments. If not, procure what you need from the Void colonies."

Colicos' eyes raised up and he glanced across to Sterling. However, he was just a shocked as the scientist appeared to be. The way that Griffin had so casually sanctioned the kidnapping of Void colonists for human experimentation was dark, even for her.

"You can go, now, doctor," Griffin added, nodding to Lieutenant Shade. The Admiral then glanced to Sterling. "Assuming you are also finished with your officer, Captain?"

Sterling was surprised to be asked, though it made for a welcome surprise. "No, you can go, Lieutenant," he said, waving Shade off.

Colicos protested, as was to be expected from the excitable genius. However, the man quickly piped down when Shade shoved her pistol into his gut and ushered him through the door.

"I guess we have our orders then?" Sterling said, once the door had swished shut. "Far Deep Nine it is. I assume you have an uncharted route for us to get there from this location?"

"You assume correctly, Captain," replied Griffin. "However, Commodore Wessel will have monitored your surge at New Danvers, so we will need to be careful."

"I thought you said they wouldn't be able to surge without the field data you provided to us?" Sterling replied, frowning.

"That is correct," said Griffin, removing an ID chip from her breast pocket, along with another device that Sterling did not recognize. "However, they will be able to scan the aperture and determine its unique configuration. This may be enough to allow Admiral Wessel to uncover details about the Obsidian Project from the Top-Secret archives."

"But they can't surge through these apertures," Sterling hit back, though he was suddenly unsure of himself, "or can they?"

"In time, Fleet Science Division would figure it out," Griffin admitted. "That is why I erased as many of the aperture locations as I could from the archives years ago, precisely for this eventuality."

Sterling huffed a laugh. "Talk about playing the long game, Admiral," he said, with admiration. "You've been planning this for some time?"

Griffin very nearly smiled, but Sterling accepted it could also have been a twitchy muscle. "It is always helpful to have a contingency, Captain. One that takes into account the very worst possible outcome, and offers a route to retribution. Even so, the less Wessel knows about the project the better."

Sterling nodded. Keeping the Wessels in the dark was a plan he could definitely get on board with. Even better would have been a plan that involved blasting them to atoms, he thought.

"Hold out your hand, Captain," Griffin said, rousing Sterling from his murderous thoughts. She removed two objects from her pocket and held them out to him.

Sterling reluctantly extended his hand, palm up, glancing nervously across to Banks as he did so. Without warning, Griffin pressed the second of the two objects into his palm. Sterling heard a sharp click and felt a stab of pain. He pulled his hand away in a reflex action and stared at it. Blood was pooling in the center of his palm from a tiny puncture wound.

"What the hell?" he protested, but Griffin did not explain her actions, or apologize for drawing blood. Instead, she pressed the ID chip into his hand, covering it with his blood.

"This ID chip is now hard-coded to your DNA," Griffin said, sitting back and placing the device that had drawn blood onto the table. "When you insert the chip into your captain's console it will program a surge vector that will return you to my location. All you need to do is activate it first."

"How do I activate it?" asked Sterling, grabbing a tissue from the center of the meeting table to mop up the residual blood on his palm.

"You bleed on it, of course," replied Griffin, coolly. For a moment, Sterling thought she might have been joking, but then he remembered it was Natasha Griffin he was talking to. There was more chance of the deck plates telling him a joke than the stern admiral. "Now, please have a number twenty-seven meal tray brought up to me in here," she added, adjusting her chair to get more comfortable. "I will eat while the repairs to the Invictus are conducted."

Sterling and Banks glanced at each other, though it seemed clear that this was their cue to leave.

"Aye, sir," replied Sterling, pushing himself out of his seat. He was suddenly unsure of whether he was on his own ship or not. As he reached the door, Banks stopped and turned back to Griffin.

"Admiral, would the other two robot-controlled ships out there be able to escort us into the Void?" she asked. "There may still be Sa'Nerra at Far Deep Nine, and the last time we were in the Void, it was crawling with aliens."

Sterling hadn't considered this option, and was keen to hear Griffin's answer.

"It is a good suggestion, Commander, but I'm afraid you will have to make do on your own," Griffin replied. "The AIs in the Obsidian Soldiers currently only respond to me. They have grown up with me, so to speak. Their behavior is too unpredictable to place under your command at this stage."

Sterling thought for a moment. "Maybe you could upgrade them with gen-fourteen code from the Invictus?" he asked. "I'm sure Lieutenant Razor would be able to assist."

Griffin looked surprised – it was another expression that did not suit her. "The Invictus is still running a gen-fourteen?" she asked. "Fleet standing orders were to downgrade to gen-thirteens."

"That's correct, Admiral," Sterling replied. He then considered how best to phrase the remainder of his response. "I may have 'overlooked' that order," he added, deftly.

"Very good, Captain," said Griffin. "Have Lieutenant Razor report to me in thirty minutes."

"Aye, sir," said Sterling. He then opened the door and stepped outside. Banks followed and the door to the meeting room swished shut. Sterling felt an immediate sense of relief, as if he'd just walked out of a police interrogation room. However, it wasn't long before he noticed that Banks was grinning. "What's so amusing?" he asked, feeling suddenly uneasy. He then hurriedly checked his pants. "I didn't spend that entire meeting with my flies down, did I?"

"No, it's worse, I'm afraid," said Banks, still grinning.

"Out with it, Mercedes," Sterling snapped. He'd already lost patience with his first officer's game.

"There's only one number twenty-seven meal tray left in the wardroom stores," Banks said, coolly.

Sterling cursed. "Damn it, really?"

Banks nodded. "I'm afraid so…"

Sterling cursed again then made a snap decision. It was one he hoped he wouldn't live to regret. "Enough is enough," he said to Banks, standing tall. "Swap her order for a twenty-eight," he added before turning and heading toward the bridge. "Admiral or not, no-one eats the last twenty-seven on this ship, but me."

THE TRANQUIL NOTHINGNESS of surge space was violently ripped away and Sterling found himself face down on his console. Alarms were wailing in his ears and he looked up at the viewscreen to see that the Invictus was spinning out of control.

"Ensign Keller, report!" Sterling called out, pushing himself upright. The deck was shaking, transmitting powerful vibrations into his body through his boots and his hands, which were clasped around the trembling captain's console.

"Helm controls restored," Ensign Keller called out. The helmsman was barely clinging on to his station at the front of the bridge.

"All stop, Ensign," Sterling called back before glancing over to his first officer and adding, "then give me a damage report."

The crew responded and within seconds the vibrations began to subside and the alarms were silenced. Instead of a blur of spinning stars on the viewscreen, Sterling could now make out a yellow sun and a greenish-blue planet in the distance.

"Answering all stop, Captain," said Keller, flopping back into his seat as if he'd just endured the world's scariest rollercoaster ride.

"Damage is minimal," Banks chimed in. "Thankfully, that felt a lot worse than it actually was. Admiral Griffin's surge computations took the sting out of the journey this time."

Sterling snorted a laugh. "It certainly didn't feel like it," he commented.

"Reactor stabilizing, Captain," said Lieutenant Razor from her engineering stations at the rear of the bridge. "The surge field generator will need a full restart, but that will only take me ten minutes."

"Ten minutes?" Commander Banks chipped in, scowling at Razor over her shoulder. "That's a sixty-minute job, by the book."

"Aye, Commander is it," Razor replied, coolly. "By the book, I mean."

Banks cast a sideways glance to Sterling, but he just smiled back at her. He was getting used to his engineer's unique way of doing things.

"Carry on, Lieutenant," Sterling said, addressing his chief engineer. "Just try not to blow us up in the process."

Sterling then peered out at the star system through the viewscreen again. "Now the only question is where the hell are we?"

He hadn't specifically directed this question to Ensign Keller, but it was his helmsman that responded.

"We're in the Oasis Colony system, Captain," Keller said.

"Oasis Colony? That's one hell of a surge," said Banks, confirming the readings on her own console. "We're actually pretty close to a regular aperture that's within surge-range of Far Deep Nine."

Then another alert chimed across the consoles of Sterling, Banks and Lieutenant Shade in unison. Sterling knew the alert tone well, but didn't need to wait long before his weapons officer confirmed his fears.

"Enemy vessels detected in the system, Captain," Shade began, as ever making her report with a calm and measured degree of urgency. "Twenty-four Sa'Nerran warships at long-range. It looks like they're attacking Oasis Colony."

"There's nothing we can do to help them," Sterling said, quick to head off any suggestions from his crew that they might render aid. "Set course for the aperture to Far Deep Nine, and try to keep as low a profile as possible. Hopefully those alien bastards will be too busy with Oasis Colony to bother with us."

Ensign Keller responded to the order then Sterling felt the thrum of the engines begin to vibrate the deck beneath his feet.

"MAUL is with them, Captain," Shade pointed out.

Most officers would have reported the presence of the Sa'Nerra's most decorated warship with a degree of fatalism or somberness. Shade, however, sounded like she was pleased that the deadly heavy destroyer was in the system. Sterling understood her sentiments, since they still had a score to settle with the warship and her commander, but that would have to wait.

"Keep a close eye on it, Lieutenant," Sterling replied. "But remember that we're not here for them. Not this time, anyway."

"Aye, Captain," Shade replied. As usual, his weapons officer hid her emotions well. However, Shade's body language still gave off enough subtle cues to tell Sterling that she was disappointed they weren't accelerating toward MAUL with their weapons charged.

Time seemed to move in slow motion as the Invictus continued its approach toward the aperture that would surge them to Far Deep Nine. A tense silence had fallen across the bridge as all eyes were on the scanners, watching to see if the Sa'Nerra reacted to their presence. Every bleep of a console caused Sterling's pulse to spike and his muscles to tense up, wondering if MAUL had detected them. It felt like sitting outside an interview room, waiting for the door to open and the interviewer to call his name.

"There's wreckage surrounding the aperture, Captain," said Commander Banks. She then tapped her console and a magnified image of the area appeared on the viewscreen. "I'd say it was perhaps a freight convoy, taking supplies either from or to Oasis Colony."

Sterling studied the wreckage on the viewscreen and on his console and didn't like what he saw. The Sa'Nerra weren't known for sneak attacks, but since Emissary McQueen and Crow had joined the ranks of the enemy, the alien's tactics had changed. And despite the presence of an alien taskforce in the system, there was still a danger from Void pirates.

"Full power to the weapons and regenerative armor," Sterling ordered, glancing across to Shade.

"Aye, sir," replied the weapons officer with a controlled measure of enthusiasm.

"You think it could be an ambush?" wondered Banks, as the Invictus entered the debris field.

Sterling shrugged. "I just don't want to take any chances. We no longer have the benefit of a COP to bolt us back together again if we take a pounding."

"Good point," replied Banks. "I keep forgetting that we're now part of the Obsidian Project, or whatever Admiral Griffin is calling her secret program now."

"I don't care what she calls those metal things, we're still the Omega Taskforce, even if we're doomed to forever be a taskforce of one," Sterling hit back.

"I'm reading a power signature inside the wreckage, Captain," Shade interrupted, snapping Sterling's attention back to the potential ambush. "The energy levels are rising. It has all the hallmarks of a ship powering up and preparing to fire."

Sterling scowled down at his console and assessed the readings. He considered his ship and crew to be superior to anything the enemy could throw at them, even MAUL. However, he also had a healthy respect for his adversary's capabilities and an awareness that the aliens had grown more cunning in recent months. As such, the ambusher was making it suspiciously easy to be seen, Sterling considered.

It was like trying to hide amongst trees while wearing a bright yellow, high-visibility jacket.

"Should I target the energy signature, Captain?" asked Shade, eagerly.

"Stand by, Lieutenant," Sterling replied, running an additional scan on his console. The results confirmed his suspicions. "There's another ship powering up in the debris cluster to our aft, port side." He sent the scan readings to Shade's console. "This one is actually doing a good job of trying to hide that fact, though."

Shade nodded. "Confirmed. Target acquired Captain."

"Pulverize that debris cluster, Lieutenant," said Sterling. "Let's not wait for our friend to show his hand."

The tempo and timbre of the thrum through the deck plating changed as the Invictus' forward plasma rail guns built to maximum power.

"Coming about on the target now," said Ensign Keller, using their maneuvering thrusters to spin the nose of the Marauder on target.

A flash of energy lit up the viewscreen and Sterling watched as the blasts of plasma tore through the debris, shredding the cover that the lurking ship was hiding behind. There was a ripple of explosions and moments later a phase-three Sa'Nerran Skirmisher limped out from behind the burning wreckage and tried to flee. Sterling could see it was badly damaged and longer a threat.

"The second ship has broken cover and is preparing to attack," Shade announced.

"Keep us out of the second Skirmisher's primary firing arc, Ensign," Sterling said to his pilot before turning to

Lieutenant Shade. "Full attack, and torpedo what's left of the first one," he added, hooking a thumb in the direction of the viewscreen. "No-one gets away with trying to stab us in the back."

"Aye, Captain," said Shade, relishing the opportunity to employ lethal force.

Sterling was then shaken off balance as plasma blasts hammered into the Invictus' hull.

"Turret fire from the second Skirmisher…" Banks called out, reading out the updates as they appeared on her console. "Low yield. No damage."

A torpedo then snaked out from their aft launcher. Sterling watched the weapon accelerate toward the alien warship like a spear. Moments later the alien vessel was consumed in fire.

"Skirmisher one destroyed," Shade reported, confirming the kill.

Another series of thumps rocked the bridge and Sterling saw a section of the ship's armor turn amber on his damage readout.

"Direct hit, port-side aft," Banks said, working on the damage control section of her console. "Regenerative armor holding at sixty-eight percent."

Sterling then heard the whir and thud of their turrets tracking the second vessel and returning fire. The viewscreen updated to show their shots landing on target and heavily damaging the Sa'Nerran warship.

"Time to wrap this up Ensign," Sterling said, focusing on the back of Keller's head. "Bring our main plasma cannons to bear and let's finish this."

"Aye, captain," Keller replied, briskly.

Straight away Sterling felt the kick of the ship's engines and thrusters altering their course. Keller was adept at throwing the Marauder-class warship into maneuvers that were frequently too sporty for their inertial negation systems to fully compensate for. The Skirmisher then came into view ahead of the Invictus. It had been expertly outmaneuvered by Keller and now had its belly exposed to their primary rail guns.

"Firing..." Shade called out, baring her teeth like a rabid wolf.

Energy raced toward the enemy vessel, punching through its center and coring it like an apple. For several seconds the Skirmisher listed out of control, energy crackling across its surface and fire spilling from the fresh holes in its armor and hull. Then the warship exploded and the Invictus was peppered with debris, though the fragments were so small it was no more dangerous than bugs bouncing off a windshield.

"Enemy ships, destroyed, Captain," Shade announced.

Sterling's console then chimed an alert. He read it without delay then cursed under his breath.

"Our little fireworks show has gotten MAUL's attention," said Commander Banks, as usual quicker to assess the updates than Sterling was. "It's accelerating toward us with two destroyer escorts. And we're being hailed."

"Ensign Keller, take us to the mouth of the aperture and prepare to surge to Far Deep Nine," Sterling said before then addressing his chief engineer. "Lieutenant, we need a way to ensure that MAUL doesn't monitor our surge vector and find out where we're going," he said. "Can we scramble our surge field?"

Razor shook her head. "I'd need time to study the technique Griffin used first," she replied, "but it's likely the same technique won't work when applied to standard surge field dynamics. If it did, Fleet or the Sa'Nerra would have already employed similar technology."

Sterling's console chimed again. The incoming communication request from MAUL was still pending. Sterling continued to ignore it, while trying to come up with another option to prevent the aliens from tracking their onward journey.

"I could try a rebound surge," Razor suggested. "It's risky, but it could work."

"You'll have to enlighten me, Lieutenant, what is a 'rebound surge'?" Sterling replied, feeling no shame in pleading ignorance on this occasion.

"It was a defensive tactic that was theorized while I was going through the academy," Razor replied. "In simple terms, we surge to a decoy location, directly to the mouth of the exit aperture, then immediately reverse engines and surge back to the original location. A third surge then takes us to where we actually want to end up."

Sterling frowned and could see that Banks looked similarly skeptical. "Is it even possible to make three surges in such quick succession, in the way you've described?" Sterling asked. "Surely, we'd just burn out the field generator, along with half a dozen power relays."

"Yes, sir, most likely," Razor replied, seemingly unfazed

by this eventuality. "However, the benefit is that the close proximity of the surges muddles the residual energy signature. Anyone following us wouldn't be able to figure out where the hell we went. It could potentially take them days to sift through the surge field data in order to work out what happened, and even then it wouldn't be conclusive."

"In the meantime, we're left stranded with our pants around our ankles and no ability to surge," Sterling countered, pointing out the one major flaw in Razor's idea.

"Yes, sir, in a manner of speaking," Razor replied, again peculiarly unconcerned. "But I can rebuild the surge field generator at Far Deep Nine in less time than it would take the Sa'Nerra to work out where we are." She shrugged. "To be honest, Captain, I've been meaning to do it, anyway. The shipyard engineers did a pretty shoddy job, all things considered."

Sterling's console chimed again. MAUL was still attempting to communicate, though this time it was broadcasting on all available channels.

"They must really want to talk to you, Captain," commented Banks, "and I have a pretty good idea who it is on the other end of the line."

"So do I," Sterling answered, not relishing the prospect of speaking to his former crewmate. He threw his hands up. "What the hell, let's do it Lieutenant," he said, making his decision. "But if we end up spending the rest of our lives on an abandoned mining research station, I warn you now that I may hold a grudge."

"I wouldn't blame you, sir," replied Razor, turning to her consoles to make the necessary surge calculations. She then paused and glanced at Sterling over her shoulder. "Though it won't be necessary, Captain. This *will* work."

Sterling nodded to his engineer. He already had faith in Razor's capabilities, but was buoyed further by her calm, measured confidence.

"Torpedoes launched," Shade then announced from the weapons control console. "Twelve inbound, accelerating hard. Time to impact, three minutes, fourteen seconds."

Sterling acknowledged Shade, then accepted the incoming communication request from Sa'Nerra Heavy Destroyer M4-U1. Moments later, the face of Emissary Clinton Crow appeared in front of him on the viewscreen. Sterling's former engineer looked distinctly pissed off.

"How did you get into the Void?" Crow demanded, dispensing with any pleasantries. "You were last monitored surging to F-sector, along with the rest of your pitiful fleet."

Sterling shrugged. "Looks like your scanners could do with a tune-up, Crow, because we've been out here the whole time," he replied.

"An obvious lie, Captain," Crow hit back. "But once we capture and turn your vessel, all your secrets will belong to the Sa'Nerra."

"Actually, I was just leaving, but thanks for the offer," Sterling said, glancing down at his console and watching for Razor's surge program to be loaded.

"You can't run from me any longer, Captain," Crow continued. "Surrender now and spare your crew the trauma of a false hope of escape. Submit to me and you can still be a part of the mighty Sa'Nerran empire."

"After careful consideration, your offer is declined," Sterling replied, still keeping half an eye on his console. "I was actually hoping it might have been McQueen on board your ship, rather than you. But I don't mind killing you first."

Crow laughed and even managed a smile. "Bravo, Captain, I always did appreciate your cavalier spirit." Then the emissary's face became as hard as the metal plate covering half of his head. "Emissary McQueen was looking forward to breaking you personally. But I see that you would prefer death instead. So be it."

The viewscreen cut off and Crow's image was replaced by a magnified view of a dozen torpedoes racing in their direction. Suddenly, the torpedoes seemed to splinter into six new sections, each section spreading apart from the others.

"Well, that's new..." commented Banks, channeling her dark sense of humor.

"We now have seventy-two torpedo fragments inbound, Captain," Lieutenant Shade confirmed. "Our point defense cannons are tracking them, but I calculate only a twenty-six percent chance we'll get them all."

Sterling turned to face Razor. "Any time now, Lieutenant," he said, maintaining his composure, despite his stomach turning over like the drum of a washing machine.

"Rebound surge program complete and loaded into the navigation computer, Captain," Razor said. Without explanation, the engineer then dropped to the deck and lay flat on her back. "This is going to get a little strange,

Captain. I suggest you lie down, or at least brace yourself."

"Understood, Lieutenant, I'll take my chances on my feet," Sterling replied, gripping the sides of his console. He knew that this came across as mere bravado, but he literally wasn't going to take their situation lying down. "Execute the surge, Ensign Keller. And everyone, hold on."

"Aye, sir," Keller replied. "Surging in ten."

"Point defense guns have failed to neutralize all the torpedoes, Captain," Shade announced. "Impact in fifteen seconds..."

"Talk about cutting it close," Sterling muttered, glancing across to his first officer.

"Surging in five..." Keller called out.

Sterling gritted his teeth and steeled himself, though he didn't have any idea what he was steeling himself against. This would be his first – and hopefully last – rebound surge. Then the ship, the bridge and his body were consumed by the aperture. His mind wandered freely for several seconds then his body exploded back onto the bridge. Moments later the ship's engines kicked into full reverse and the surge field generator built to a crescendo for a second time. The disorientation that resulted from a regular surge was usually fleeting. However, on this occasion, there was no time for the dizziness to dissipate before Sterling was again consumed into nothingness. His mind again wandered, but this time his thoughts were muddled and confused. He saw Ariel Gunn in front of him. Her lips were moving, but her words made no sense. Then her head exploded and in its place another head grew, like a flower sprouting from a bulb. A face formed and Sterling saw that it was Mercedes Banks. Sterling was then thrown back into reality for a second time and again the engines kicked hard. Still disorientated and confused, Sterling fell to the deck, his head spinning and stomach sick. He felt his body hit something hard, then he was pulled back into the surge dimension for a third time. The face of Mercedes Banks appeared to him again, her lips moving as Ariel Gunn's had done, but like the friend that he had chosen to kill, Banks' words made no sense. Then Banks' Fleet uniform melted away and she was suddenly naked. Sterling tried to look away, but he couldn't. She reached out to Sterling and pulled him closer, the power of her grip inescapably strong.

"Join us, Lucas," Banks commanded, as Sa'Nerran armor grew over the top of her body, forming a skin-tight cocoon.

"Never!" Sterling yelled. He tried to struggle, but it was futile.

"Join us," Banks said again. But this time it was the face of Lana McQueen speaking the words.

Sterling tried to scream but he was suddenly mute. He tried to push McQueen away, but it was impossible to overcome the power she held over him. The emissary laughed then released Sterling of her own choice and took two measured paces backward.

"You will join us, or she will die," McQueen said, pointing to a shadowy figure to her side. Sterling couldn't see the figure's face, but he knew it was Banks simply from the curve of her body and the flow of her hair. "You're not strong enough to kill her, Lucas. You never were. And that is why you'll lose…" The former fleet captain then smiled at him before her head exploded, showering his face in hot flesh and bone.

Sterling screamed again, but this time the sound of his voice filled his own ears. He realized that he was on his back on the deck of the Invictus, staring up at the ceiling. Alarms were ringing out all around him, but all he knew was that he was still alive. He was tired, tormented, battered, bruised and sick to the very pit of his stomach – but he was alive.

You won't beat me… Sterling thought, as he lay there, waiting for his strength to return. *You will never beat me…* Then, for the first time, Sterling realized that the 'you' he was referring to was not Crow, or McQueen, or even the Sa'Nerran empire as a collective. It was himself.

Sterling had barely set foot on the Far Deep Nine mining research station before the stench of decaying bodies assaulted his senses. Even for someone accustomed to the smell of death, it took Sterling by surprise.

"I never thought we'd be back here again," said Banks, stepping beside Sterling. She too then scrunched up her nose and held a hand over her face. "We might need to send a cleaning crew though here first, though."

Colicos entered the docking area next and immediately bent double, hacking and coughing like he was about to throw up. Shade was close behind, weapon in hand.

"Get a hold of yourself, doctor," Sterling ordered, showing the scientist no sympathy. "The sooner you finish your work, the sooner we can all get off this station. Just think of the smell as your incentive to work fast."

"This is intolerable!" Colicos complained, though he was still gagging so badly it sounded like he had a sponge in his mouth. The scientist staggered over to the wall and propped himself up against it, clasping a hand to his mouth. Sterling had thought that the scientist was acting up on purpose, but the longer this hacking and gagging routine continued, the more it appeared genuine.

"I'll assemble a team to clean up the dead, sir," said Lieutenant Shade. She still had her plasma pistol aimed at Colicos, despite his apparent helplessness. "What do you want to do with the bodies of the commandoes?"

"They're just rotten meat now, Lieutenant," Sterling replied, stepping over the body of a dead Sa'Nerran warrior. "But we should honor them in the manner of their choosing. See to it," Sterling added.

"Aye, Captain," Shade replied.

Sterling watched Shade step away and tap her neural interface to make the necessary arrangements. All the while the weapons officer continued to watch Colicos like a vulture watching a crippled animal, waiting for it to fall and die. Sterling had witnessed and participated in too many horrors to believe in a higher power. Certainly, if one existed then Lucas Sterling would not be in its good graces. However, he respected the wishes of those who did believe, regardless of which god or gods they worshipped. In truth he didn't know whether any members of his crew were spiritual people, but he would respect their various funeral customs, whatever they were. This was despite him believing that such occasions were a pointless waste of resources and manpower. A sentimental outpouring of emotion – energy that could better be spent on more important tasks. However, he also knew that hope was a powerful ally, and that the loss of hope could be as crippling as any injury or disease. If it provided comfort to his crew to honor the dead in a specific manner then so be it. And so, for their sake, he would do what was expected of him.

Sterling continued to watch his officers and crew set to work and took a moment to reflect on the events of the last few hours. It had taken the crew of the Invictus a full hour to fully recover from the deleterious effects of Lieutenant Razor's experimental 'rebound' surge maneuver. Twenty injuries had been reported in the aftermath and more than half the crew had to be treated for nausea and intense headaches. Mercifully, the injuries were minor – mostly cuts and bruises from falls due to the extreme dizziness and nausea that the triple-surge had caused.

Mercifully, the disorientation the surge had caused had also spared Sterling the embarrassment of his bridge crew hearing his panicked cries. Sterling's intense experience had actually roused his senses sooner than the others, allowing him to return to his feet and man his station before his officers. For a time, the nightmare scenes he had witnessed remained strong in his mind. However, as was always the case, Sterling was soon able to regain mastery over his emotions and bury these darker thoughts deep in his psyche.

It wasn't all good news, though. As Lieutenant Razor had stated, the 'rebound' surge had burned out their surge field generator and left the ship momentarily defenseless. Fortunately, once the rest of the bridge crew were back at their posts, an analysis of the system showed that the Sa'Nerra had long-since departed. As a result, Far Deep

Nine, like the other installations in the system, was completely deserted. The destruction of the Sa'Nerran mining ship had apparently removed any reason for the aliens to continue their occupation.

"Penny for your thoughts?" said Banks, snapping Sterling back into the moment.

Sterling smiled at her. "I'm just thinking that I hope this pays off," he replied, glancing over at Colicos, who was still propped up against the wall, looking clammy and pale. "Because if Colicos can't do what we need, I'm not sure we have another card to play."

"There is only one other," replied Banks, folding her arms. "We stand and fight the Sa'Nerra, right down to the last ship and the last commando. If that's not enough, then maybe it's just our time."

Sterling shook his head. "These alien bastards don't get to decide when it's our time," he replied, glaring over at Colicos. "That cowardly piece of garbage got us into this mess, and he's going to get us out of it."

He advanced toward Colicos, who was finally beginning to recover. However, Sterling's rapid advance quickly turned the scientist's complexion more ashen again.

"Come on, doctor, no rest for the wicked," Sterling said, grabbing the man by the collar of his tailored shirt and yanking him toward his old lab.

"Really, Captain, such brutishness does not become you," Colicos protested. The scientist managed to shake off Sterling's hold on him and step away, angrily straightening his shirt collar as he did so. "I will make my own way there, thank you."

"Then get a move on, doctor," Sterling hit back, giving him another gentle shove. "Or I'll have Commander Banks drag you to the lab by your hair. And I promise that you won't be able to shake her off quite so easily."

Colicos glanced over to Banks, who merely smiled and flashed her eyes at him. "This endeavor is pointless," Colicos said, continuing to protest. However, he was also now making his way swiftly toward the lab. "I don't know what you expect me to achieve in just a few days. It took me years to progress my research to the level where neural control was possible."

"Then you've already done all the hard work, haven't you?" replied Sterling, shoving Colicos in the back again to remind him he was still there. "Besides, we may not even have a few days, so I'm going to need this neural blocking device within eighteen hours. Twenty-four at the most."

Colicos spun around, red-faced. "That's impossible!" he screeched. "Even for a man of my brilliance."

"If you're so brilliant then it shouldn't be any trouble, should it?" Sterling hit back. "Just get it done, otherwise I'll leave you here to rot with the rest of these corpses."

James Colicos continued to protest for the remainder of their short journey to the lab. For the most part, Sterling managed to filter out the scientist's babbling, though by the time they reached the laboratory space he was still close to shooting the man and being done with him there and then.

"Get to work, doctor," Sterling said, shoving Colicos in front of the nearest workbench. "I don't care what you have to do, and which bodies you have to pull out of cold storage to do it. Get me that neural control blocker, and while you're at it, figure out how to fix my chief engineer's brain too. You have eighteen hours to do both, otherwise you're going to become a permanent resident."

Colicos looked ready to protest again, but Banks took a pace toward him, muscles bulging inside the sleeves of her tunic. The scientist's jaw snapped shut and he quietly shuffled away to another part of the lab.

"I want a security detail on him around the clock," Sterling said, turning to Lieutenant Shade, who had followed Colicos like a shadow. "He doesn't so much as take a crap without a commando watching him, understood?"

"I beg your pardon!" Colicos exclaimed, but Sterling ignored the man.

"And he doesn't sleep until he's done," Sterling went on, still addressing Shade. "I don't care if you have to whip him, stick him with a cattle prod or pump him full of stims to keep him working. Whatever it takes, is that clear?"

"It will be my genuine pleasure, Captain," Shade said, drilling into the scientist with her eyes. Colicos still appeared to be reeling from the prospect of a commando watching him go to the bathroom.

Ordinarily, the sadistic nature of his weapons officer's reply might have perturbed Sterling. However, on this occasion, he hoped that Shade did have to resort to more arcane and medieval techniques in order to motivate the scientist. It was as much as the man deserved.

"Commander Banks and I are going to check the station for any supplies and equipment," Sterling continued. "Keep me apprised of any developments."

"Aye, sir. Would you like me to assign you a security escort?" Shade replied.

"No, this place is dead," Sterling said, noticing another rotting corpse at the far end of the lab. "Besides, your commandoes have enough to deal with recovering the bodies and watching that asshole." Sterling nodded toward Colicos as he said this. The scientist folded his arms and muttered something under his breath. Sterling couldn't quite catch what Colicos had said, but he was certain it wasn't complimentary. Sterling then rejoined Commander Banks and the two of them began to head out of the lab.

"If you're looking for useful supplies, Captain, then I suggest you check storage sub-level two," Colicos called out.

Sterling stopped and turned to face the scientist. "What's your definition of 'useful supplies', doctor?" he replied, curious and suspicious as to why the man was suddenly trying to be helpful.

"It's where I stored the food I brought here from Oasis Colony, along with the tools and components that I will require for this impossible task you have set me. Your engineer might also find them of use when it comes to rebuilding your surge field generator."

"I'll check it out," Sterling replied, still more than a little suspicious. "Anything else down there that I should be aware of?"

"Nothing that concerns you, Captain," Colicos snapped.

Sterling sighed then glanced at Banks. "See if you can persuade our resident genius to loosen his tongue," he said, returning his gaze to the scientist. "Perhaps a couple of broken toes will do."

Banks moved toward Colicos and the scientist jolted back, knocking into a workbench and scattering its contents onto the floor.

"Fine, fine!" Colicos called, holding up his hands. "Really, Captain, you are most uncivilized."

"What else is in sub-level two, doctor?" Sterling asked. "The truth this time."

"A substantial supply of silver, if you must know," Colicos reluctantly answered. "Which is all mine and not to be requisitioned by you or Fleet!"

Sterling snorted and shook his head. "The Void colonies are all but gone, doctor, so I don't think you'll be needing spending money any time soon," he hit back. "Besides, Commander Graves and Lieutenant Razor can made good use of silver in medical and engineering applications."

"Even so, it is mine," Colicos snapped, his tone forceful and insistent. "You may be a brute, but I trust you are also not a common thief. If you want or need it then you must trade for something I want."

"And what might that be?" said Sterling. He was genuinely curious about what appealed to Colicos more than wealth and status.

"I want my own quarters," the scientist hit back. "I want my dignity and, eventually, my freedom."

"Pull off this impossible task, doctor, and I'll grant you your own quarters," Sterling replied, considering that to be a fair bargain. "However, assuming we all live through this, your ultimate fate is not mine to decide." Colicos' eyes narrowed, but for once the scientist kept his mouth shut. "Now, is that everything we need to be aware of down there?" Sterling added. He was impatient to leave – he'd spent more than enough time in Colicos' presence as it was.

"Yes, Captain, that is all," Colicos replied. The man then turned his back to Sterling and began to pick up the tools that he'd knocked onto the floor earlier. "Now, if you'll excuse me, I apparently have a lot of work to do."

Sterling turned to Banks and extended a hand toward the exit, inviting his first officer to take the lead. "After you, Commander," he said. "Let's go and explore the dungeons."

STERLING TURNED the handle and pushed open the manually-operated steel door that led onto sub-level two of Far Deep Nine. The tarnished hinges groaned and Sterling found himself needing to push harder to drive back the years of accumulated grime that was gathering underneath the door. As he entered, boots sticking to the tacky floor tiles, yellow ceiling lights flickered on and hummed softly. A thick layer of dust obscured the light diffusers, causing the room to remain in gloomy darkness.

"I think whatever is stored down here probably rotted away years ago," said Commander Banks, stepping through door after Sterling and scrunching up her nose. "It smells like damp and decay."

Sterling pressed on into the storage room and ran his finger through the dust that had settled on top of a stack of metal crates.

"Well, at least we can be pretty sure the Sa'Nerra never plundered these stores," Sterling said, rubbing the tacky black grime between his fingers. "So maybe we'll find something useful down here, after all." He raised his left forearm and accessed a schematic of the sub-level on his computer. "The main storage area appears to be a few sections along," he added, wiping his hand clean on the seat of his pants. "We should probably start there and work our way back."

Sterling and Banks moved through the subterranean maze, popping open the lids of every container and crate they came across along the way.

"This feels like opening presents on Christmas morning," Banks said, lifting the lid on another crate and peering inside.

"You must have received some pretty crappy gifts then," Sterling said, sifting through the contents of a barrel-shaped container, which was filled with an assortment of spare parts for the machinery on the station. "Most of the stuff in these crates is junk."

"Actually, I never really experienced Christmas, so I wouldn't know," Banks replied, moving on to another container.

Sterling remembered that Banks had been orphaned as a child and had spent her childhood bouncing around various orphanages and foster homes, before signing up to Fleet at age sixteen. Sterling had also spent his youth moving from place to place, never settling anywhere for long. Despite their short tenure on the ship, the Invictus had ironically felt like more of a home than either of them had experienced before.

He moved on to another crate and found a collection of

power cells. "Here you go then, a gift from me to you," he said, picking out one of the cells and offering it to Banks.

Banks smiled as she took the cell, clutching it to her chest like a teddy bear. "Really, Captain, you shouldn't have," she said, sarcastically, before tossing the cell back into the crate. "I mean you really, really shouldn't have."

Sterling laughed and the two officers continued to inventory the stores, in time discovering several crates that contained items of value. These included meal trays and medical supplies, along with several crates of electronic and mechanical components that could be adapted for use on the Invictus.

"Wow…"

Sterling glanced over his shoulder to see Banks staring down into a square chest about the size of a food hamper. Her face was lit by something from within, as if the crate had an internal light source.

"Is that a good 'wow' or a bad 'wow'?" Sterling asked, moving beside his first officer and peering into the chest. "Wow…" he then said, as it became clear what the box contained.

"There's enough silver in here to buy an entire cruiser at one of the shipyards on the Void planets," Banks said, digging her hand into the chest and allowing the thin silver bars to slip through her fingers.

"Make sure Razor takes this one, and keeps it well hidden from Colicos," Sterling said, inspecting one of the shiny bars like a magpie eyeing up a piece of jewelry. "If we can't make Colicos pay with his life, we'll make him pay with his fortune instead."

"Aye, sir," Banks said, enthusiastically, remaining mesmerized by the vast quantity of silver in front of her.

Sterling left his first officer to admire the hoard and continued to scour the room, using the flashlight function on his computer to supplement the subdued, yellow overhead lighting. Moving along the far wall, he suddenly felt a chill wash over his body and he physically shivered.

"Did someone just step on your grave?" Banks said, closing the lid of the chest and glancing over at Sterling.

Sterling hugged his body and rubbed the tops of his arms. "Whoever is was must have been an Eskimo," he replied. "It's freezing over here."

Banks moved closer, tapping commands into her computer as she approached. "It's not you," she said, eyes still on her screen. "The temperature drops sharply here, by over ten degrees."

Sterling scowled then moved closer to the wall, running his hand across the surface.

"The wall feels colder here too," he said, making use of his physical sense of touch while Banks continued to scan the area using more twenty-fourth century methods.

He crouched and ran his hand down the wall almost to where it met the floor. He felt a cold breeze drift over his skin, making the hairs on the back of his hand stand on end.

"There's definitely something behind this wall," said Banks, still focused on her computer. "But whatever it is, it's not on the architectural plan."

Sterling heard a sound, like a knife clattering onto the deck in the wardroom, and he froze.

"Did you hear that?" he whispered to Banks.

His first officer nodded and instinctively they both went to neural comms. Then another sound filtered into the room, closer than the first.

"Lieutenant, do you have anyone on sub-level two?" Sterling asked his weapons officer over the neural link.

"Negative, Captain, we're all on level one," Shade replied. Her voice was distant. The dense structure of the research station was interfering with neural communications. "Do you need assistance, Captain?" she added. There was another sound, this time clearer and more distinct. Footsteps. "Negative, Lieutenant, but stand by," Sterling replied, tapping his interface to close to link. He then nodded to Banks and they both drew their weapons.

"I'll circle around to the right," Banks said through the link, though she had already begun to move away.

Sterling nodded, then headed directly toward the source of the noise, staying low with his weapon held ready. He saw a shadow flicker across the deck and moved into cover, watching the intruder creep further into the room. Suddenly, the shadow turned and came directly toward him. His heart leapt in his chest and he sprang out of cover, weapon raised.

"Don't move!" Sterling called out, aiming the weapon at the silhouetted figure's head.

Banks appeared out of nowhere a moment later, pistol also trained on the intruder. The figure froze and its hands shot toward the ceiling.

"Don't shoot, it's just me," a panicked voice cried.

Sterling advanced and activated the torchlight on his

computer, shining it into the intruder's face. He cursed and breathed a sigh of relief. It was Ensign Keller.

"What the hell are you doing down here, Ensign?" Sterling said, lowering his pistol to his side. "I nearly blasted your head off!"

"Sorry, Captain, it's just that everyone else is busy and I was at a loose end," the helmsman replied, rushing through his words. "I bumped into the scientist, James Colicos, and he said you were down here. So, I thought I'd lend a hand."

"You might have let us know that first," said Sterling as Banks stepped out of the shadows, glowering at the ensign.

"Yes, sir," Keller replied, standing to attention. "Sorry, sir."

"Well, since you're here, you may as well make yourself useful," replied Sterling. He started walking back to the false wall they'd discovered earlier. "It looks like there's something back here. We could use some help finding a way through."

Keller appeared intrigued and hurried over to the wall. He rested his hand on the surface then began to trace the same line Sterling had done until he discovered the air gap near the floor.

"Maybe we can just force it?" said Keller, looking at Banks.

Sterling nodded to his first officer and she rested her hands on the wall and braced herself against it. The metal groaned and Sterling saw the panels flex, but the wall did not move.

"Try over here," said Keller, who had traced the path of

the cold breeze further along the wall. "There's a seam here."

Banks dusted off her hands and moved to the section of the wall that Keller had indicated. This time she pressed her back against the surface and leaned into it, digging her heels into the deck. The muscles in Banks' thighs rippled and the wall began to slide back.

"Keep pushing," said Sterling, joining in with the effort.

"Don't just stand there, Ensign," Banks said, speaking through gritted teeth. "Push!"

Through the combined effort of all three officers, the wall slid open more freely, driving back a thick layer of black grime in the process. Sterling dusted off his hands then shone his torchlight inside the opening. Unlike the storage areas they'd worked their way through previously, the room was completely empty. Then as Sterling stepped further inside, the light from his torch shone on a corridor that led deeper into the research station. Sterling examined the new space more closely, recognizing the style of architecture at once.

"This looks like Sa'Nerran design," Sterling said, shining his light around the room. "My guess is that they added this section after driving out the human colonists."

"Why though?" said Ensign Keller. "What is this place?"

Sterling shrugged. "I don't know, but there's only one way to find out."

"Should we call for backup?" Banks asked.

It was a reasonable precaution, though Sterling could tell that his first-officer had only asked the question out of protocol. The glint in her eyes suggested she was eager to continue exploring.

"I think three of us is enough for now," Sterling replied. He had the same itch to continue. He felt like an archeologist in ancient Egypt, discovering the tombs of the Pharaohs for the first time. "Weapons out and ready, though. We don't know what to expect down there", he added in a more cautionary tone. The stories of ancient tomb raiders also included tales of booby-traps and ancient curses. While he knew that these were apocryphal, at least when it came to ancient Egypt, an alien addition to an abandoned research station was another matter.

Sterling led the way down the steeply sloping corridor, until it eventually widened into a larger space. It was now pitch black and also freezing cold. Sterling hugged his jacket tighter around his chest, but the cold had already begun to creep into his bones.

"Over here," said Banks, who had moved over to the far corner of the room. "It looks like more storage containers."

"Check out the other corner, Ensign," Sterling said to Keller.

The helmsman nodded and disappeared into the darkness. Sterling swept his torchlight over to where his first officer was standing and cautiously approached. As he got closer, he could see rows of the containers Banks had described, lined up alongside each other with narrow gaps between them.

"Can you scan inside them?" asked Sterling, while examining the container next to the one Banks had found.

"I've tried, but the readings are inconclusive," Banks

said. Her face was brightly illuminated by the computer screen. Set against the pitch-black backdrop of the room, it gave her a ghostly, disembodied appearance. "I'm picking up some low-level power readings, and the temperature of these containers is twenty degrees warmer than the ambient temperature in here."

Sterling frowned and ran his hand along the top of the container. It was wet with condensation. Then he shone his torchlight onto the surface and his heart leapt inside his chest for a second time. Staring up at him from inside the container was a Sa'Nerran warrior in hibernation stasis.

"I think I've found something!" Ensign Keller called out.

"Nobody touch anything!" Sterling shouted back, but it was already too late. Moments later, lights blinked on inside the room, temporarily blinding him. The thrum of power generators began to rise.

"We have to get out of here, right now!" Sterling called out. However, he had barely made it three paces before a door dropped down from above, sealing the exit.

"Crap, these are Sa'Nerran stasis pods," said Banks, squinting down at the container to her side, while shielding her eyes from the overhead lights. "There's a warrior inside this thing."

"And we're trapped in here with them," replied Sterling. He tried to force the door that had sealed them inside the room, but it wouldn't budge. Cursing he ran back to Banks.

"See if you can get that open," he said, nodding toward the exit. "Otherwise, we'll have to cut through.

"Captain, I don't think we'll have time," said Ensign Keller, hurriedly backing toward him.

White clouds of gas had erupted from beneath the stasis pods. Sterling grabbed Keller and dragged him clear of the mist, though it still stung his eyes and burned his throat.

"We only have a couple of minutes before these things activate," croaked Sterling, coughing into his sleeve. "We have to destroy the pods before the warriors come out of hibernation."

The covers of three stasis pods at the far end of the room shot open. Long, leathery fingers rose out of the mist and Sterling heard the distinctive hiss of the alien language.

"I can't get the door open," Banks said, returning to Sterling's side, breathing heavily. "Cutting through is our only option."

Sterling cursed again then grabbed Keller's arms and turned the ensign to face him. "Start cutting, Ensign," Sterling said, grabbing the helmsman's pistol and adjusting the power setting. "We only need a hole big enough for us to crawl though, understand?"

"Aye, Captain, I'm on it," Keller said, as Sterling slapped the weapon back into his hand.

"It would be quicker with two people cutting," Banks pointed out, as four more pods opened, spilling more white gas into the room. It was now impossible to see more than ten meters in front of them.

Suddenly, Sterling saw a warrior approach out of the haze. Its yellow eyes were dry and bloodshot and its leathery, gray skin was wrinkled and tight, like the fingertips of someone who'd spent too long in the bath. Sterling raised his pistol and blasted the warrior in the head, adding the smell of burned alien flesh to the heady mixture of odors already filling the room.

"I think we're going to need every last shot we have," Sterling replied, as more hisses filled the room. "And even then, it might not be enough."

A SECOND SA'NERRAN warrior advanced through the fog and Banks raised her weapon and fired. The blast carved a chunk out of the alien's neck and it went down hard. However, behind the body, Sterling could already see more aliens clawing themselves out of stasis pods and advancing toward them.

"Reduce the power setting on your pistol to the lowest you can get away with," said Sterling, flicking the dial on his pistol down by two notches. "We only need to hold them off long enough for Keller to cut us an exit."

Banks nodded and made the adjustments before firing at a third warrior. This time the blast burned a hole in its head three inches deep. The warrior initially appeared confused and reached up, pressing a long finger inside the cavity and touching its freshly singed brain. Then it fell forward, like a felled tree.

"These things are giving me the creeps," said Banks,

dropping to one knee and sweeping her pistol around the room. "It's like they're damned zombies or something."

"It's stasis sickness," replied Sterling, tapping his neural interface and trying to reach out to Lieutenant Shade. "If a human had been woken that quickly, they'd already be dead." Sterling then focused on the link, but he couldn't make the connection.

"Hurry, Ensign, I can't reach Shade to call for backup," Sterling said, glancing back to his helmsman. Keller had so far managed to cut through a meter section of the door. "We're on our own down here."

"The metal is thick, sir, it's going to take some time," Keller called back. Sweat was pouring off his face from the heat of the cutting beam.

"Time is the one thing we don't have, Ensign. Work faster," Sterling ordered.

Suddenly another warrior staggered through the haze and Sterling raised his pistol, ready to fire. However, the warrior fell as if it had been smashed in the back with a sledgehammer. He checked on Banks, but she was engaging two other warriors across the other side of the room.

"If we're lucky, these things might drop dead without us needing to kill them," Sterling called over to his first-officer.

Two more warriors then advanced and this time Sterling was forced to fire. The first blast struck the warrior's chest, but the alien continued on. Sterling cursed and fired again, killing the warrior with the second shot.

Damn it, aim for the head... Sterling thought, chastising himself for wasting a shot. He knew he perhaps had at most twenty more before his power cell was empty.

"Cap...n...is th... you?"

Sterling received the words through his neural link, but the signal kept cutting out, like a weak FM radio.

"Lieutenant Shade?" Sterling replied, moving around the room in an attempt to get a stronger link. "If you can hear me, we need you, right now."

"Wha... is your... loc...n?" the voice replied. Sterling couldn't be sure that it was his weapons officer on the other side of the link, but so long as he could reach someone, he didn't care who it was.

"Sub-level two, north perimeter," Sterling replied, closing his eyes in an attempt to focus harder on the link. "Send a squad, now!"

"Aye..." came the single word reply before the link was severed.

Sterling cursed then opened his eyes to see a Sa'Nerra warrior charging at him through the mist. Raising his weapon, he blasted the alien at close range. The energy hammered into the warrior's hip, but its momentum carried it on and Sterling was tackled to the deck, his pistol spiraling from his grasp. A second later, the warrior was on top of him, clammy, leathery fingers clasped around his throat. The alien was so close that he could taste its foul breath and see every line of detail in its shriveled, grey skin. Sterling broke the hold, finding it easier than he expected to overpower the creature, then spun the alien onto its back. Grabbing the sides of its head, Sterling drove his thumbs into the warrior's yellow eyes, causing them to explode like pus-filled balloons. The warrior hissed wildly, but Sterling didn't let go. Using his hand-hold he repeatedly hammered the alien's head against the metal deck until its body became limp.

With no time to recover, Sterling was grabbed from behind and he felt the clammy grasp of more alien fingers digging into his flesh. Thudding an elbow into the alien's ribs, Sterling threw the warrior over his shoulder. It landed hard on the deck, already looking half-dead. Recovering his pistol, Sterling blasted it in the head at point-blank range then spun around to cover his rear.

"Commander, report!" Sterling called out into the haze. The room was now equal parts vapor from the stasis pods and smoke from the burning bodies of dead aliens.

"I'm already on my second cell," Banks called back.

Sterling then saw his first-officer backing toward him through the smoke. He was about to go to her when a warrior rushed out of the haze and drove its shoulder into Banks' gut, pushing her deeper into the smog. Sterling set off in pursuit, but was tackled by another alien. He fought the creature, but this warrior was far stronger than the one he had easily overpowered. Leathery fists pounded into Sterling's face, forcing him to raise his arms to block the blows. The warrior switched up its attack, hammering him in the gut instead. Winded, Sterling was unable to retaliate, allowing the alien to continue its assault with relentless brutality. Then then fizz of a plasma pistol pierced his ears and the warrior suddenly went limp and slid off his body.

"Captain, are you okay?" asked Ensign Keller, dropping

to a knee by his side and offering Sterling a hand. Sterling took it and Keller hauled him to his feet.

"I'm fine, Ensign," Sterling replied, clutching his ribs with one hand and recovering his weapon with the other. "Now get the door open, or we're dead."

"My cell is empty," Keller replied. "That last shot used everything I had left."

Sterling thrust his pistol into the ensign's hand. "Then use this, instead," he said, shoving the helmsman back toward the door. "I'll strangle these bastards with my bare hands if I have to."

Keller ran back to the door while Sterling headed into the fog, looking for his first officer. "Mercedes!" Sterling called out. Through the gloom, he could hear the hiss of alien warriors and human grunts of pain. "Mercedes!" Sterling called out again, feeling panic rising in his gut.

A warrior flew over his head, missing him by inches. Banks appeared through the smoke; her hands drenched in dark crimson Sa'Nerran blood. As she got closer, Sterling could see that her eyes were wild. He knew he wouldn't get any sense out of her at that moment, but he didn't need to. All he needed was her brutality.

Standing back-to-back, Sterling and Banks fought off more warriors. Recovered from his earlier battering, Sterling focused on the weak points of the aliens' anatomy, cracking knees and hammering his elbows in the backs of their necks. Banks, in contrast, displayed no such finesse. She had given herself over to rage and blood lust, resorting to cracking bones and tearing out the throats of the warriors that were foolish enough to stand up to her. Yet, despite their efforts, the enemies continued to come, and soon Sterling's strength failed him.

"Ensign, report!" Sterling called out, dropping to one knee, gasping for breath. "We can't hold them for much longer."

"It's no use, sir!" Keller replied. "The metal is too thick. This cell is depleted too."

Sterling cursed and backed up against the wall. Five more warriors were approaching through the bitter-tasting smoke, all advancing cautiously on account of the bodies piled up around them.

"Then get on your feet, Ensign," Sterling said, spitting blood onto the deck. "If you're going to die in here then die with your hands wrapped around their throats."

Keller tossed the expended pistol away then rose up and raised his guard. Sterling glanced across to his young helmsman and was impressed to see there was no fear behind his eyes. There was only anger and frustration and a will to survive.

Maybe we can still do this... Sterling told himself. *We've faced worse odds.*

Then the dark silhouettes of three more warriors appeared in the distance and Sterling felt his conviction waver. Five on three was perhaps manageable, even in their battered and exhausted condition. Eight on three, though, was impossible, even with Mercedes Banks at his side. However, it no longer mattered how many there were. All that mattered was how many of the alien bastards they could kill before they fell. Sterling sucked in a lungful of the foul air and prepared himself to attack.

"Captain Sterling, please respond."

It was Opal Shade, reaching out through the still-open neural link. The connection was strong.

"Hold here!" Sterling called out to Banks and Keller, barring both from advancing with his outstretched arms. He then focused on the link. "Lieutenant Shade, tell me you're outside the door?"

"Aye, Captain, what is your condition?" Shade replied, as cool as ever.

"Just blast through the damned door and get in here!" Sterling called back. He could now see the yellow of the warriors' eyes. The aliens were hissing in harmony, like some sort of chant. "Everyone, get down!" Sterling yelled, throwing himself to the deck.

Moments later, Sterling's body was blanketed in a shower of sparks and he felt hard chunks of metal land on his back and legs. Plasma blasts then raced inside the room, thudding into the bodies of the warriors that had come so close to ending his life. Shade charged in, almost stepping on Sterling in the process and continued to unload into the room. Four commandoes followed, each with 'Homewrecker' heavy plasma rifles in hand.

Sterling pushed himself up and withdrew into the corridor outside the smoke-filled room, still coughing and holding his bruised side. Likely he had a cracked rib or two, but all considered he'd gotten off lightly, he told himself. Banks then appeared with Keller at her side, closely followed by Lieutenant Shade.

"Thank you, Lieutenant, that was too close," Sterling said, resting against the wall to regain his breath.

"I'll have a team sweep through sub-levels one and two to check for other hidden spaces, sir," Shade said. "My guess is that the Sa'Nerra were using Far Deep Nine to store reserve forces close to Fleet space. It would allow them to quickly gather reinforcements, without having to return to their half of the Void."

"What's the betting that asshole Colicos knew about this place all along?" said Commander Banks.

Sterling's first officer was covered in blood, but Sterling could tell from its color and thickness that it was not her own. As usual, Banks' resilience and strength had resulted in her suffering few injuries.

"That's something I intend to find out," replied Sterling. His loathing for the traitorous scientist had reached a new high.

Sterling was about to set off back up the sloping corridor to sub-level two when he felt a link form in his mind from Commander Graves. Frowning, he stopped and allowed the connection to take hold.

"What's up, Commander?" Sterling asked. His medical officer was the last person he'd expected to hear from at that moment.

"Captain, we have a situation," Graves said, sounding unusually ill-at-ease. "Five warships have surrounded the station and locked weapons onto the Invictus."

Sterling pressed his eyes shut and shook his head. "Sa'Nerran?" he asked, fearing the worst. "Is it MAUL?"

"No, Captain," Graves replied. "They are ships from

the Void. A man from the lead vessel said you would remember him."

"Who is it, Commander?" asked Sterling. There was a brief pause before Graves answered, though he had a sinking feeling he already knew what was coming.

"He says his name is Marshal Masterson."

STERLING REACHED the docking area of the research station and found Marshal Masterson senior already waiting for him. There was a shuttlecraft docked at one of the ports adjacent to the Invictus and through the viewing gallery windows, five aged warships loomed outside. The lawman himself was also flanked by a dozen other men, some of whom Sterling could see were his deputies. However, at least half of the men did not wear the silver star on their jackets, which suggested they were guns for hire.

"Well, well, it seems you've been in the wars, Captain," said Masterson, smiling at Sterling.

Sterling caught a reflection of himself in a window and he realized he made for a sorry sight. His uniform was dirtied with grime and his face bore the tell-tales cuts and bruises of a recent fight.

"I've been in a war nearly my whole damned life,

Marshal," Sterling hit back. "In case you've missed the news, the Sa'Nerra are winning."

"Like I give a damn about Earth," Masterson replied, shrugging. "My only war is with you Captain, and it's a war I plan on winning."

The open threat prompted Lieutenant Shade to aim her weapon at the Marshal. The dozen other men behind the lawman then brandished their weapons too, followed soon after by Shade's remaining commandoes. It was a classic Mexican standoff.

"Easy there, Captain," said the Marshal, holding up his hands in an attempt to calm the situation down. "We could very easily end this in a shootout right now, and likely neither of us would survive. But I have the guns of five warships trained on your vessel. If they don't hear from me then your precious little ship gets annihilated."

"Your archaic taskforce is no match for the Invictus," Sterling hit back, though in truth he knew he was outgunned.

"Come now, Captain, let's not play games," the Marshal replied, smiling again. "Your ship might survive long enough to disable two or at best three of my ships, but we both know it can't best five, not without being crippled or destroyed itself."

"How the hell did you find us, anyway?" Sterling said. He was already bored of their posturing.

"You didn't think I'd let you escape judgement for your crimes, did you?" Masterson replied. "I've been tracking your movements these past few weeks and months and setting up aperture relays in case you showed up. It's cost me every penny I had, but now I see it was money well spent." Masterson then looked around the docking area of the research station and turned up his nose. "Though I honestly didn't expect I'd finally corner you here, of all places."

Just at that moment, James Colicos strolled into the docking section. He was peering down at a personal data assistant in his hand and hadn't noticed the standoff in the room.

"This is really rather fascinating," Colicos began, still oblivious to the group of armed men and women. "It appears that your Lieutenant Razor was on to something with the idea of a firewall. I believe I can easily refine her technique to assist with her injury, in addition to..." Colicos finally looked up and saw Marshal Masterson and the group of armed men. The scientist glanced across to Sterling and the others, mouth hanging open.

"James Colicos?" the Marshal said, squinting at the scientist as if he were a hundred meters further away than he was. "Last I heard you were dead."

"Yes, I get that a lot," replied Colicos, dryly.

Colicos then seemed to grasp the seriousness of the situation, though Sterling noted that the man also appeared strangely unafraid.

"Oh, thank you for coming to rescue me, Marshal," Colicos began, lowering the PDA to his side and hustling toward the lawman. Sterling tutted and shook his head, realizing that Colicos was trying to twist the sudden development to his advantage.

"Hold it right there," barked one of the deputies,

training his firearm on Colicos instead of the commandoes. The scientist stopped sharply, glancing nervously at the weapon before shooting Masterson a saccharine smile.

"I trust that you will punish Captain Sterling to the fullest extent of the law for abducting me," Colicos added, making a show of sounding desperate and wounded.

The Marshal frowned. "I'm not here for you, Colicos," the lawman said. "But since you're wanted for the kidnap and murder of a dozen colonists, I'll take you in too."

Masterson then nodded to one of his deputies who swept forward and grabbed Colicos by the arm. The scientist dropped the PDA and tried to fight off the deputies, but his struggles were weak and ineffective.

"I need him, Marshal," Sterling said, advancing into the center of the room. The weapons of the deputies then swung back to cover him. "Colicos' work is vital to the war."

"Your war, Captain," Masterson hit back. "And I don't give a damn about his work, either. He'll face judgement, just the same as you."

Colicos continued to protest until one of the deputies clocked him over the back of the head with the barrel of his pistol. The scientist fell limp in the deputy's arms.

Sterling cursed. He was backed into a corner with no way out. The Marshal was right that the Invictus couldn't take out all five of his ships, certainly not when the enemy vessels already had their weapons locked and ready to fire. And if they started shooting, the chances were that none of them would make it out of the docking area alive.

"So what happens now, Marshal?" said Sterling, taking the lawman's earlier advice and cutting to the chase. "We could kill each other right now or cut a deal. I don't have time to indulge your personal vendetta."

Marshal Masterson tutted and wagged a finger at Sterling. "Not a vendetta, Captain. Justice," the lawman replied. "You can only outrun justice for so long before it catches up with you, as it has done now."

Sterling huffed a laugh and shook his head. "I thought you said not to play games, Marshal," he hit back. "At least half of those ships out there along with the men behind you aren't Marshals or deputies. They're mercenaries, and since when do Void Pirates dispense justice?"

"Since you killed my other deputies and also tried to kill me," Masterson hit back, his tone becoming bitter and resentful. "Needs must, Captain. Justice must be served."

"And who exactly are you dispensing judgment on behalf of, Marshal?" Sterling continued. "The Sa'Nerra have likely wiped out Oasis Colony by now. The other colonies will be next." Sterling threw his hands out wide in despair. "And all because of one man's petty need for revenge."

"Enough!" snapped Masterson, the sudden sharpness of his tone causing the deputies and mercenaries to grip their weapons more tightly. The room was a powder keg waiting to explode. "You will face my judgement, Captain, and you will face it now. The only choice you have is to accept my justice willingly and spare the rest of your crew, or have them die alongside you."

Sterling sighed. He didn't believe for one second that Masterson would let the rest of his crew live. The lawman would know, just as he did, that if left alive, Banks would take the Invictus and hunt the Marshal and his deputies down to the last man. From several bad options, Sterling realized he was only truly left with one. They all had to fight and take their chances.

"Fine," Sterling said, taking a step back so that he was alongside his first officer. Sterling then met Banks' eyes and communicated his intentions with a simple look. No words were required, either verbal or through a neural link. His first officer's hand then tightened around the grip of her pistol. When cornered, every creature acted on instinct, Sterling realized. And the instinct of an Omega officer was to fight and win at any cost. "Here is my choice, Marshal," Sterling said, turning back to the lawman. Then, as his muscles twitched, ready to draw his pistol and shoot Masterson, the station was rocked by a powerful explosion. Sterling and the others were thrown off balance and the room was bathed in an intense orange glow. Shielding his eyes against the glare, Sterling saw that one of the Marshal's ships had exploded in space.

"What the hell?!" the Marshal cried, raising a communicator to his wrist.

A ship roared overhead, providing Sterling with the answer to the question Masterson was about to ask his crew. It wasn't Invictus that had destroyed the mercenary vessel, but something just as dangerous. MAUL then turned and swopped back toward the docking area, annihilating a second mercenary ship. The Sa'Nerran heavy destroyer then unleashed a flurry of blasts at the Invictus, striking the Marauder cleanly on the aft section. Sterling had no way to know the extent of the damage, but he knew his ship wouldn't be able to withstand a close-range assault from MAUL for long.

"Get back to the ship!" Sterling cried, opening fire at the group of lawmen and mercenaries, all of whom had been distracted by MAUL's sudden attack.

Banks and Shade also opened fire and moments later, plasma was flashing back in their direction. A commando was hit and went down, but Sterling's crew were more disciplined and maintained their composure, while the Marshal's deputies and hired-guns fled in panic.

"Come back, you cowards!" Masterson cried, as the lawman backed toward his shuttle. The Marshal was holding Colicos in front of him and using the scientist as a shield. "Stop running and fight!"

"We have to get Colicos back," Sterling called out to Lieutenant Shade. "We can't do anything without him."

His weapons officer nodded and tried to advance, but a volley of bullets slammed into her armor and forced her back. Shade gritted her teeth and forced herself up, ready to try again when another explosion shook the docking area, knocking everyone to the deck.

"Fight them you cowards!" Masterson yelled, retreating inside his docking port, still with his weapon pressed to Colicos' neck.

The deputies rallied and began to fight back, killing

another commando. Sterling cursed and returned fire, blasting the shoulder of one the deputies and severing the man's arm. Outside, the three remaining mercenary and Void Marshal vessels were taking the fight back to MAUL. Sterling knew it would buy some time, but not much. MAUL would make short work of the older vessels before training its guns on the Invictus.

"Everyone, get back to the ship," Sterling said, slapping Banks on the shoulder.

"What about Colicos?" Banks said while continuing to lay down suppressing fire.

"If Masterson gets away then we follow," Sterling called back, blasting a hole in another deputy's gut. "If not, we improvise."

Banks, Shade and Sterling moved inside the umbilical, while the remaining commandoes used their 'Homewrecker' heavy plasma rifles to drive the deputies and mercs back. Suddenly, Sterling realized that Keller wasn't with them. He looked around the docking section for his ensign then spotted him, crouched behind cover in the center of the room. Sterling cursed and tapped his neural interface.

"Ensign, get back here, now!" Sterling called out in his mind.

"Sir, the PDA!" Keller replied through the link.

Sterling then saw the data device that Colicos had been holding when he'd entered the room. It was barely a couple of meters in front of his ensign, but there was no way he could reach it without putting himself directly in the line of fire.

"Keller, leave it and get back here, that's an order, damn it!" Sterling called out. However, Keller had already made his move.

Sterling was helpless as he watched Keller dart out and grab the PDA. Spinning on his heels, the helmsman then sprinted toward Sterling and the others. *Come on, you can make it!* Sterling thought, willing his ensign on. Then he saw Marshal Masterson raise his pistol.

"Ensign, get down!" Sterling called out, but the flash of plasma had already left the barrel of the lawman's weapon. The top of Keller's head was blown off, splattering the deck with scorched bone and brains.

"No!" Sterling yelled, pounding his fist against the metal wall of the docking port.

The PDA flew through air and skidded to a stop at Sterling's feet, but in the heat of the moment, he no longer cared about the device or the secrets it contained. He marched out into view and opened fire at Masterson's forces, killing three deputies before they'd even seen him coming. Sterling then focused his fire onto Masterson, clipping the lawman's shoulder. The Marshal roared with pain, ducked out of sight and was gone.

"Captain, we have to go," Banks cried, grabbing Sterling's arm to make sure he didn't continue his frenzied assault. Sterling tried to shake her off, but Banks' grip was literally irresistible. "Lucas, now!" Banks cried again, dragging Sterling back into cover. "MAUL is coming, we have to go!"

Sterling cursed and thumped the wall with his fist another three times in an attempt to release his aggression and regain his focus. Then he grabbed the PDA at his feet and ran inside the Invictus with Banks still at his side, tapping his neural interface as he went.

"Get us out of here, Commander," he called out to his doctor and temporary bridge commander.

The docking hatch slammed shut and moments later the Invictus detached and spun away from the station. Through the docking bay windows, Sterling could see MAUL pressing its attack on Masterson's vessels. There was another explosion and a fierce orange glow as the fourth of five aged warships was destroyed. Then MAUL turned its guns on the Invictus.

"Graves, maximum acceleration, now!" Sterling called out through the link, but he could see it was too late. MAUL had them dead to rights.

Sensing an opportunity to escape, the last of Masterson's ships tried to turn and run. The old gen-one frigate's engines ignited and it accelerated directly in front of MAUL at the instant the Sa'Nerran heavy destroyer opened fire. The older vessel was obliterated, but MAUL was too close to evade the burning wreckage. The alien vessel ploughed through the debris, which struck it like a dozen wrecking balls all at once. MAUL spun out of control and its engines flashed out.

"Captain, MAUL has been disabled," he heard Commander Graves call out over the link. "What is our destination?"

Sterling looked over to the station and saw Marshal Masterson's shuttlecraft blasting hard toward the aperture.

"Pursue that shuttle, Commander," Sterling said,

slumping down against the docking hatch. All he could think of was Keller's head exploding and Marshal Masterson's face as the lawman pulled the trigger. "I don't care if it flies into the heart of the Sa'Nerran empire. Wherever that ship goes, you follow."

CHAPTER 18
IN PURSUIT OF REVENGE

The flames that had engulfed the viewscreen suddenly cleared as the Invictus pierced the atmosphere of Oasis Colony. Save for the sound of Sterling's finger tapping on the side of his console, the bridge was silent. It had remained that way for the majority of the journey from Far Deep Nine to the planet that Marshal Masterson's shuttle had escaped to. Commander Banks had temporarily taken over the helm control station. It was strange not to see her at his side, Sterling mused, but it was even stranger not to see Ensign Keller at his post at the front of the bridge. He was as much as fixture as the viewscreen itself. Now he was just dead meat.

Sterling knew he was a cold-hearted bastard - it came with the territory – but Keller's death had hit him hard. Not that he'd shown it. No-one on the ship had shed a tear over the ensign's death, and Sterling knew that no-one would. His crew would deal with Keller's loss in their own ways, in the privacy of their quarters and their own thoughts. In contrast, Sterling's way of dealing with Keller's death was going to be very public. He was going to tear Marshal Masterson apart with his bare hands. He was going to make sure the so-called lawman understood the consequences of killing one of his officers. Despite all the talk of justice, Masterson merely wanted to avenge the death of his son. Sterling would make the lawman truly understand the nature of vengeance.

"We're receiving a communication request," announced Lieutenant Shade. She had assumed the monitoring of comms channels while Banks was at the helm. "It's from the Bismarck."

Sterling was wondering when the former Fleet Lieutenant would contact him. Christopher Fletcher's ship had shown up on the scanners immediately after the Invictus had surged into the system. The Bismarck was the reason that the Sa'Nerra were no longer at Oasis Colony – Fletcher had surged in and cleaned house. However, he hadn't done it alone. Accompanying Fletcher's modified gen-one destroyer, were the twelve other mutineer ships plus another fifty more. The new additions were all a hodge-podge mixture of Fleet and Sa'Nerran warships salvaged from battles fought decades ago. Lieutenant Razor had detected residual surge energy that suggested an even greater number had originally been present for the battle. However, regardless of the exact strength of Fletcher's forces, it was clear it had been enough. Dozens of Sa'Nerra warships now littered the orbit of Oasis Colony, and an operation had already begun to reclaim the salvageable vessels to add them to Fletcher's already powerful fleet.

"Put Fletcher through, Lieutenant," said Sterling, glancing over to his weapon's officer. He wasn't in the mood for a conversation with anyone, but he was intrigued to hear what the old veteran had to say.

"Captain Sterling! I must admit I'm surprised to see you back at Oasis Colony," Fletcher began, jovially. Sterling couldn't help but smile. It made a nice change to receive a message from someone who wasn't trying to kill him. "The last report we received said the Sa'Nerra had taken G-sector and cut Fleet off from the Void."

The former fleet officer appeared in good spirits, displaying the confidence and buoyancy of a man who had just been victorious in battle. Sterling knew the feeling well, though at that moment he couldn't recall it. He felt only a numb sense of pain, like a nagging headache that wouldn't go away.

"It's complicated, Captain," replied Sterling, choosing to address the man according to his current status, rather than his old Fleet rank. "And I'm afraid I don't have time to explain right now."

Fletcher nodded. "Understood, Captain. Keep your secrets," the former fleet officer replied, offering a wink of reassurance to highlight he was only joking. Sterling, however, was also in no mood for jokes, and Fletcher appeared to recognize this at once. "Is this matter anything I can assist with, Captain Sterling?" he asked, taking a much more earnest tone.

"I'm tracking a Void Marshal down to the planet's surface," Sterling said. He felt he had no reason to keep secrets from the man. "He has someone I need. And he's also responsible for killing one of my officers."

The older man sighed and nodded. As a former Fleet officer, Sterling knew he had at least some understanding of how he was feeling at that moment. However, Fletcher's own history of loss and pain allowed the man to have greater empathy for his situation than most.

"We monitored a shuttle heading toward Sanctum Spaceport," Fletcher replied. "A word of warning, though, Captain. If it's Ed Masterson you're after, he's made Sanctum his own private law-enforcement base. I hear he bankrupted himself hiring mercenaries from all over the Void in order to find you."

"We met them already," said Sterling. "They're all dead."

Fletcher nodded. "I'd like to say I'm sorry to hear that, but in all honestly that would be a lie," the former officer admitted. The man then became more earnest again. "Which of your officers was lost, Captain?"

"My helmsman, Ensign Kieran Keller," Sterling replied, feeling his mouth suddenly go dry. The memory of Keller's head being blown off pushed its way to the front of Sterling's mind. Rage swelled inside him and he clenched his teeth, fighting hard to bury his emotions and keep a tight lid on his anger. He needed to save his energy and his aggression for the moment he had his hands wrapped around Masterson's throat.

"I'm sorry to hear that, I enjoyed meeting him," Fletcher replied, coming across as heartfelt and sincere. "I hope you get your man, Captain. The Marshals no longer serve a useful function, and haven't for some time now. If we all survive this then I'm going to make some changes in the Void."

Sterling glanced down at his console, observing the movements of Fletcher's rag-tag fleet. The salvage operation had been organized with military precision. Judging by their initial scans, it also looked like Fletcher had only lost four ships in the battle.

"Based on what you just accomplished here, Fleet could use you back on the front line, Captain Fletcher," Sterling said, feeling nothing but admiration for the man. "It seems that your original family of thirteen ships has grown somewhat over the years."

Sterling knew he was pushing and had made the comment as casually as possible, hoping Fletcher's jubilant mood would loosen his tongue.

"That it has, Captain," Fletcher replied, allowing a thin smile to curl his lips, "but my days with Fleet are long past. The Void is my home now. Should the Sa'Nerra destroy Earth and come looking for a fight here, I aim to be ready."

Sterling nodded. He admired Fletcher's courage and determination, as well as the man's clear aptitude for battle and for command. However, despite the impressive victory he'd won at Oasis Colony, the cold truth was that he didn't stand a chance against the Sa'Nerran invasion armada. It seemed wrong to throw cold water on Fletcher at a time when he was riding high from his victory, but Sterling was not one to pander to false hopes. He trusted that Fletcher would want to know what they were facing.

"If the Sa'Nerra come, I don't doubt that you'll give

them one hell of a fight, Captain Fletcher," Sterling said. "But the alien armada is hundreds strong, with a capital ship that can destroy a small moon. If they come, you will not be able to stop them." Fletcher bristled, but didn't immediately reply. Age and experience had allowed the man to stymie a natural urge to pridefully refute Sterling's assertion. Instead, Fletcher was contemplating his words carefully. "Believe me, Captain, I don't mean to rain on your parade," Sterling added, while the older man continued to reflect on what he'd said. "I only want to give you the truth, wholly unvarnished."

Fletcher sighed and nodded. "I guess we'd better all hope that Fleet prevails then," he replied, though it was clear to Sterling that the old officer had little faith in such an outcome. "Be careful down at Sanctum, Captain," Fletcher added. "Masterson isn't the sort of man to negotiate, or to back down."

"Thank you, Captain Fletcher, but I have no intention of doing either," Sterling replied. "The time for talk is long gone. Now it's fight or die, for all of us."

One of the Bismarck's crew walked up behind his commander and whispered something into Fletcher's ear. The older man nodded then turned back to Sterling.

"I'm afraid I must go, Captain," Fletcher said. "However, I hope our paths cross again, in better circumstances."

"As do I," Sterling replied, offering the man a respectful nod. "Good hunting, Captain Fletcher."

"And to you also, Captain Sterling," Fletcher returned the gesture. The image of the Bismarck's commander then cleared from the viewscreen and was replaced with a view of Sanctum Spaceport.

"Ten minutes until we're on the ground, Captain," said Commander Banks, swiveling the pilot's chair around to face Sterling. "What's our strategy when we arrive?"

Sterling's hands balled into fists. "We go in hard and kill anyone who stands in our way," he said. Then he glanced across to Lieutenant Shade. "I want every commando we have left on the deck the moment we land," he said, watching the eyes of his weapon's officer sharpen as he spoke. "Colicos is our target. We have to get him back."

"And what about Masterson?" Banks asked. "Shall we leave him to you?"

Sterling shook his head. "I don't care who kills him, or how he dies, but let me make one thing absolutely clear." Banks, Shade and Razor all came to attention as Sterling said this. He met the eyes of his officers in turn before fixing his gaze onto Commander Banks. "We don't leave this planet until Masterson is dead at my feet. Call it revenge, call it whatever you like, I don't care. This time, it's personal."

Smoke poured into the sky above Sanctum City, billowing up from the remains of hundreds of buildings that were still burning. Fire ships buzzed all around the city, doing what they could to put out the infernos, but the Sa'Nerra had left few parts of the metropolis untouched. Chris Fletcher's intervention had ensured that the city and its population had not been entirely eradicated. Even so, Sterling found the scale of the alien bombardment of the planet to be shocking, and Sterling did not consider himself a man who was easily shocked.

"Do another pass around the city with scanners on maximum, then approach Sanctum Spaceport nice and slow," Sterling said to Banks, who was still piloting the Invictus. "But be ready to press the pedal to the metal at the first sign of trouble. We don't know what other tricks Masterson has up his sleeve."

"Aye, Captain, though so far it looks pretty dead down

there," Banks replied, easing the Marauder back around to begin her scanning run.

Sterling had studied and seen footage of Sa'Nerran attacks on the Void colonies during his time at the academy. However, the bulk of the heavy fighting on the ground had occurred during the first two decades of the war, all of which was before his time in the Fleet. The footage and reconstructions of the conflicts didn't do justice to the reality, Sterling realized in that moment. The scene in front of him was truly apocalyptic in nature. Thousands of mutilated and burned bodies littered the blackened streets. Dotted in amongst all the death and destruction were a few individuals and families who had somehow escaped the bombardment. Ironically, these small clusters of life appeared incongruous to their surroundings, like they were travelers visiting a long-dead, alien world. Sterling was not even sure they were the lucky ones. Huddled together, weeping in front of the charred remains of their homes and loved ones, they had lost almost everything. *Death would have been a mercy...* Sterling thought as he and the rest of the bridge crew continued to observe the scene in silence. *It's the only mercy those alien bastards are ever likely to grant.*

The worst of it was that the destruction of Sanctum, along with the other cities on Oasis Colony, had been achieved by a relatively small alien force. Sterling knew that should the Sa'Nerran armada reach Earth, the result would be destruction on a scale orders of magnitude greater than he was witnessing at Sanctum. It was a reminder of the importance of their mission. It was a validation of everything he had done, and would yet still do, in order to ensure the Sa'Nerra were defeated.

"Coming up on Sanctum Spaceport now, Captain," said Commander Banks. Then Sterling's first-officer huffed a laugh. "I'll be damned, the hotel is still standing. How the hell can that monstrosity have survived while everything else burned?"

"It just goes to show that there is no justice on this planet," Sterling replied, thinking of Masterson's constant claims that he was on the side of the law.

"Then let's dispense some natural justice of our own," Banks replied, glancing at Sterling over her shoulder. In her eyes, Sterling saw the same hunger for retribution that growled inside his own gut.

"I'm reading three gen-one fleet frigates on the deck, surrounding the hotel, sir," said Lieutenant Shade. "The vessels are heavily modified and adapted."

"Are they Masterson's?" asked Sterling, cocking his head towards the weapons console.

"Negative, Captain, they don't read as belonging to the Void Marshals or their deputies. In fact, I'm not detecting any kind of transponder ID at all."

Sterling nodded and returned his gaze to the viewscreen. "That means that they're mercenaries or Void Pirates," he said. "More of Masterson's hired guns."

"Confirmed, sir, I'm detecting Masterson's shuttle on the ground too," Shade added. His weapon's officer then highlighted the shuttle on the viewscreen. It was nestled between two of the frigates.

"I'm reading elevated power readings from the

warships and the shuttle, sir," said Lieutenant Razor from the rear of the bridge. "They're getting ready to take off or shoot at us, or more likely both."

Blasts of plasma erupted from two of the grounded mercenary frigates, striking the Invictus across the belly.

"Regenerative armor holding at eighty-nine percent," Shade reported as another blast lashed the ship. "Eighty one percent."

"Destroy those ships," replied Sterling, steadying himself against his console, "but leave the shuttle intact. I need Masterson to believe he at least has a fighting chance of escaping."

"Aye, sir, loading firing pattern now," said Lieutenant Shade.

A cloud of dust was kicked up as one of the frigates engaged its thrusters and begun to lift off the ground. *Oh no you don't...* Sterling thought, waiting for his weapons officer to pull the trigger. *There's no escape for any of you, not this time.*

"Firing," Shade called out.

Sterling felt the thump of rail guns resonate through his console and watched as the energy tore through the hull of the escaping frigate. The vessel exploded like a grenade, smashing windows and pockmarking the hotel with fragments of burning debris.

"The second ship is powering up," Razor said.

However, Sterling could already see on his console that their turrets had locked on. The second ship was then peppered with dozens of smaller, more tightly-focused blasts of energy. It was like being hit by a sawn-off shotgun at close range. Fires and electrical arcs erupted from the hull breaches and the ship collapsed onto the hard standing, adding more smog to the already thick, polluted atmosphere over Sanctum. Men and women ran from the vessel, covering their mouths and firing wildly at the Invictus with hand held weapons. Some made it inside the hotel, but others were consumed in flames as smaller explosions continued to pop off all over the vessel.

"The last ship is making a run for it," Banks called out from her station. "It obviously doesn't have the heart for a fight."

Sterling knew that the ships and the crews on Sanctum had played no part in the raid at Far Deep Nine. Yet they were still outlaws and bandits and also in the employ of Marshal Masterson senior. He recalled Fletcher's promise to make changes to the Void Colonies, should any of the planets survive the war. However, Sterling thought there was no reason to wait until after the conflict had ended to eradicate the scum and riff-raff.

"Target their engines and fire," Sterling said. "All weapons."

"Aye, sir, locking on," Shade replied as the mercenary frigate began to climb, its engines burning brightly. The nose of the Invictus then tipped up, bringing the might of its primary rail guns to bear. "Firing..."

Sterling watched the flashes of energy tear through the black sky above Sanctum, then rip through the frigate like a knife through tissue paper. The split halves of the ship exploded, spewing flaming debris for miles around. Some of the wreckage smashed into some of the few buildings that had survived the bombardment relatively unscathed. Most of it thudded harmlessly into ground that was already burned black. Collateral damage didn't mean much now, Sterling thought, as the smoke trail from the crashed ship began to dissipate. Sanctum was already a wasteland. The structures and the survivors that were still standing were just as dead as the rest of the city – they just hadn't realized it yet.

"Set us down in front of the hotel and keep our turrets trained on that building," Sterling said. He then turned to his weapons officer. "I want everyone you have on the deck in full combat gear in two minutes."

"Aye, sir, they're already standing by," Shade replied, jumping down from her station. She was like a live, exposed circuit, humming with energy. Battle was the only thing that made Opal Shade truly come alive.

"The target it Colicos," Sterling reminded his weapons officer. "I don't care if he's missing limbs, so long as he's still breathing and his mind is intact. See to it."

Shade nodded and hurried off the bridge, while Sterling tapped his neural interface and connected to Commander Graves. He opened the link to allow Banks to monitor. "Commander, ensure that the medical bay is ready to receive wounded, then report to the bridge," he said.

"Aye, Captain," replied Graves. Sterling was about to close the link when his medical officer spoke again. "If possible, please also retrieve some enemy casualties. We are currently low on artificial blood plasma, I can harvest what I need from the battlefield dead."

Sterling huffed a laugh and shook his head. "Understood, doctor, there will be no shortage once we're through, I promise you that," he replied, closing the link.

"He's a dark one alright," commented Commander Banks.

"I have a feeling I'm heading to an even darker place than Graves inhabits," Sterling said. He wasn't even sure why he'd said this or what he expected Banks to say in reply. Perhaps he was looking for her to validate his actions, or perhaps he was looking for her to reign him in. However, his first officer's reply left no doubt as to her perspective.

"Whatever it takes, Lucas," Banks replied, coolly. "If that means channeling the darkness inside of us, then that's what we do."

Sterling felt the thump of the Invictus' landing struts touching down. Banks disengaged their engines and slid out of her chair. "We're down and secure, Captain."

Sterling nodded. "Then suit up, Commander. The Omega Directive is in effect."

THE CARGO RAMP of the Invictus hadn't even hit the
asphalt at Sanctum Spaceport before small arms fire began
to rain down on the Marauder-class Destroyer. The ship's
turrets returned fire, hammering blasts of plasma through
the ground-floor windows of the hotel, and within seconds
the incoming shots stopped. Sterling smiled; whatever
weapons the mercenaries and deputies had to hand was no
match for the Invictus.

Lieutenant Shade moved out first, leading her squad of
six commandos. A second squad then moved up along the
far side of the hotel. The thump of the heavy boots was
swiftly followed by the boom of plasma hand-cannons and
the rapid buzz of "Homewrecker" heavy plasma rifles.
Sterling waited patiently for his weapons officer and her
squads to disperse, then stepped calmly down the ramp
with Commander Banks at his side. He was in no hurry.
Marshal Masterson was cornered with nowhere to run.

The only place the lawman was headed any time soon was straight to hell.

"He'll probably be holed up on the upper level of the main foyer of the hotel," said Banks as they both strode out on the asphalt with the Invictus at their rear. Like Shade and the commandoes, they had donned full combat armor, though both had forgone wearing helmets. Sterling wanted Masterson to look him in the eyes and know who had killed him. "Masterson and his mercs and deputies will have their weapons trained on the main entrance," Banks continued. "We should probably try to find another way inside."

"You're right, we probably should do," Sterling replied, checking the power setting on his Homewrecker rifle as he walked. Then he glanced across to his first-officer. "But I'm not sneaking around after this guy. This is going to be a straight-up power play, agreed?"

Banks nodded. "Suits me just fine, Captain."

Like Sterling, Banks was also equipped with a heavy plasma rifle, though she had a plasma hand-cannon slung over her back too. Sterling had preferred a different choice of secondary weapon. Attached to his belt was one of the serrated, half-moon blades the clean-up squads had recovered from a fallen Sa'Nerran warrior on Far Deep Nine. Now it was his to wield in anger.

Plasma blasts and screams filled the air around the hotel as Shade and her commandoes tore through the mercenaries and Void Deputies with ruthless aggression. It was a ferocity that Shade usually reserved for their true enemy – the Sa'Nerra – but on this occasion her brutality was warranted. Masterson had killed one of Sterling's own, and for that the lawman would receive no quarter.

Sterling climbed the stairs of the hotel and stepped onto the veranda. It was clear that the door had been barred from the inside. Ordinarily, it would have been enough to at least slow down any attempted incursion into the building. However, the occupants of the hotel hadn't accounted for Mercedes Banks.

"I think you should knock," said Sterling, extending a gloved hand toward the door.

"If you insist," replied Banks, taking a couple of steps back in order to get a run-up to the door.

Sterling pulled a stun-grenade from his belt and moved to the side of the hotel's entrance. The weapon had been enhanced by his talented chief engineer, who had insisted the grenade was now powerful enough to stun the occupants of a football stadium. Sterling nodded to his first-officer and steeled himself, ready to toss the grenade inside once the way was cleared.

Banks stormed forward and thumped her boot into the door, focusing every ounce of her genetically-superior strength into breaking it down. The door caved in like it was made of Styrofoam and plasma blasts and bullets immediately soared through the opening.

"Your turn!" Banks called out as she drew back into cover.

Sterling tossed the stun-weapon inside and ducked into cover, pressing his hands to his ears. Despite being outside the hotel when the weapon detonated, it still felt like someone had popped a giant balloon next to his head. The torrent of plasma and conventional arms fire coming through the door stopped and Sterling wasted no time in advancing. Raising his rifle, he marched inside the hotel, blasting holes into the stunned mercenaries at point blank range. Banks moved in a second later, heading to the opposite side of the main saloon area, unleashing powerful blasts of plasma at armed men and women on the balcony level. Soon the room was filled with smoke and the stench of burning human flesh. Sterling knew that it would not be the last time he was assaulted by the revolting odor before the day was won. The difference was that this time he didn't care.

Bodies continued to fall as Sterling advanced further inside the hotel. A Void Deputy sprang up from behind the bar and shot him at close range with a firearm. The bullet ricocheted off his armor and thudded into the ceiling. Sterling aimed his plasma rifle at the deputy and squeezed the trigger, blasting a hole straight through his chest. The deputy's eyes widened with horror and the man staggered back, touching his fingers to the cauterized wound. Seconds later he was dead.

"Kill them!" a voice shouted into the room. "Damn it, kill them now!"

Sterling looked up and saw Marshal Ed Masterson on the upper-level balcony at the rear of the saloon. The lawman was bookended by two deputies, who immediately opened fire at Sterling. He moved into cover, but not before a blast struck his thigh. The thud of the impact was followed swiftly by a burning pain. Cursing, Sterling checked the wound and saw that the armor on his leg had been melted through. However, it had served its purpose and spared him from serious injury.

"Mercedes, cover me!" he called out. He was too wound-up to use neural communications. Besides, on this occasion there was no need for stealth, he realized. The whole city – or what was left of it – would have heard the battle by now.

Banks moved out and fired up at the balcony, the powerful blasts of plasma driving the lawman back and through an open doorway. At the same time, Sterling rushed through an archway that led to the upper floors of the hotel. Bodies were hunched in the corner, cowering as the sound of more plasma blasts echoed around the hotel. Sterling recognized one of the women as Dana, the owner of the establishment.

"Where is he?" Sterling asked the woman, while keeping a watchful eye on the landing at the top of the stairs.

Dana scowled at Sterling, apparently not recognizing him. Then her features softened and she shot up, grabbing him by the arm.

"Oh, thank god, I thought you were the Sa'Nerra," Dana cried, hugging Sterling's arm tightly.

Sterling shook off the proprietor of the hotel then peered into her relieved eyes. "Masterson. Where is he?" he asked again, showing no compassion for the woman, who was clearly traumatized. Dana appeared shocked that Sterling has so brusquely shrugged her off. However, there must have been something in his eyes that told the woman he was in no mood to be trifled with.

"He's in the honeymoon suite on the third floor," Dana said, nodding toward the stairs. "That bastard has damned near taken over the place. He's not paying what's due, mind you."

"How many deputies or mercenaries does he have up there with him?" Sterling replied. He wasn't interested in the woman's ridiculously misplaced grievances. He only wanted to get his man.

"I don't know, five or six, maybe," Dana shrugged. "If you kill him, make sure you leave me enough silver to cover his check."

Sterling huffed a laugh and shook his head. The city had just been razed by the Sa'Nerra and its population mostly reduced to ash, yet Dana was more concerned about her profits.

"Once Masterson is dead you can take whatever you want from his cold, dead, corpse for all I care," Sterling replied. "But I suggest you use the money to get off this world, before the Sa'Nerra come back."

"And go where?" Dana replied, practically screeching the words at him. "Where the hell can any of us go that those alien bastards won't follow?"

Sterling didn't have an answer for her. The truth that if the Sa'Nerra broke through the Fleet lines and destroyed Earth, nowhere was safe.

"As far away as possible," Sterling replied, giving the only answer he could. "And don't come back."

Dana took two steps back from Sterling, looking dazed

and confused. He assumed the hotel owner had wanted some form of reassurance that everything was going to be okay. Perhaps even a rousing speech, filled with heroic hyperbole about how Fleet was going to kick the aliens back to where they came from. However, these would have been a lies and false hopes. The Void Colonists would all have to settle for reality sooner rather than later. All Dana had to do was step outside her own front door to see it for herself.

"The main saloon is clear," said Banks, moving through the archway and covering their rear. She ejected the power cell from her rifle and reloaded.

"Masterson is in the honeymoon suite, third floor," replied Sterling, glancing up at the landing area.

Banks backed up closer to Sterling and also peered up the stairwell. "It looks tight up there," she said, slinging her heavy plasma rifle and equipping the plasma hand-cannon instead. "We should be prepared for more close-quarters action."

Sterling nodded, slinging his rifle and drawing his pistol instead. His hand touched the handle of the Sa'Nerran half-moon blade, and he contemplated whether to use it instead. However, he left the weapon attached to his belt, knowing that the time would soon come when its blade would be wet with blood.

"Shade and the commando squads have secured the perimeter and Masterson's shuttle," Banks said, turning to Sterling and tapping her neural interface to close her link to the weapons officer. "Half of the mercs and deputies fled. Shade requests that she be allowed to pursue."

"Order Shade to run them down, all of them," Sterling replied, setting a foot on the bottom stair. "We'll deal with Masterson personally."

"Aye, sir," Banks replied, tapping her interface and relaying the command to the Invictus' weapons officer. Sterling guessed that his weapons officer would likely consider it to be the best order she had ever received. When it came to Opal Shade and killing, it was more than just her duty - it was her profession.

"Let's move," said Sterling, heading up the stairs in the lead, pistol held ready.

After the raucous gun battle in the saloon, a strange stillness had fallen over the hotel. All Sterling could hear was the creaking of floorboards beneath his feet and the sound of his own breathing, heavy and laden with anticipation. Reaching the third floor, Sterling then heard the groan of floorboards from somewhere up ahead. He signaled to Banks and both of them moved more cautiously onto the landing of the hotel's upper level. They pressed their bodies to the wall next to the archway leading into the third-floor corridor, ready to move out. Suddenly, the stillness was shattered by the fizz of plasma weapons opening fire at close range.

The wall crumbled as whomever was on the other side shot blindly through it in an attempt to ambush them. Banks was hit and fell, tumbling down the stairs to the landing below, but Sterling didn't have time to check if she was hurt. Charging through the opening, he came face-to-face with three mercenaries, each of them still firing blindly through the wall. Sterling shot the closest at point blank range, carving a chunk out of the man's chest and destroying his right shoulder. A blast fizzed past Sterling's ear, so close it scorched the hair on the side of his head. Sterling shot again, destroying the second man's abdomen. The mercenary collapsed onto Sterling and knocked his pistol out of his hand just as the third attacker opened fire. The blast melted through the body that was still draped across Sterling and he felt the energy burn his ribs. Roaring with pain and anger, Sterling used the dead man as a battering ram, driving the remaining mercenary against the wall before tossing the corpse aside. The final mercenary raised his pistol, but Sterling caught the man's wrist and managed to wrestle the barrel of the weapon away. The pistol fired and the fizz and bright flash of light temporarily stunned him. Sterling took a punch to the face and staggered back, giving the mercenary the space to take aim. The man squeezed the trigger, but the weapon did not fire. The cell was empty.

Sterling spat blood onto the floor, more enraged than he was injured, then drew the half-moon blade from his belt. The mercenary tossed the empty pistol and pulled a machete from a sheath before coming at him again. Sterling parried the mercenary's initial attack and countered with a thumping left hand. The punch was so hard and struck so cleanly that it crushed the man's nose. Dazed from the impact, the mercenary staggered back and blindly swung at Sterling, but this time the assault was slow and contained little power. Dodging the strike, Sterling swung the alien blade and opened the mercenary's throat. He watched the man croak and splutter, hands desperately trying to stem the flow of blood. Then the mercenary's body thumped into the floorboards, blood spewing from the gaping wound like a crimson fountain.

Sterling lowered the blade to his side as Banks raced around the corner, plasma hand-cannon raised and blood trickling from a cut to her eye. She saw the dead bodies on the ground and raised an eyebrow at Sterling.

"Do you still need me?" Banks said, filling the awkward silence with a prime example of her misplaced, dark humor.

"How about you take the lead this time?" said Sterling, dabbing the back of his fist to his throbbing jaw.

He switched the Sa'Nerran blade to his off-hand and recovered his plasma pistol as Banks moved ahead. His first officer followed the narrow corridor to the first guest-room door. Coordinating with Sterling, Banks turned the handle and pushed the door open before bursting inside, hand-cannon raised. However, the room was empty. Sterling cursed and they both moved on, trying each new door in turn. He knew that behind one of the doors was Marshal Masterson and James Colicos, but which one he had no idea.

"Where the hell is the honeymoon suite, anyway?" said Banks, as another room turned up a blank.

"How would I know? I've never been married," Sterling hit back, crabbily. He was getting frustrated. The one man he wanted to find was the one man that had so far evaded him. "Just look for the biggest room."

Suddenly the door to a guest room flung open and a

deputy leaned out, pistol raised. Banks beat the man to the trigger, the boom of her plasma hand-cannon assaulting Sterling's ears. The deputy was reduced to a smear on the door then Banks moved inside.

"Don't shoot, don't shoot!"

Sterling moved up and saw another deputy on his knees, hands pressed to his head and weapon tossed away in front of him. Banks had her plasma hand-cannon jammed into the back of the lawman's head.

"Which room is Masterson in?" demanded Sterling, cutting to the chase.

"Take a right at the end of the corridor, then it's two doors along on the left," the deputy said. The man's voice was shaky and weak and he was unable to meet Sterling's eyes. "I swear that's where he is, now please don't kill me."

Sterling glanced at Banks, the look in her eyes as cold and ruthless as his own. There was a silent understanding between them. It was the understanding that they had both already descended to the darker parts of their psyches, and that there was no turning back.

Sterling left the room and a moment later the hand-cannon boomed for a second time. His first officer then emerged beside him, her armor wearing a fresh coat of blood.

"Now we finish this," said Sterling, following the directions the deputy had given them. "We can go in hard and fast." He locked eyes with his first officer to ensure he had her full attention. "If you see Masterson and can take the shot before me, do it. Is that clear?" He wanted the Marshal for himself, but he wasn't about to let his own desire for vengeance get in to the way of their mission. He needed Colicos more than he needed the satisfaction of making the kill.

"Understood," replied Banks, firmly. "You can count on me, Lucas."

Sterling nodded. "I know I can," he replied, still holding her eyes. "I've never trusted anyone more. Even myself."

Banks moved up to the door that the deputy had indicated and held her cannon ready. Sterling got into position too and drew in several, long deep breaths.

"On my order," whispered Sterling.

Banks took a pace back, preparing to kick in the door. Sterling crouched behind her, ready to engage the mercenaries or deputies he expected to be inside.

"Now!"

Banks smashed open the door before dodging aside to allow Sterling a clean shot. Plasma blasts raced over Sterling's head and he shot back, killing two deputies and wounding a third. He could see Masterson at the rear of the room, holding Colicos in front of him as a shield.

"Go!" Sterling called out and Banks rushed inside, blasting another deputy in the chest and coating the wall with his charred entrails. Sterling moved in moments later, but there was no-one left to kill. No-one besides Marshal Ed Masterson.

"Stop right there or he dies!" Masterson yelled, pressing the barrel of a plasma pistol to the side of Colicos' head. "If you want him, you have to let me go."

"Fine, let him go then," Sterling lied. "I don't care about you, Marshal. I just need Colicos."

The Marshal laughed, though the lawman's voice was shaking more than his hands. "I'm not stupid, Captain," the man hit back. "You don't get him until I'm safely on board my shuttle with the engines running."

Sterling stepped away from the door and motioned toward it with the blood-stained, Sa'Nerran blade. "Lead the way, Marshal," he replied, casually. "Like I said, I don't give a damn about you."

Masterson scowled at Sterling, his ever-changing expression a kaleidoscope of suspicion and mistrust. However, the man was desperate and Sterling knew it. The lawman would take any option other than a plasma blast to the head. Then, as soon as Masterson had got close-enough or had let down his guard even for a millisecond, Sterling would take him out. And if he didn't get the chance, he knew that Banks would. Either way, Masterson would not leave the room alive.

"No tricks, Captain," Masterson said, ushering Colicos toward the door. The scientist was petrified with fear, but as far as Sterling could tell, Colicos was uninjured.

"No tricks, Marshal," Sterling answered, maintaining a strict poker-face. "Your shuttle is outside. I'll order my commandoes to let you through."

Sterling nodded to Banks, and she made a show of tapping her neural interface and pretending to relay the order. However, Banks knew just as well as he did that the lawman had only seconds left to live. The Marshal's skeptical eyes flicked to Banks then back to Sterling, but the ruse worked. Masterson clung on to the faint hope of survival like an infant clinging to its mother. Suddenly, there was the thump of bootsteps outside, growing rapidly closer. Masterson froze, pulling Colicos tighter and digging the barrel of his weapon into the scientist's temple. Sterling felt his heart thump harder in his chest and continued to watch Masterson like a hawk, while Banks covered the door.

"What's going on? I said no tricks!" Masterson yelled.

A split-second later, a Void Deputy burst through the door, weapon raised. There were two blasts of plasma. The first shot was fired by the deputy and the second was from Banks' hand-cannon. Two bodies hit the deck, leaving Marshal Ed Masterson standing alone between the Fleet officers, covered in the blood and brains of James Colicos and the deputy.

Sterling snarled a curse into the air then threw down his weapons and advanced on the Marshal, clasping his hands around the lawman's throat. Masterson tried to claw Sterling's hands away, but the older man was quickly overpowered. Dropping to his knees, Masterson croaked and spluttered, his eyes imploring Sterling to stop, but the lawman's cries only made him want to increase the pressure further. Hands and arms burning from the exertion of strangling the Marshal to death, Sterling pulled Masterson closer, so that they were nose-to-nose.

"Die you cowardly son of bitch!" Sterling roared into the man's face, which had already begun to turn blue. Masterson's tongue bulged out from his mouth, but Sterling held on until the last gasps of air escaped the lawman's lungs. It was barely louder than the whistle of the breeze brushing past the windows of the honeymoon suite. It was a weak raspy whisper, closer to the sound of a Sa'Nerran hiss than a human word. Then when all the life had been choked out of the man, Sterling threw the dead body of Marshal Masterson Senior to the floor and spat on it.

STERLING STARED down at the body of Marshal Masterson, muscles still burning and chest still heaving. He then looked over at the body of James Colicos, splayed out by the lawman's side, and cursed. The entire left side of the scientist's head had been blown away by the deputy's wayward shot. Not even Commander Graves, with all his macabre and experimental medical treatments, could do anything to save the man. Colicos was dead, and with him went all hopes of reversing the effects of the Sa'Nerran neural weapon.

"What the hell do we do now?" Said Commander Banks. She was still covering the door, in case another panicked deputy rushed inside.

Sterling climbed to his feet and turned his back on the dead scientist. There were only two options on the table, as far as he could see – fight on or give up. And the one thing he knew for sure was that Captain Lucas Sterling was never going to give up. He'd rather die.

"Now we head back to Griffin and give her the bad news," Sterling said, reaching down to pick up his pistol and the Sa'Nerran blade he'd used to such devastating effect earlier. "I just hope she has a plan B."

"We still have the personal data assistant that Colicos was using on Far Deep Nine," Banks replied. "Perhaps Razor can glean something from that?"

"Perhaps," Sterling admitted, allowing for the possibility that Graves or Razor could make use of the scientist's early data. However, he was not optimistic. Sterling then felt a neural link form in his mind. He could see from the expression on his first officer's face that she had received the connection too.

"Captain, we have just monitored a number of inbound surges in the system," said Commander Graves, giving his report in his usual, clinical style. "Thirty Sa'Nerran warships are approaching Oasis Colony. One of them is MAUL."

"Understood, Commander, we're on our way back to the ship now," Sterling replied. "What's their ETA?"

"MAUL is approaching more slowly, sir. It appears to have engine damage," Graves went on. "The other vessels surged in through a different aperture. They will be in orbit in forty-two minutes."

The subdued nature of Graves' report belied the significance of the information he had delivered. It meant they had to leave and leave quickly.

"Inform Lieutenant Shade then get ready to depart as soon as everyone is back on-board," Sterling said.

"Aye, Captain."

Sterling hooked the Sa'Nerran blade to his belt then nodded to Banks, who cautiously checked the landing outside the door.

"Has your business with the Marshal been resolved, Captain?" Graves asked, out of the blue. Sterling hadn't closed the link and didn't realize that his medical officer hadn't done so either.

"If you mean is the bastard dead then yes," Sterling replied, casting his gaze back to Masterson's grotesque, blue face.

"Did he suffer, Captain?"

The question caught Sterling off-guard and by the perplexed look on Banks' face, she felt the same.

"Yes, he suffered, Commander," Sterling replied. "I saw to it personally."

"Good, I am glad," came the reply, though the commander's voice was as lukewarm and unenthusiastic as it always was. "I'll get the ship ready. Graves out."

Sterling felt Graves leave his mind then he frowned over at his first officer. "What the hell was that about?" he asked.

"Keller," Banks replied, without hesitation. "Graves was fond of him."

Sterling sighed and nodded. He remembered that the young ensign enjoyed Commander Graves' company and was fascinated by his ghoulish tales of medical experimentation. However, he didn't know that Graves also liked Keller. These sorts of details always seemed superfluous to him, like the names of the commandoes that frequently fought and died under his command. He knew he should care more about the minutiae of his officers' lives, like other Fleet captains, but that wasn't who he was. Did that make him a worse captain or a worse human being, Sterling wondered? In the end, it wasn't for him to judge. It wasn't his job to be anyone's friend. His responsibility was to lead his crew and ensure they did their duties so that humanity survived. Ensign Kieran Keller had never faltered in this task and for that the young man had earned Sterling's respect and gratitude.

Banks moved out onto the landing first, hand-cannon aimed along the corridor. Alarms were now blaring outside the hotel, like the old air-raid sirens that sounded during the blitz in World War Two. Whatever remained of Oasis Colony's early warning system had obviously picked up the Sa'Nerran vessels too.

"Maybe Fletcher is still close and could help us out?" said Banks, checking the stairwell, which was also clear.

"We monitored him surging out of system just before we touched down," Sterling replied, hurrying down the wooden steps in pursuit of his first-officer. "Likely, an alert signal would have already been sent through the aperture relays, but whether he'll make it back in time is anyone's guess," he added, moving through into the saloon. Dana, the hotel's owner was there, dragging the dead bodies into a pile in the center of the floor. She glowered at Sterling and Banks as they moved through, but didn't speak a word to either of them.

"What about the other ships in the system?" said Banks, still keeping a wary eye on Dana.

"They might be able to hold of the Sa'Nerra until

Fletcher returns," Sterling said, moving up to a window and checking outside. "But we need to be long-gone before MAUL gets here. That ship may be damaged, but it's still a killer."

"They're all dead, if that's what you're worried about." Sterling glanced behind to see Dana looking at him, hands pressed to her hips. "Your soldiers killed them all," the owner of the hotel continued. "The deputies I mean... all the damned lot of them. Who the hell is going to protect us now?"

Just at that moment the enormous doorman who Sterling and Banks had encountered the first time they'd visited the hotel stepped onto the porch. The floorboards groaned under the man's immense weight.

"Did you do this?" the man asked, directing the question to Commander Banks.

Banks shrugged. "With a little help, yes."

The huge man nodded. "Good," he replied before stepping inside the hotel and planting himself in an armchair. "The Marshals were all bastards, anyway. Good riddance."

Sterling snorted a laugh then glanced back at Dana. "There you go, he's your protection," Sterling replied, nodding toward the giant.

"He's no good against aliens in space through, is he?" Dana hit back. Then her features suddenly softened and she smiled at the giant. "Though, if you want to be head of security, Cotton, I'll pay you double."

"Okay," the huge man shrugged, pushing himself out of

the chair and leaning against the bar instead. The counter top looked on the verge of collapsing.

"Your name is Cotton?" said Banks, raising an eyebrow at the man.

"It's because I'm so gentle," Cotton replied, though the broad grin on the man's face suggested it was perhaps more of a nickname than the giant's actual name.

"Put your trust in Christopher Fletcher," Sterling said in response to Dana's rebuttal. "And listen to Cotton too, he knows what he's talking about. The Marshals and deputies are gone and good riddance to them." He turned to leave, but the proprietor of the hotel had more to say.

"And I suppose you're gone too, right?" Dana said, storming toward Sterling and blocking his path. "The Sa'Nerra come and you Fleet types run away and leave us here to die, just like you did before." She spat at Sterling's feet. A globule of spittle landed across the toe of his boot and began to slowly dribble onto the wooden floor. "You're all the same. Cowards!"

Banks stepped to Dana, eyes burning and fists clenched, but Sterling raised a hand and she backed away.

"We're nothing like the rest of Fleet," Sterling hit back, glaring at Dana. He didn't care what she thought of Fleet, but to call him a coward was a worse insult than spitting on his boots. "But the war won't be won here, not today. So, you're on your own."

Dana recoiled from Sterling, clearly taken aback by his candor. Sterling imagined that the hotel owner had been expecting a strong rebuttal of her accusation, followed by a string of empty promises that Fleet would never abandon them to the Sa'Nerra. Dana deserved the truth. It was the least he could offer her.

Sterling felt a link forming in his mind and he tapped his interface to open the channel.

"Christopher Fletcher's squadron of thirteen warships had just entered the system, captain, along with reinforcements," said Commander Graves.

"Reinforcements? How many?" asked Sterling.

"Thirty-two vessels at the last count sir," Graves replied. Sterling shook his head. His medical officer had somehow managed to make this good news sound anticlimactic. "The bulk of the Sa'Nerran taskforce has broken off to intercept Fletcher's forces. However, two Skirmishers remain on a heading to this planet, along with MAUL, though the heavy destroyer is an hour behind them."

"Understood, Commander, are Shade and her commando squads back on board?"

"Affirmative, Captain," Graves replied. "However, there were two fatalities and four other casualties. The injuries are nothing I cannot repair."

"We'll be there soon, Commander, Sterling out," Sterling tapped his interface to close the link. He then returned his attention to Dana, who was still speechless after Sterling's frank comeback. "Put your trust in Fletcher," Sterling reiterated. "If you're not going to take my advice and leave this planet then be prepared to fight. And don't give up, because I sure as hell won't."

"Giving up ain't our style Captain, not in the Void," Dana said, returning to the work of collating the bodies.

She screeched at Cotton to help her and the giant man reluctantly joined in, hauling bodies onto the pile with remarkable ease.

"I like him," said Banks, with a wry smile. Then she hooked a thumb at Dana. "Her, not so much."

"Come on, Commander, I think it's time we checked out of this hotel," said Sterling, stepping onto the veranda.

The smell of the burning city hit him like an ocean wave. The air was acrid and thick, but there was also a coppery, metallic taste to the smoke that Sterling was far more familiar with. It was the taste of death. The crackle of the fires and hum of the fire-ships hovering overhead was soon drowned out by the roar of the Invictus engines and thrusters. Sterling and Banks strode up the cargo ramp of their Marauder-class Destroyer, which quickly whirred shut behind them, sealing them off from the planet's rotten air. However, Sterling could still taste it on his tongue and smell it in Banks' hair as she moved ahead of him and hit the call button for the elevator. The ship had lifted off the hard standing before the elevator had even arrived on deck one. The momentary delay between the engines kicking in and the inertial negations systems working to compensate for the acceleration was still something Sterling could detect with absolute precision. Like the dull shine of the deck, the artificial gravity, and the feel of the ship's cool metal to the touch, it told him that he was home.

The elevator door swished opened onto deck one and Sterling moved out with his first officer by his side. Traversing the short distance along the corridor to the bridge, he entered to see Commander Graves already standing down from the command platform, waiting for him.

"We are underway, Captain, weapons and regenerative armor at full power," Commander Graves said.

"Thank you, Commander," Sterling replied, stepping up to his console. "You can return to the med bay and tend to the wounded."

Sterling's medical officer acknowledged the order and quickly departed without another word. Glancing right he noticed that Lieutenant Shade was already at her post. She was splattered with blood and the scars on her armor told the story of the battle she had just fought. However, she appeared uninjured and also curiously at ease. For Opal Shade, the calm always came after the storm, not before. He shot her a respectful nod, which his weapons officer returned before issuing her report.

"Two phase-two Sa'Nerran Skirmishers on an intercept course, Captain," Shade said, bringing up an image of the vessels on the viewscreen.

Sterling removed the ID chip that Admiral Griffin had given to him, containing the coordinates for their rendezvous point. He pressed the chip to one of the many open wounds on his body, smearing his blood across the device before inserting it into his captain's console. The chip activated and the co-ordinates of a suitable long-range aperture appeared on the display.

"Here's our heading, Commander," said Sterling, sending the information to the helm control console. Commander Banks had just slipped into the seat.

"We won't make it to the aperture threshold before

those Skirmishers intercept us," Banks said, working at her console. "But we will make it through before MAUL has a chance to ruin our day again."

"Target those two Skirmishers and prepare to take them out," Sterling said, addressing his weapons officer. "If they want to die here then so be it."

The captain's console then chimed an incoming message. He glanced down and saw that the request was coming from MAUL. Sterling was in no mood to fence with the Sa'Nerran Emissary, but he also wanted Crow to know he was alive and still in the fight. Accepting the communications request, he straightened his aching back and waited for Crow's image to appear on the screen.

"I grow tired of this chase, Captain Sterling," said Emissary Crow. There was a fresh scar to the side of the man's face, and in the background, Sterling could see that the bridge of the ship had taken heavy damage.

"Then stop chasing me, asshole," Sterling hit back. "The war is in Fleet space not here. Surely a man of such great importance as yourself has better things to do than scurry around the Void chasing down one little Marauder?"

"I am not needed on the front line, Captain," the Emissary replied, taunting Sterling with his smile. "Thanks to all the turned Fleet ships that have joined our cause, we are already more than enough to crush your fleet and your planet."

"Then don't let me keep you from joining in the fun," replied Sterling, glancing down and checking on the range to the Skirmishers.

"I'm afraid Emissary McQueen has other plans for you, Captain Sterling."

"What the hell is that supposed to mean?" Sterling found the emissary's cryptic statement to be genuinely perturbing and was eager to learn its meaning.

"You'll find out soon enough," the emissary replied, still with the same provocative smile. "In any case, I will gain far more enjoyment from turning your ship and crew so that they can witness the end of your civilization as obedient drones."

Sterling laughed and shook his head. Then he gripped the sides of his console and leaned in toward the screen, glaring at Crow with hateful eyes.

"It's true that you might destroy Fleet, and you might destroy Earth too," Sterling admitted, feeling strangely indifferent about the prospect of both. "But I promise you this, Crow. The war will end with the Sa'Nerra on their knees, not humanity."

"Really, Captain, I would expect bravado such as this from Fleet admirals, but not from a cold-hearted killer such as yourself," Crow hit back.

"It's not bluster, asshole," said Sterling, "it's a promise."

Crow's eyes narrowed. "We will see, Captain," the emissary snarled. "But first, you have to get past me."

The transmission was cut at the source and the image of Crow faded. "Fire as soon as we're in range," Sterling ordered, his fingers turning white from the pressure of gripping his console.

"Surge generator charging, Captain," Commander

Banks reported from the helm control station. "We'll reach the aperture threshold in thirty seconds."

The two Skirmishers launched torpedoes and opened fire with their plasma cannons. Sterling felt the thump of the impacts on the hull and saw the damage control panel light up in his peripheral vision. However, he remained focused on the enemy vessels, as if the ship's weapons were reliant on his eyes to lock onto their targets.

"Optimal range... now," announced Lieutenant Shade. "Firing all weapons."

A barrage of plasma raced out toward the alien warships and both Skirmishers were struck cleanly across their bows. Shade had targeted the command centers of the older-model warships and scored direct hits. It was the equivalent of a headshot, crippling the ships without needing to inflict significant damage.

"Enemy vessels both disabled, sir," said Shade, the flicker of a smile crossing her lips. "We're clear to surge."

Sterling nodded, but felt no elation at the victory. It was two ships out of hundreds that still lingered in Fleet space, waiting to descend on earth and turn it to ash. With a way to defend against the Sa'Nerran neural weapon and stop their warships from being turned, Fleet might have had a chance. However, that hope had died with James Colicos in Sanctum City on Oasis Colony. What came next, Sterling didn't know. What he did know was that he wasn't giving up the fight. Not now. Not ever.

THE INVICTUS BURST back into normal space at the co-ordinates that Admiral Griffin had supplied for their rendezvous. As with previous surges through the experimental, long-range apertures, the experience was jarring and deeply unpleasant. This time, however, Sterling had just about managed to remain standing, sparing him the indignity – and pain – of falling on his ass on the cold metal deck. Even so, it took a full minute before the nausea and dizziness had eased enough that he could get his bearings and find out where in the galaxy Griffin had sent them.

"All stations, report..." Sterling said while massaging his throbbing temples with thumb and forefinger.

"We've suffered some minor structural damage and a dozen secondary systems are down on decks four and five," Razor began. The ship's chief engineer was reading the analysis on her screens at the rear of the bridge, though her voice, along with her long legs, were still unsteady. "The surge field generator is offline, but it isn't damaged," Razor continued, after pausing to suck in a series of long, slow breaths to help steady herself. Even so, Sterling still thought she looked like she was about to be sick. "And there are a dozen other red lights on the damage control board, but none are anything we need to worry about right now."

Sterling nodded then glanced across to his first-officer's console before remembering she was still at the helm. In his befuddled state he'd also forgotten that Keller was dead, and was expecting to see him sitting in front of the helm controls. The shock of him not being there was jarring. Then the memory of Keller's gruesome death resurfaced like a whale breaching out of the ocean. Sterling cursed Masterson's name into the air, taking some small comfort from knowing the lawman was dead by his own hands.

"Any idea where we are, Commander?" Sterling said, leaning on his console for support while peering at the back of Banks' head.

"I don't have an exact fix yet, but it looks like we're somewhere between F-sector and G-sector," Banks replied. "I do know that we're not close to any of the inner colonies; this really is the middle of nowhere."

Sterling's console then chimed an alert and he checked it, feeling his pulse begin to race. In addition to their own frazzled brains the scanners had also been unreliable since the surge. He frowned at the data, which suggested there was a cluster of objects a few hundred kilometers directly ahead, though Sterling couldn't tell if they were ships, asteroids or something else entirely.

"Lieutenant Razor, can you clean up the scanner resolution?" Sterling asked, glancing over his shoulder at the engineer. "Something is out there and I'd like to know what."

Razor was silent for a few moments while she worked. Then she tutted and shook her head before turning to face the command station. "That's the best I can do right now, sir," the engineer said, clearly frustrated by her inability to provide a better response.

Sterling checked his console again, but other than the scanners indicating that the objects in question were not rocks, he was no wiser than he had been before.

"Well, there's certainly something out there," Sterling said, tapping a new series of commands into his console. "And if our scanners can't tell us what they are then perhaps the good old mark-one eyeball will do a better job."

Sterling finished his sequence of commands, manually aiming their optical scanners at the area in question. A blurry, magnified image of the cluster of objects appeared on the viewscreen. He scowled at the image then returned to his console, adjusting the parameters one by one until the image began to resolve more clearly. Suddenly, Banks let out a long, low whistle.

"What on earth is that?" she said, eyes fixed on the collection of warships and space station components that were now showing clearly on the viewscreen.

"I have no idea," replied Sterling, also marveling at the spectacle.

"Scanners are back online," Razor announced from her

station behind Sterling. "But they're only telling me what we can already see."

"It looks like some sort of damned ship's graveyard out there," commented Banks. "Where the hell has all this stuff come from?"

"Griffin has clearly been busy," said Sterling, alternating his gaze between the updated scanner readings and the viewscreen.

Spread out in front of the Invictus were dozens of warships in various states of disassembly, and at least as many space station components. The station components appeared to be Fleet designs spanning at least three decades. Sterling could see sections of what looked like old command outposts married to much more recent shipyard components. There even appeared to be an old Fleet Gatekeeper built into the hodge-podge structure.

"I'm detecting around a hundred ships in total, sir, all of which have been stripped down for salvage," Razor reported. "There are also six gen-one repair ships and what looks like a KT-400 mobile repair platform."

"A KT-400?" said Sterling frowning at Razor. "Those things haven't been in service since before you were born."

"That's correct, sir," Razor replied. "Though it was an excellent piece of equipment and far superior to the KT-500 and KT-610s that replaced it."

Sterling raised an eyebrow. "I'll take your word for it, Lieutenant," he replied, recalling Lieutenant Razor's fondness for all things tools and machinery.

"The gatekeeper that's integrated into the main

structure is actually the Stalwart," Razor continued, unperturbed by Sterling's slightly sarcastic response to her geek-level historical knowledge. "If you recall, captain, the Stalwart used to be the gatekeeper for G-sector."

"That I do remember, lieutenant," Sterling replied. He was a senior lieutenant at the time the Stalwart was decommissioned. Then he remembered that Griffin – a Rear Admiral at the time – had been responsible for the decommissioning operation.

"It's clear that Admiral Griffin had been playing an extremely long game," commented Sterling, sweeping his eyes across the sprawling space city. "She must have been planning this for decades."

Sterling's console chimed another alert, but Razor was quick to provide an update before he could check it.

"I'm detecting another structure to the rear of the main installation, sir," Razor said. The viewscreen then updated to show what looked like a long scaffold, which was set apart from the rest of the pick-and-mix style station. "There are fifty-two warships docked to the structure," Razor went on, zooming the display in onto one of the onyx-black ships. "I'm picking up subtle variations in design and configuration, but broadly speaking they are similar to the vessels we saw with Admiral Griffin. And judging from their material composition, I'd say they were constructed from the parts of the other ships that litter the space surrounding the installation."

"Obsidian ships," said Sterling, looking at a detailed scan of one of the vessels on his console. As with the other warships they'd encountered, they were small and powerful, like the Invictus. And Sterling guessed that they were also all crewed by Griffin's neurotic Obsidian Soldier robots.

"We're receiving a communication request from the station, Captain," said Banks, swiveling her seat to face the command deck. "It's the Admiral," she added, flashing her eyes at him.

"Let's not keep her waiting then," Sterling replied. As usual, the prospect of speaking to Griffin caused flutters in his gut. It was a sensation he'd never been able to shake off – like the feeling of being sent to the principal's office and waiting to be called inside. Submitting to the urge to fix his disheveled appearance, Sterling straightened his back and went to smooth down his tunic. However, his hand merely scraped across the hard, synthetic fabric of his armor. He'd forgotten he was still wearing it.

"Are you going to dock, Captain, or just lurk around outside for the remainder of the war?" said Admiral Griffin, as pugnacious as ever.

"Honestly, Admiral, I was waiting for an invitation," Sterling replied. "Or at least some confirmation that this isn't an abandoned Sa'Nerran outpost or some other alien command post."

"It is not, Captain, as you can well see," Griffin hit back. "You are cleared for docking, port two." The helm control console registered the arrival of the docking data with a brief chirrup and Commander Banks began steering the Marauder on course. "I must admit I did not expect to see you back so soon," Griffin went on. "I assume this means your mission was either a spectacular success or a spectacular failure."

Sterling sucked in his cheeks then sighed through his nose. Griffin was going to find out sooner or later, so he figured he may as well let her have the bad news now.

"Colicos is dead," Sterling began. Griffin's eyes closed and her jaw clenched. It was perhaps the first time in his life that he'd seen her lost for words. "We had a run in with a Void Marshal on Far Deep Nine, then Emissary Crow showed up," Sterling went on, using the silence to get the rest of his story out. "The Marshal took Colicos and we tracked him to Oasis Colony, but Colicos was caught in the crossfire and killed."

A tense silence followed Sterling's announcement, during which time Griffin merely glared into his eyes through the viewscreen. Sterling didn't even dare to blink.

"That is an unfortunate development, Captain," she eventually replied. Sterling had envisaged Griffin's reaction to be akin to a volcano erupting. In contrast, the understated nature of her reply came as a welcome relief, despite also being more than a little perplexing.

"We did recover a PDA with some of Colicos' early analysis, but I don't expect it to turn up much," Sterling went on, if only to fill the silence. "However, we have to face the fact that finding a way to reverse the effects of the neural weapon is no longer a possibility."

"Come aboard, Captain, and we will discuss the next steps," Griffin replied, still with remarkable cool. She looked ready to terminate the conversation when her eyes drifted off to the side of Sterling. "Where is your first-officer, Captain?" Griffin said, brow furrowed into a frown.

"She's at the helm, Admiral," Sterling replied. A wave of repressed anger then flooded through his body, knowing what he would have to say next. "Ensign Kieran Keller was also killed in action on Far Deep Nine."

Sterling was about to tell Griffin that his ensign had given his life in the best tradition of the service, and that his death had been worthy. However, he realized that Griffin wouldn't care and it would have been a waste of breath.

"I understand, Captain," the Admiral replied. As expected, she offered no condolences or asked any questions regarding the circumstances of Keller's death. To Griffin, Keller was just another statistic. "An Obsidian Soldier will meet you at the dock and bring you to me," she went on. "Only you and Commander Banks need attend our meeting. The rest of your crew can assist with repairs to the Invictus, aided by my facility and soldiers."

"Understood, Admiral," Sterling replied. He was about to enquire further about the mysterious 'facility' that Griffin had just mentioned, but the Admiral had already severed the link.

"That went surprisingly well," said Banks as the Invictus crept closer to the space station. "I was half-expecting the Admiral to bite your head off."

"So was I," Sterling admitted. "The fact she didn't means she has a plan B. And whatever it is, it must be big."

"Maybe she has her own secret army of turned Sa'Nerran warriors that she plans to unleash against the alien armada?" suggested Banks, turning to dark humor to fill the vast gulf in their knowledge.

Sterling snorted a laugh. "I guess anything is possible," he replied, staring out at the bizarre space station in the middle of deep space. Then a chill ran down his spine, wondering whether Banks might in fact be correct.

STERLING WATCHED one of Admiral Griffin's robotic "Obsidian Soldiers" march toward him and Commander Banks as they waited at the docking port. The pace of the machine's advance and its ominous appearance felt threatening and Sterling's hand instinctively moved toward his sidearm. The robot eventually stomped to a halt a few meters in front of him, though it was still a few seconds before he allowed his hand to relax away from the grip of his pistol.

"Admiral Griffin has ordered me to deliver you to her," the Obsidian Soldier announced. The machine used the same synthesized voice as the gen-fourteen AI on the Invictus. However, the robotic soldier lacked the cheerful demeanor of his ship's computer, coming across as flat, aggressive and terse. In many respects, It sounded just like Admiral Griffin, which Sterling figured made a lot of sense, considering who its commander was. "Follow me," the robot commanded before spinning on its metallic heels and marching away again.

"Yes, sir..." commented Sterling, raising an eyebrow at Commander Banks as the robot rapidly departed.

"They appear to be a little short on charm," Banks replied. "I wonder where they get that from..."

Sterling decided to allow his first officer a little leeway, rather than chastise her for the snarky comment about Admiral Griffin. This was mainly because he had been thinking the exact same thing. Then he noticed that the Obsidian Soldier had already nearly marched out of their sight.

"Come on, we'd better hurry before we lose the damned thing," Sterling said, setting off in pursuit of the Obsidian Soldier at a brisk pace. He eventually had to jog the length of the first corridor just to catch up with it.

The robot continued on in silence, leading Sterling and Banks through the interior of the station. Their journey lasted only a couple of minutes, but in that time, Sterling noted that they had passed through three distinctly different eras of space station design. It felt like some sort of clever museum exhibit, showing Fleet architecture through the ages. The final section was one that Sterling recognized. It was the command section of a Gatekeeper-class mobile weapons platform.

The Obsidian Soldier moved up to the door of the command center and pressed its hand to the entry pad. The lock mechanism appeared to interface with the machine then the door swooshed open.

"Go inside," the robot said, extending its claw-like fingers through the opening.

"Only if you say, please," Banks replied, squaring off against the machine. The Obsidian Solder angled its dome-shape cranial section at Sterling's first officer and focused its optical sensors on her face.

"Go inside," the machine said again.

Sterling was surprised to hear that the robot's second command was delivered more assertively, to the point of being borderline aggressive. It was clear from the fierce expression on Banks' face that the directive had not gone down well with her.

"Come on, commander," he said, ushering his first-officer away from the machine before she decided to tear it to pieces. "Let's save the lesson in manners until another time."

Banks glowered at the machine for a moment longer before moving inside. Sterling followed, keeping half an eye on the robot soldier as he did so. He knew that the machines were on their side, but at that moment it certainly didn't feel that way. Sterling then spotted Admiral Griffin at the far end of the old Gatekeeper's Combat Information Center, and moved toward her. She was staring out through a window at the docking scaffold containing the Obsidian Ships.

"Welcome to Obsidian Command," said Admiral Griffin, turning away from the oval-shaped viewing window and meeting Sterling's eyes. The robotic warrior stepped inside the CIC and the door closed behind it.

"Does the robot have to stay, Admiral?" Sterling hooked

a thumb at the machine. "I feel like it's only waiting around to rip my head off."

"I can assure you it is not, Captain," replied Griffin, stopping just short of rolling her eyes at Sterling.

"Good, because I'd hate to have to blast the damned thing into scrap," quipped Sterling.

Then without warning, the robot advanced, thrusting its claw-like hand toward Sterling's throat. "Hostile intent detected," the Obsidian Soldier announced, its tone suddenly darker and more menacing. Sterling froze as the robot's blade-like finger was pressed against his neck. "Shall I terminate this human?"

Banks sprang into action, catching the robot's arm and forcing its deadly claws away from Sterling's throat. The gears and motors of the Obsidian Soldier whirred and groaned as the super-human officer overpowered it and drove it back. The Obsidian Soldier then tried to grab Banks with its other hand, but she anticipated the attack and caught the machine's forearm. Sterling had no doubt that his first officer would win the contest of strength, but he wasn't willing to risk it. Drawing his pistol, he pressed it to the machine's domed-shaped head and slipped his finger onto the trigger.

"Back off, right now!" Sterling snarled at the machine, adding pressure to the trigger.

"That will be all, soldier," Griffin said, her own voice belying the seriousness of the situation.

The Obsidian Soldier immediately stood down and took two swift paces backward. Without another word it turned its back on Sterling, opened the door and marched outside. Sterling waited until the door had closed again before lowering his weapon and turning back to the Admiral. Banks, however, remained focused on the door, her chest rising and falling rapidly and hands balled into fists.

"Forgive me, Admiral, but what the hell was that all about?" Sterling snapped, holstering his pistol. For once, he didn't care about adhering to protocol – he needed answers.

"Please, Captain Sterling, get a hold of yourself," Admiral Griffin replied, still remarkably unperturbed by the whole situation. "The Obsidian Soldiers are merely adjusting to their updated coding. Generation-fourteen AIs are as close to sentience as we've ever come, but they're also more than a little unpredictable, as I'm sure you're aware," Griffin continued. "This was why they were removed from service in favor or the more reliable, but less intelligent gen-thirteens."

"Admiral, my ship-board AI has a tendency to be annoying, but it's never tried to slit my throat," Sterling hit back.

"The Obsidian Soldiers are merely protecting me," Griffin replied, shrugging off Sterling's protests. "They are like children in many ways, still learning and adapting. I have already updated their code to include your ship's personnel records, but the process of familiarization will take some time. They will obey your commands, eventually."

"*Eventually?*" replied Sterling. Griffin's casual dismissal of the robot's actions was not reassuring. "Just how long are we talking, Admiral? And how many of my crew will it slaughter before it figures out that we're on the same side?"

"The Obsidian Soldiers are not your concern, Captain," Griffin hit back. Her cold blue eyes had sharpened and her posture had stiffened. It was clear to Sterling that the topic of conversation was now closed. "We are here to talk about the next phase of your mission."

Sterling straightened to attention. He still had more to say, but he knew the Admiral well enough to understand when to talk and when to just shut up and listen.

"With James Colicos gone, we can no longer devise a method to reverse the effects of the Sa'Nerran neural control weapon," Griffin continued. "While Lieutenant Razor may glean something of value from Colicos' PDA, the chances of success are slim. As such, I am compelled to move to the next phase of my contingency plan."

Griffin stepped up to the central computer in the CIC and activated it. A holo-schematic of the space station and adjacent docking scaffold was then projected from it. Sterling and Banks stepped up to the console and examined the image, seeing the full scale of Griffin's installation for the first time.

"How did you get all of this equipment out here without anyone noticing, Admiral?" said Sterling, marveling at the scale and complexity of the installation.

"Everything you see here is built from decommissioned or salvaged Fleet vessels and space-installations," Griffin replied. "My position allowed me to select which ships and crews were responsible for the mothball operations. As far as Fleet and the official records were concerned, everything here was recycled or scrapped."

"Presumably you had help, Admiral?" Sterling added. "You couldn't possibly have done all this alone?"

Griffin had always hinted that she had other allies, besides Sterling and McQueen, at least prior to her ascension to Emissary. However, the Admiral had also always been cagey about who these people were. Now that all of her cards were on the table, Sterling was hoping that Griffin would finally drop her veil of secrecy.

"I did not do this alone," Griffin eventually replied, after a moment of pause to consider how much she was willing to reveal. "However, all those who assisted in this endeavor are now dead, except for one."

"Captain Blake of the Hammer, right?" Sterling had always assumed Blake was in on Griffin's plot, though he'd never had it confirmed.

"Correct, Captain."

Sterling nodded, grateful for a straight answer for once. However, Griffin's unexpected candor had revealed another darker possibility. She had explicitly said that her co-conspirators were all dead. Not dead *or* turned – just plain dead. In ordinary circumstances, he wouldn't have pressed Griffin on the matter. However, these were far from ordinary circumstances, he realized.

"If Captain Blake is the only one left, how did the others die?" Sterling asked, feeling his pulse race as the words escaped his lips.

"Most died in battle, but some were neutralized on my order," Griffin said, without hesitation or a flicker of remorse. The frank and sudden response caught Sterling off-guard and he was momentarily lost for words. "That is what you actually meant to ask, isn't it Captain?"

"Yes, Admiral, it was," Sterling admitted. He wasn't surprised by Griffin's answer, though he wasn't quite sure how he felt about it either. If she was willing to kill members of her own Omega Taskforce then it meant even his own crew wasn't safe. *Then again, that is the whole point of the Omega Directive...* Sterling considered. *The needs of the mission come first, no matter the cost.*

"As you know, the needs of the mission must come before all else, Captain," Griffin said, as if she'd just read Sterling's mind. "You know this better than anyone. Those who threatened to expose my plan and reveal the existence of this installation had to be eliminated. It was not desirable, but it was necessary."

Sterling sighed and nodded. As unpalatable as Griffin's admission had been, he understood it. In fact, he accepted and even agreed with it. The question of whether it was possible to do good through prosecuting acts of evil was one that Sterling had always wrestled with. It was the classic case of "the ends justifying the means". Moralizing was something best left to historians. If future generations viewed Sterling and Griffin as figures to be despised and vilified then so be it. At least that would mean humanity had survived. There, however, still one question Sterling needed an answer to.

"And what about us, Admiral?" Sterling said, deciding he'd pushed Griffin so far that he may as well push her the whole way. "Is there an Omega Directive for me and my crew too?"

This time Griffin did hesitate before answering, if only for a moment. "If it should ever become necessary, Captain, then yes," she admitted. "But it cuts both ways," she was quick to add. "The mission comes first. It comes before you and it comes before me. Should I ever become compromised, the Omega Directive remains in effect, and I expect you to do your duty. Is that understood?"

"Perfectly, Admiral," Sterling replied, straightening to attention.

Griffin sighed then pressed her hands to the small of her back. "Now, is that enough answers for you, Captain? Shall we continue?"

Sterling nodded. He appreciated the Admiral's honesty. In a world where trust was in scant supply, perhaps their shared honesty – no matter how harsh or unpalatable the truth happened to be – was the only bond that mattered.

"So, what is our next mission, Admiral?" Sterling asked, moving the discussion on. He'd heard all he'd needed to hear.

"Now we strike back, Captain," Griffin said, appearing to grow by several inches as she spoke.

Sterling frowned. "You want to mount a counter-offensive?"

"The original intention of the Obsidian Project was to create a strike force capable of hitting at the heart of the Sa'Nerran empire," Griffin went on. "This has not changed."

"Admiral, fifty robot-piloted ships plus the Invictus are not enough of a force to attack Sa'Nerra itself," Sterling pointed out. "There must be another option."

"No, this is the only move we have left," Griffin replied, flatly. "Let me be clear, Captain," the admiral continued, her eyes sharpening further, so that Sterling could almost feel them cutting into him. "Whether Earth stands or falls is out of our hands. Adding the Obsidian Ships to our current Fleet will make no difference to the outcome. The Sa'Nerran armada will reach Earth and Fleet will make its last stand."

"You believe the Sa'Nerra will win?" said Commander Banks.

From her tone, Sterling knew that his first-officer was surprised by Griffin's statement, and Sterling understood why. Griffin was pugnacious almost to a fault. However, while she had no love for the political classes, including some of the other Admirals – Wessel most of all – she was fiercely proud of the officers who fought on the front lines. To believe Fleet would fail was perhaps the most shocking admission Griffin had yet made.

"Without a defense against the neural control weapon, our defeat is all but assured," Griffin replied, turning her sharp eyes to Banks. "Remember that our forces will not only be fighting the Sa'Nerra, but also all of the Fleet ships that they have captured and turned against us. Eventually, Fleet will be fighting against itself. It is a no-win situation, Commander. It is foolish to believe otherwise."

Banks nodded, though Sterling could see that hearing Griffin's clinical analysis had been difficult. However, as hard it had been to hear, it was again simply the truth, unvarnished and laid bare.

"Fine, so we attack Sa'Nerra and to hell with the odds," Sterling said, deciding to embrace their new destiny with open arms. "There's only one problem, Admiral. We don't actually know where the Sa'Nerran homeworld is."

Sterling hated to put a downer on the occasion, but he considered this to be a fairly sizable fly in the ointment.

"That was the case, but it is not any longer," Griffin replied, coolly, managing, not for the first time, to shock Sterling into silence. "The location of their planet was contained within the data you retrieved from the Sa'Nerran gatekeeper. I now know exactly where it is, and how to get there."

Admiral Griffin's bombshell that she knew the location of the Sa'Nerran home planet had given Sterling a renewed sense of hope. He had believed that all hope of winning the war against the Sa'Nerra had died with James Colicos. However, while it may no longer have been possible to stop the aliens' invasion of Earth, Griffin's contingency plan still provided the possibility of victory. Even if that victory came at a terrible cost.

"If we can launch an assault against the Sa'Nerran home world while the aliens are still amassed in Fleet space, we can give those bastards a moment of pause," Sterling said, balling his hands into fists. "It might even be enough to make them turn for home."

"Whether our attack forces the Sa'Nerra to withdraw from Fleet space or not, makes no difference," Griffin replied with feeling. "We'll hit them hard and we won't stop hitting them until there's nothing left of the Sa'Nerran empire but a memory."

"An eye for an eye," Banks added, glancing over at Sterling. "Maybe we can't defeat their armada, but if Earth is going to burn then we can sure as hell make sure that Sa'Nerra burns too."

Electricity raced down Sterling's spine. His mission had so far revolved around finding a defense against the Sa'Nerran threat. The Invictus had always been on the back foot, running from the enemy rather than toward it. Like Banks, Sterling preferred a straight-up fight. Now they had an opportunity to strike back and Sterling was itching to take it. Yet, there was another flaw in Griffin's plan. It irked him to raise it, but if they were going to attack the Sa'Nerran homeworld then he wanted to be sure they had every chance of success.

"We're all in, Admiral, but it's still the case that those fifty ships out there plus the Invictus won't be enough to assault Sa'Nerra," Sterling pointed out. "We're going to need a hell of lot more firepower."

"Astute, as always, Captain," Griffin said. She almost sounded proud of him, and Sterling couldn't help but feel his chest swell. "That is precisely why you will not attack Sa'Nerra with just the Obsidian Fleet."

Not for the first time during the course of the meeting, Sterling frowned at the Admiral. "Unless you've developed some sort of cloaking technology, I don't see any other ships out here, Admiral," he replied. "At least not ones that aren't in pieces, anyway."

"The ship we need is not here, Captain," Griffin said. She tapped a sequence of commands into the CIC computer. A moment later a holo-image of a Fleet Dreadnaught appeared in front of them.

"You're giving us the Hammer?" said Banks.

"No, the Hammer is deployed in defense of F-Sector," replied Griffin. "And even if we could get on-board, Captain Blake does not control the unconditional loyalty of enough of the crew to mount a full insurgency."

"Then which ship is this?" asked Banks. "The Hammer is the only Dreadnaught in the fleet."

"Incorrect, Commander," replied Griffin, stiffly. "This is the Fleet Dreadnaught Vanguard."

Sterling's brow was now so tightly furrowed that it was giving him a headache. "But the Vanguard was lost. No-one has seen or heard from it in close to two years."

"The Vanguard was infiltrated by the Sa'Nerra and captured," Griffin answered. "Captain Jericho was originally assigned to the Obsidian Project. I ensured he took command of the Vanguard after the project was disbanded. He was, unfortunately, turned during the Sa'Nerran assault."

Sterling raised his eyebrows and waited patiently for Griffin to continue. It appeared to be the day for secrets to be revealed, he realized.

"The Sa'Nerra succeeded in surging the Vanguard into the Void," Griffin went on. "However, there was a malfunction in the surge field generator resulting from damage sustained during the battle. The ship ended up lost."

"Might I assume you've now found it again?" Sterling

asked, studying the holo-imagine of the powerful warship. It was hard not to be awed by the Dreadnaught-class, Sterling thought. It was the rhino of the warship world, combining imposing size and thick armor plating. More importantly, the mighty ship carried enough armaments to level a planet, which made it ideally suited for their new mission.

"I have known the location of the Vanguard for some time, Captain," Griffin replied, letting another secret slip out as casually as a hair stylist discussing the weather. "By chance, an aperture relay probe from the Vanguard was discovered in the Void a few months after the vessel disappeared. Unfortunately, its memory storage cells had become heavily corrupted and fragmented. Fleet scientists were unable to recover any useful data from it, and so it was boxed and stored."

"I'm guessing this probe was another one of your clandestine acquisitions, Admiral?" said Sterling, offering a knowing smile. As much as Griffin irked him and even sometimes scared him, he couldn't help but admire her gall and tenacity.

"It took over a year to reconstruct the memory cells to a sufficient degree to glean any useful information from the probe," Griffin went on. "And by the time I learned anything of value, I already knew that the War Council would not countenance a rescue mission."

"So, what happened to it?" asked Banks, sounding as intrigued as Sterling was to learn the Vanguard's fate.

"The information is patchy, but it appears that the Vanguard's crew mounted a fight-back against the Sa'Nerran boarding party," said Griffin. The Admiral seemed relieved and even happy to be finally telling another living, breathing human the story. Sterling knew all too well that keeping secrets was a lonely occupation. "The ship's first-officer, Commander Alicia Cannon, eventually opened all of the ship's airlocks and docking garages and vented everyone into space. Her own crew included."

Banks let out a long, low whistle. "That's dark, especially for someone who wasn't an Omega officer."

"It prevented a powerful weapon from being captured by the enemy," Griffin replied, coolly. "It was not dark, Commander Banks. It was necessary."

"She would have made an excellent Omega Captain, that's for sure," commented Sterling.

"Indeed," the Admiral replied, wistfully. "Such a waste."

"So, where is the Vanguard now, Admiral?" Banks added, staring at the image of the vessel like a kid staring at a toy in a shop window. "Can we still reach it from the apertures we have access to?"

"It is adrift, but salvageable," Griffin replied. "However, the only way to reach it within any reasonable timeframe is from an aperture in F-Sector, close to F-COP."

Sterling huffed a laugh. "There's always something," he commented, mostly to himself. "Heaven forbid something might be easy for a change."

"I'm afraid that reaching the aperture and successfully surging into the Void is only part of the challenge, captain," Griffin added. "The vessel has been drifting for a long time. It will take you several weeks to reach it. And even when you do, and even assuming you can bring it back online, you can only return via the established, regular apertures. The Vanguard is far too large to surge through the experimental, long-range gateways."

Sterling rubbed the back of his neck. It seemed that for every possible solution that presented itself there were two new problems.

"Let's just assume we can re-take the Vanguard," Sterling said, erring on the side of optimism. "We don't have nearly enough crew on the Invictus to man a ship of that size. And it's also not an easy thing to hide. If we jump back into the Void in a dreadnaught, someone is going to notice."

Griffin raised an eyebrow. "I have a solution for the first problem, Captain." She operated the CIC computer and a schematic of an Obsidian Soldier appeared on the holo. Sterling and Banks both shot wide-eyed looks at one another as they realized what Griffin was suggesting.

"You want to crew the Vanguard with these robotic psychopaths?" Sterling dearly hoped he had misinterpreted Griffin's intentions.

"As ever, Captain, your keen observations are most impressive," Griffin replied, this time with obvious sarcasm.

"No offense, Admiral, but one of those things almost slit my throat a few minutes ago," Sterling hit back.

"And as I already explained, they will learn and adapt," Griffin said. She was clearly not going to take no for an answer. "These machines do not eat or sleep and one unit is capable of performing the functions of three or four human crewmembers. I will assign one hundred Obsidian

Soldiers to your command. That will be a sufficient skeleton crew to operate the Vanguard and bring it home."

Sterling blew out his cheeks and shrugged. "What the hell. I guess getting murdered by these lunatic machines beats spending the rest of my life in Grimaldi."

"That's the spirit, Captain," replied Griffin, deadpan.

"That only leaves the issue of where we hide a four-kilometer-long warship," Sterling said, feeling the sting of Griffin's snarky comebacks. "Because as you've already highlighted, we can't use a long-range aperture to surge to this base."

"Call me crazy, but I think I have a solution," Commander Banks chipped in. "May I, Admiral?" She pointed to the CIC computer.

Admiral Griffin nodded and Banks set to work on the computer. A few second later the image of a massive space-dock appeared on the holo. It took Sterling a few moments to realize what it was, but then the penny dropped.

"The Sa'Nerran shipyard inside the ring-system at Omega Four?" Sterling asked.

Banks smiled and nodded. "The aperture relays we deployed in the system showed that the shipyard is still there, and there hasn't been a single Sa'Nerran vessel in or out of the system for weeks." She shrugged. "It's the perfect hiding place, and it also has the facilities we need to repair the Vanguard and any other ships we need. We only need to swap out the alien computer system and the whole damn thing is ours."

Sterling knew that swapping out the Sa'Nerran computers for Fleet systems wouldn't be as trivial as Banks had made it appear. However, he couldn't deny the idea had merit. And with the resources of a Dreadnaught at their disposal, it was certainly possible.

"It's a long-shot, but then so is every option we've got right now," replied Sterling. He looked back to Admiral Griffin. "I think it could work."

"Excellent, then it's agreed," Griffin said, as ever seemingly undetered by any challenge she was presented with. The Admiral then shut down the CIC computer and returned to the spherical viewing window. Sterling took this to mean that the meeting was coming to its conclusion. "You will depart as soon as repairs to the Invictus have been completed," the Admiral added. "I'll have one of the Obsidian Soldiers escort you back to your ship."

"No thanks, Admiral, I think we can make it back on our own," Sterling said. He had no intention of allowing the machine another opportunity to skewer him.

"As you wish, Captain," Griffin replied, still peering out through the window. "You are dismissed."

Sterling flashed his eyes at Banks and turned to leave. Just at that moment the doors swished open. Sterling almost went for his pistol again, assuming it was an Obsidian Soldier returning to finish the job. However, rather than an onyx black killing machine, the new arrival was Lieutenant Shade.

"Apologies for the intrusion, but I have urgent news," she reported.

Griffin turned to face Shade, eyes sharpening once more.

"Why didn't you just inform us over neural comms,

Lieutenant?" asked Sterling, wondering why Shade had chosen to relay urgent news in person.

"I have a neural blocker enabled in this room, Captain," Griffin cut in. "I do not like secrets."

Sterling almost laughed out loud at the absurd irony of Griffin's statement, but just managed to reign in the urge. "Go on, Lieutenant," he said to Shade.

"Aperture relays report that F-sector is under attack, sir," Shade continued. The revelation left Sterling numb, like the heat had just been sucked out of the room. "The Sa'Nerra have committed their entire invasion armada to the attack."

Sterling cursed. "Then we don't have any time to waste," he said, glancing back at Admiral Griffin. "How soon can you have the Obsidian Soldiers loaded onto the Invictus?"

"They have already been loaded on board, Captain," said Griffin. Her response implied that she thought this fact should have been obvious.

"Then we have to leave right away, whatever state of repair the Invictus is in," Sterling said, turning to Banks. "If the Sa'Nerra take control of F-Sector, we'll have no chance of reaching the aperture. But the battle will be a perfect distraction."

Banks nodded. "I'll get the ship ready to depart right away," she said before turning to Lieutenant Shade. "You're with me, Lieutenant." Shade moved to Banks' side and the two officers hurried out of the CIC.

Sterling was about to leave too when Griffin spoke up. "Good luck, Captain Sterling." If he hadn't known better, he would have said there was a warmth and familiarity to the Admiral's voice that implied a level of concern for his wellbeing. "I will move what I can of my base to Omega Four and see you there."

Sterling nodded. "I'll be there, Admiral," he replied. "I don't know when or how, but I swear that I'll bring the Vanguard home."

Griffin nodded. "I'll be waiting, Captain. Good hunting."

Sterling saluted the Admiral then marched out of the CIC. He knew that the task ahead seemed impossible, but he also held true to the idea that the greater the stakes, the greater the reward. If he could recover the Vanguard and get it to Omega Four then they would have a weapon that was capable of pulverizing a planet from orbit. *It's time to fight fire with fire...* Sterling thought as he continued to march back to the docking port. He would rain fury onto the alien's homeworld until their planet was reduced to nothing but rubble and ash.

STERLING WATCHED the battle raging in F-Sector on the viewscreen, his face painted red by the low-level alert lights on the bridge. Sterling was no stranger to combat, but he'd never seen anything on the scale of the battle unfolding before him. Hundreds of warships occupied the space surrounding F-COP and dozens more were surging in every minute. The fighting was already heavy, but so far there was no sign of the Titan – the super-weapon commanded by Emissary McQueen herself.

"Tactical analysis, Lieutenant," Sterling said to his weapons officer, though he kept his eyes focused on the battle. "How do we weave our way through the chaos out there to reach the aperture we need?"

Shade entered a sequence of commands into her console and the viewscreen switched to show a tactical analysis of the battle. Their target aperture was highlighted on the screen, located within the ever-expanding perimeter of the battlefield, beyond F-COP. Sterling cursed, realizing that there was no way to reach it without flying into the combat zone.

"Looks like we have no choice but to fight our way through," said Commander Banks. She was still at Keller's former station at the front of the bridge. Sterling had requested she continue her temporary role as pilot; he needed someone at the helm that he could trust.

"If that's the case then so be it," replied Sterling, also realizing there was no other option. "Maybe we can even take a few of these alien bastards down before we surge." He turned to Shade. "Find us a route in, Lieutenant," he said, adding a note of caution, "but no heroics. We can't afford to take heavy damage out here."

"Aye, sir," Shade replied, already working at her console. A course projection then appeared on the screen. "I suggest this route, Captain," the weapons officer added, nodding toward the screen. Clearly, she had already been working on the plan before Sterling had asked her to plot a route.

Sterling studied the course, finding it to be surprisingly nuanced for his usually gung-ho weapons officer. Rather than find every opportunity to engage the enemy, Shade had plotted a course that would take them in behind the Fleet Dreadnaught Hammer. They would then be able to use the massive dreadnaught for cover while they waited for an opening to make their run for the aperture.

"Good work, Lieutenant," said Sterling. "Though, if I'm honest, I'm surprised you didn't suggest we just charge headlong at the closest cluster of enemy warships."

"This isn't the battle I'm interested in, Captain," replied Shade, as cool and collected as always. "The real fight will be at Sa'Nerra. I want to be there to see their cities burn and their space stations crumble."

"You'll get your chance, Lieutenant," replied Sterling, meeting the eyes of his warmongering weapons officer. Shade had spoken with feeling and it was a sentiment he shared. "We all will, so long as we can get through this."

"Course laid in, Captain," said Commander Banks. "But there's a squadron of Skirmishers and Sa'Nerran Light Cruisers between us and the Hammer," she continued, as the Invictus powered toward the battle. "The Samson and Typhoon have engaged them, but they're taking heavy fire."

"Then let's give them a hand," said Sterling, highlighting two of the enemy ships on his tactical screen. "Fire at will, Lieutenant."

"Aye, sir," Shade replied, staring at the targeted enemy vessels like a hungry wolf.

As the Invictus powered toward the battle, the Typhoon was caught in the crossfire from two Skirmishers and driven out of position. The Skirmishers swooped in behind it, sensing the kill.

"New target," said Sterling, highlighting the enemy vessel on his console for Banks and Shade to see.

"Adjusting course," replied Banks.

Sterling felt the engines kick hard before the inertial negation systems compensated. Banks may not have had Keller's deft touch at the helm, but she was every bit as aggressive – if not more so. The Skirmishers rapidly came into view ahead of the Invictus, the speed of their approach seeming to catch the enemy off-guard. Flashes of plasma lit up the viewscreen as Shade fired the main plasma rail-guns, striking one of the phase-three Skirmishers square across the back. The vessel exploded instantly, showering them with fiery debris. Powering through the debris field, Shade unleashed a volley of plasma at the second Skirmisher, damaging the alien vessels' engines and causing it to fall back. The alien ship was then pummeled by a devastating attack from the Samson and obliterated in an instant.

Sterling's console chimed and he saw that a message had come through from the Fleet Destroyer Typhoon on the open channel.

"Thanks for the assist, Invictus," the captain's voice said. "Though I have to say, I'm surprised to see you here and on our side. Fleet has you listed as an enemy combatant. I almost ordered my weapons officer to target you."

Sterling huffed a laugh. "No problem, Typhoon, and thanks for the heads up," he replied, silently cursing the Wessels as he did so. "Do me a favor and let the others know we're on the same side."

"Will do, Captain, Typhoon out," the voice replied before the comm channel clicked off.

"It's going to be hard enough reaching the aperture with just the Sa'Nerra to deal with," commented Banks. The sizable form of the Hammer was now visible ahead of them. "I hadn't figured that our own damned ships might be gunning for us too."

"I think it's time I had a little chat with Captain Blake,"

said Sterling, opening a comm channel to the Hammer. "Hopefully, he's still on our side. Or on Griffin's, at least."

The Invictus was rocked by another plasma blast, forcing Banks to take evasive action. Sterling saw that two Sa'Nerran Destroyers had broken off and were now in pursuit.

"Keep those alien destroyers off our ass, Commander," Sterling said to Banks, as the face of Captain Blake appeared inset on the viewscreen.

"What is it Captain Sterling, I'm a little busy?" snarled Blake. As Sterling's former commanding officer, the two men knew each other well, and while they shared a grudging respect for one another, there was also no love lost between them.

"I need you to give us cover," Sterling replied as another blast rocked the ship.

"Port side ventral armor holding at eighty-two percent," Lieutenant Razor called out from her station at the rear of the bridge. "Minor damage reported to deck four primary power relays. I'm returning to engineering, Captain."

Sterling acknowledged his engineer, who then hurried off the bridge, before focusing back on Captain Blake.

"We're on a special assignment from Admiral Griffin," Sterling went on as his crew continued to fight the pursuing destroyers. "I think you know the sort of assignment I'm talking about."

The Invictus turned hard, bringing its main rail guns to bear on the first of the two destroyers. Shade returned fire catching the alien ship across its aft section, destroying its engines and sending the vessel spinning out of control.

"Griffin has been stripped of rank and branded a turned enemy of the United Governments, Captain," Blake replied, coolly. "And, for that matter, so have you."

Sterling cursed. He didn't have the time or patience to fence with Blake. "Look, Captain, are you going to help us or not?" He tapped his console and sent the co-ordinates of the aperture directly to Blake's captain's console on a secure, private channel. "I need to reach the coordinates I've just sent to your console and I need to get there in one piece."

Blake's eyes dropped to his console. His brow scrunched into a scowl before he stared back at Sterling through the viewscreen. "I know where you're going, Captain, and it's a wild goose chase," Sterling's former CO replied. "I've sent probes and recon shuttles out there looking for what Griffin is sending you to find. It's not there."

Sterling was suddenly thrown off balance as the Invictus turned hard to avoid a barrage of plasma blasts from an advancing heavy cruiser.

"We're generating a lot of attention, Captain," Banks called out from the helm control. "We could really use some cover about now."

Sterling acknowledged Banks, then focused back on Captain Blake. Right now, the captain of the Fleet's flagship was his only hope.

"We have recent data that suggests otherwise, Captain, but there's more," Sterling continued. "Is this channel secure?"

Blake sighed and appeared to hit a button on his console. Sterling saw a red rectangle appear around the Hammer's name on his comms display.

"It is now Captain," Blake replied. "Say your piece."

"The Obsidian Project is still a go, Captain Blake," Sterling said, laying all his cards on the table. "We have a plan to..."

"Don't say anymore, Captain," Blake interrupted, cutting Sterling off with the precision of a scalpel blade. "Whatever I know the enemy can know."

Sterling nodded. "The bottom line is that I'm all out of friends. I need your help if I'm going to pull this off."

"You never had any friends, Sterling," Blake hit back. "Apart from one. But you killed her, don't you remember?"

Blake's words had intended to hit hard and Sterling felt his verbal assault land like an uppercut. Ariel Gunn flashed back into his mind and he felt physically sick. He opened his mouth, wanting to respond and to fight his corner, but no words came out. He'd never even considered that Blake had been sour with him about what happened to Gunn. Yet his former CO's bitterness was now clear, and Sterling could hardly blame him. Gunn was one of Blake's officers, but he'd never considered them to be close. Sterling was still stuck for any way to respond to Blake when his former CO threw him an unexpected lifeline.

"But while you have no friends out here, you do still have an ally, albeit a reluctant one." The captain of the Hammer then operated his console and new coordinates arrived on Sterling's screen. "Form up alongside the

Hammer and stay within the sectors I've just sent you. I'll make sure we give you cover, without accidentally blowing you to hell. Not that you don't deserve it."

Sterling sent the co-ordinates to Banks' console and his first officer immediately adjusted course. He then turned back to Blake and forced down a dry swallow.

"Thank you, Captain Blake," Sterling said. "And for what it's worth, I'm sorry that what went down had to go down on your ship. And I'm sorry Gunn had to die." Then he realized something – it was something he'd always known, but never admitted to anyone, perhaps not even himself. "But I'm not sorry about what I did, Captain. I probably deserve the special place in hell you've already assigned to me, and if that's my fate then so be it. But I did what I had to do, and I'd do it again. Nothing is going to stop me from completing my mission, Captain. Nothing and no-one."

There was brief silence while Blake studied Sterling through the viewscreen. Then the captain of the Hammer simply nodded.

"That's why she chose you," Blake said, "and that's the only reason I'm helping you now. Good hunting, Captain Sterling. Hammer, out."

The image of Captain Blake disappeared from the viewscreen, which was now dominated by the formidable bulk of the Fleet Dreadnaught Hammer. The massive capitol ship's cannons were pounding plasma out into space all around them, providing a shield of searing energy that prevented any enemy vessels from getting close. Sterling checked his console and saw that the Hammer was heading to the co-ordinates he'd sent to Captain Blake. They were riding along with the Dreadnaught like a barnacle on a whale's back.

"We're in position alongside the Hammer," said Banks, using the moment of respite from the battle to take a breath and glance back at Sterling. "We'll have to break out from cover to reach the Aperture, but for now we're protected."

Sterling nodded. "That's one thing that's gone right, at least," he commented, resting forward on his console. An alert then chimed and he cursed himself for potentially jinxing their good luck.

"We're receiving a message," Banks said. Then she cursed too. "It's from the Venator."

Sterling sighed and shook his head. "What the hell is it with that guy, anyway?" he commented.

"I just don't think he likes you very much, Captain," said Banks, with a slight smirk.

"Thank you for that keen observation, Commander," Sterling replied, scowling at Banks through the tops of his eyes. He then sighed again and threw out his hands. "What the hell, put him on the viewscreen, Commander." He straightened his back and stared at the screen. "Let's hear what he has to say this time."

"Aye, sir," Banks replied, spinning back to face the viewscreen. Moments later, the face of Commodore Vernon Wessel appeared. To say the man looked enraged would have been an understatement, Sterling considered.

"Captain Sterling, you are hereby under arrest, charged

with treason!" Wessel snarled at him. Sterling had seen his former academy classmate mad before, but this was on a whole other level. "You are to surrender to me at once or be destroyed."

"With the greatest respect, Commodore, kiss my ass," Sterling replied. Wessel's face went red and the man looked like he was about to explode like an overinflated balloon. Sterling abruptly cut the channel before Wessel had a chance to yell whatever string of expletives he was building up to bawl at him through the viewscreen.

"He won't be happy about that..." commented Banks.

"I really don't give a damn," Sterling said as more flashes of plasma raced past them from the Hammer. "Unless that asshole wants to run the gauntlet and come at us while we're protected by the Hammer, he can just sit out there and stew for all I care."

Sterling's console then chimed another alert. He cursed, expecting it to be Wessel again, but when he checked his console, he saw that it was an all-ships priority alert from F-COP. Then a massive flash lit up the viewscreen. However, this wasn't the flash of plasma, it was the flash of a ship surging into the system.

"New contacts..." Lieutenant Shade announced. As usual, she was quicker with her analysis than Sterling had been. "Multiple new alien warships."

"On screen," said Sterling, feeling his hands tighten around the sides of his console.

The viewscreen updated and the colossal form of the Sa'Nerran Titan dominated the screen. The vessel immediately set a course directly for F-COP, flanked by dozens of smaller cruisers. However, in amongst them was another vessel that Sterling recognized. It was a vessel they'd faced before, more than once. Flying in formation with the Titan was MAUL. Then the battle-scarred Heavy Destroyer changed course. It had locked directly on to the Invictus and was coming at them hard.

STERLING PEERED down at the scanner readings, seeing alien warships closing in on the Invictus from in front and behind. Ahead was MAUL, no doubt still commanded by an irate Emissary, Clinton Crow, Sterling thought. To their rear was the Fleet Marauder Venator, commanded by an even more irate Vernon Wessel. Sterling didn't know who wanted his head more – the enemy or the side he was supposed to be fighting for.

"The Titan is charging it aperture-based weapon," said Lieutenant Shade. "It's locked on to F-COP."

Suddenly, the Hammer began to veer off-course. It was now heading directly for the Titan, as was half of the Fleet.

"What the hell..." said Sterling, trying to raise Captain Blake on a comms channel to get an explanation. He then tried to reach the officer through a neural link. However, on both occasions, his request was denied

"I've intercepted a Fleet-wide broadcast," said Shade,

scowling down at her console. "New orders to take down the Titan were just transmitted."

Sterling snorted. "I guess we're no longer on Fleet's Christmas card list," he said. The fact they had not also received the message was no accident. Sterling assumed that Wessel would made sure they were cut off. "Stay with the Hammer for as long as you can, Commander," he ordered, calling over the helm control station. "Then break for the aperture and run like hell."

"Aye, Captain," Banks replied, adjusting course to remain inside the protective perimeter of the Hammer's firing solution.

Sterling then felt a link forming in his mind. It was weak and unfamiliar. He checked the status of the neural comms network and saw that the signal was being relayed from the Hammer. He selected the channel and boosted it through the Invictus' neural relays as best he could. Even so, it still required immense concentration to form the link.

"Captain Sterling, I don't have much time..." came the voice of Captain Blake. "The Titan is preparing to destroy F-COP. If it succeeds, F-sector will fall and the fleet will be forced to withdraw to the solar system. I have to try to stop it."

Sterling closed his eyes and focused harder on the link. It was slipping away by the second. "I understand, Captain, and thanks for getting us this far. We'll take it the rest of the way."

"If you find the Vanguard then don't come back here, Captain," Blake went on. Through the intimacy of the link Sterling could feel the man's fear. It was like Blake knew he was about to die and was speaking his final words. It was unexpected and more than a little disquieting. "Fleet is compromised..."

"Captain, I'm reading a massive amount of neural energy being generated by the Titan," announced Shade. "The level is off the scale..."

Lieutenant Shade's sudden statement broke Sterling's concentration and his grip on Blake's mind wavered.

"Neural energy?" Sterling asked Shade, unsure whether he'd heard her correctly. "Is it trying to scramble our neural comms?"

"Unknown, sir, but the field is concentrated around the central emitters array on the front of the vessel," Shade replied.

"Captain, you must listen..." continued the voice of Blake in his head.

Sterling peered down at his console, trying to understand the new readings from the Titan while also trying to maintain his link to Blake. It was demanding all the mental strength Sterling had left to conduct a verbal and neural conversation simultaneously.

"I'm still here, Captain," replied Sterling through the link, fighting against the searing pain that was now cutting through his temples from ear to ear. "How has Fleet been compromised?"

"... has been turned..."

Sterling recoiled from his console, suddenly focused purely on the mind of Captain Blake. "Say again, Captain, who has been turned?" Sterling said. He waited for Blake to answer, but he could feel the link fading fast. "Captain the link cut out. Tell me who has been turned!"

The link deteriorated further and Sterling hammered his fists against his console, desperately trying to reach out to Blake again. However, it was no use. The link was too weak. Sterling cursed and stared at the neural energy data from the Titan on his console, trying to understand its meaning and purpose. Then it suddenly all made sense to him. It was like staring blankly at a Magic Eye image only for the hidden picture to suddenly appear in front of him, as clear and crisp as a spring morning.

"Mercedes, get us away from the Hammer now, maximum acceleration!" Sterling called out to Banks.

Sterling knew that his first officer would be confused by the order, but he also knew she wouldn't question it. He was banking on this implicit trust between them to save their lives, because he knew that any hesitation, no matter how slight, could be fatal. The Invictus turned a split-second later and Sterling was forced to grip the sides of his console to compensate for their sudden, ferocious acceleration. Then as the dreadnaught slipped into the distance behind them, a massive burst of neural energy was projected from the Titan. It grew and expanded like an ice cream cone until it completely enveloped the Hammer and several ships close to it. Sterling was gripped by a searing pain inside his head, focused around his neural interface. Despite the connection being weak, he was still linked to Captain Blake on the Hammer, but now the nature of the connection had altered. It was like he was linked to an entirely different person.

Blake's fear had gone, and had been replaced with the sort of unflinching certainty that Sterling had never experienced before. No human being is ever one-hundred percent certain of their actions. There is always some doubt, always some fear. Humans are built to second-guess themselves and to be cautious. Bravery is an ability to go against human nature and the will to survive. The mind of Captain Blake was devoid of these basic human traits, and Sterling realized why. Blake had been turned. Suddenly the link between the two captains was severed, releasing Sterling from the tortuous agony that had been gripping his mind. It had been like having a strip of razor-wire wrapped around his brain.

"Captain, what's wrong?" said Banks. She was half out of her seat, preparing to run to his aid. It was only then Sterling realized he was face down on his console.

"The Hammer has been turned," Sterling replied, pushing himself upright again. "The Sa'Nerra have developed a way to project the neural control signal."

"The entire ship?" Banks said.

"I can't be sure, but I know Blake has gone," replied Sterling. "I could feel his mind changing."

Banks and Sterling returned their attention to the viewscreen. The Hammer had already veered away from the Titan and was turning its guns on F-COP and the rest of the fleet instead. The Invictus was rocked by an explosion and Sterling was thrown to the deck.

"The Venator is firing at us," Shade called out. "Armor integrity down to twenty-six percent. Hull breaches on decks two and three, sections four through eleven."

"Return fire!" Sterling called back, clawing himself

back to his feet. He opened a direct channel to the Venator and put Wessel on the screen.

"Are you insane?" Sterling yelled at the Commodore. "The Hammer has just been turned. F-COP is about to be annihilated and you're shooting at *us*?"

"Surrender, Captain!" Wessel roared back. "My mission is your capture, not this battle."

Sterling cursed and closed the channel. "Take them down, Lieutenant," he roared. "Ram the bastard if you have to!"

The Invictus' plasma cannons fired and the Venator was struck cleanly. Sterling saw explosive decompressions along the rival Marauder's port side and knew the damage was serious, but he didn't have time to assess the tactical situation. With the Hammer joining the alien Armada, F-COP was lost, which meant they were running out of time.

"I'm reading another energy build-up from the Titan," Shade called out.

Sterling cursed. "The neural weapon again?"

"Negative, this is different," Shade replied. "We've seen it before. It's the aperture projection array."

"Full speed to the aperture," Sterling called over to Banks. The ship was then struck again and consoles blew out on the bridge. Sterling steadied himself against his console, ignoring the damage control readings, and turned to Shade. "Press our attack on the Venator, Lieutenant, they're hurt."

"That wasn't the Venator, Captain," Shade answered. "That was MAUL."

Sterling checked his console and added the image of

the Sa'Nerran Heavy Destroyer to the viewscreen. It somehow looked even meaner than he remembered it.

"Put the Venator between us and MAUL," Sterling called out, acting on an idea that had just popped into his head. "With any luck, one Marauder looks like any other to Emissary Crow."

The Invictus banked hard towards Wessel's ship and swooped underneath the belly of the Venator. It was so close that Sterling physically ducked, as if the ship was about to take his head off. There was an intense flash of light, so bright that the viewscreen had to automatically polarize to avoid the intensity of the glow from hurting the crew's eyes.

"The Titan is firing," Shade called out.

Sterling focused the main section of the viewscreen onto F-COP and watched as a circular column of energy began to burrow through the center of the station. The Titan tipped up its nose, carving a furrow into the city-sized combat outpost like a blowtorch melting through ice. Moments later, F-COP detonated, enveloping a dozen nearby ships in flame along with it. Debris was spewed out in all directions, colliding with Fleet and alien ships alike.

"Fleet Admiral Rossi has ordered all ships to retreat," Shade announced. "The message was broadcast in the clear."

Sterling tapped his neural interface and reached out to Lieutenant Razor in engineering. He widened the connection to allow his bridge crew to monitor.

"Lieutenant, I'm going to need another one of your miracle rebound surges," he said through the link. "We can't allow MAUL or the Venator to know where we're headed."

"Aye, sir, I'm already on it, but there is a problem," Razor replied.

"When is there ever not a problem, Lieutenant?" replied Sterling, shrugging even though Razor obviously couldn't see him.

"Our target surge vector is already way beyond safety margins," Razor went on. "And I'm talking my own margins, here, captain, not the conservative ones that Fleet supplies."

The Invictus was slammed by another plasma blast and Sterling saw more sections turn amber on his damage control console.

"Cut to the chase, Lieutenant," he said through the link. "We don't have much time."

"It'll work, but the margin of error widens with each surge," Razor replied. "We could end up a long way from where we need to be."

"Anywhere is better than here, Lieutenant, just get it done," Sterling hit back.

"Aye sir, I'm transmitting the program to the helm control console now," Razor replied, and the link was severed.

"We'll be within range of the aperture in sixty seconds," Commander Banks called out.

The bridge was hammered again and Sterling's console exploded, showering his face with hot sparks that burrowed into his flesh. He slammed his fist on the broken terminal and turned to Shade.

"Enough is enough. Take that bastard out!" Sterling growled. The aggression from Sterling only seemed to fuel Shade, like a boost of nitrous oxide in a street racer. The Invictus turned hard, bearing down on the Venator nose-to-nose. *Let's see who flinches first, asshole,* Sterling thought as the two ships hurtled toward each other. "Hold your course and prepare to fire," Sterling called out.

"Fifteen seconds to impact," Commander Banks announced. "The Venator is not turning."

"He will," Sterling replied. "Wessel doesn't have the balls."

"Five seconds..." Banks called out, the stress showing in her voice. "The Venator is thrusting away."

"Fire!" Sterling yelled.

Plasma flashed out ahead, striking the engine section of the enhanced Marauder-class vessel. The Venator cartwheeled out of control and soared overhead, missing the Invictus by barely a meter. Then Sterling saw another ship coming in behind them. It was MAUL.

"The Venator is heading straight for MAUL," Shade said, anticipation building in her voice. "I don't think they've seen it."

"Come on, hit it," Sterling said, urging the two ships to obliterate each other. It would literally be a case of killing two birds with one stone. Then at the last moment, MAUL ignited its thrusters and pushed itself higher. The Venator spun past and its nose raked across the belly of MAUL, like a Katana blade slashing through Samurai armor. Explosions rippled across the hull of the alien race's top killing machine and it too spun out of control.

"MAUL is disabled," Shade said, her hands closed into fists.

The viewscreen lit up again except this time it wasn't a weapon firing or a ship surging in – it was the Venator detonating in a ball of orange flame. Banks whooped and hollered then hurled curses at the flaming mass of debris. Sterling kept his composure, but inside he was ready to explode with the same ferocity.

"Rebound surge program ready," Banks reported, managing to put a lid on her emotions, at least partially. "Not that anyone is left who'd want to follow us."

"Ship launching from the Titan, Captain," Shade announced.

Sterling cursed and glowered at Banks. "You were saying?" he said, his voice thick with sarcasm. "What was the name of your dog again? Jinx wasn't it?"

"Hey, don't blame the dog!" Banks hit back, jabbing a finger at Sterling.

"It's a new configuration," Shade went on, ignoring the misplaced jostling between the ship's two senior officers. "It's looks like a Skirmisher, but it's bigger. It's also fast."

"On screen, Lieutenant," said Sterling.

An image of the new vessel appeared. It was slightly larger than the Invictus and significantly larger than a phase-three Skirmisher. However, the design similarities between the new alien vessel and a Skirmisher were readily apparent.

"It's a phase-four," said Sterling, recognizing the layout from Fleet intelligence briefings. "Fleet calls it the Raven-class. It's fast and powerful."

"And it coming after us," added Commander Banks, with a cautionary tone.

"It can come at us all it likes, it's not going to catch us," Sterling replied. "Not this time."

Sterling heard the helm controls chime an alert and he knew they were ready.

"Rebound surge in twenty..." Banks called out.

Sterling moved over to the first-officer's console and checked the Fleet status report. Two hundred and eighty-two Fleet vessels had been destroyed and fifty-seven captured and turned, including the Hammer. The Sa'Nerran net losses were ninety-seven. The numbers told the story. Fleet – and humanity – was heading towards its end.

Sterling gripped the console and steeled himself for the surge, knowing it would sap every last ounce of strength that he had left. Yet no matter how weak he felt or how battered and bruised his body became, he knew he'd get up again. And he knew he'd find the Vanguard and bring it back into the fight. The war for Earth may have been lost, but if humanity was to suffer then he'd see to it that the Sa'Nerra suffered just as greatly. Perhaps in the end that meant no-one really won. *An eye for an eye,* Sterling thought, remembering the comment Banks had made. *Perhaps that will have to be good enough.*

There was a flash of light and Sterling was consumed by nothingness. The Invictus had surged out of Fleet space, perhaps for the very last time.

STERLING WAS STOOD on the balcony overlooking the cargo hold of the Invictus. Lined up in rows beneath him like the terracotta army were one hundred of Admiral Griffin's Obsidian Soldiers. All of them were currently offline and Sterling much preferred them that way. Despite Griffin's insistence that the thinking machines would get used to Sterling, the thought of activating the robotic warriors filled him with dread.

"Penny for your thoughts?"

Sterling glanced behind to see Commander Banks standing on the balcony. She was smiling at him, and he couldn't help but smile back. "You'll need more than a penny," replied Sterling, returning his weary eyes to the robotic army at their feet. "One hundred would probably do it."

Jinx the beagle trotted up beside Sterling's leg and peered up at him with wide, brown eyes. Her tail was wagging so fast it was a blur.

"Can I help you, acting Ensign?" asked Sterling.

"She just wants some attention from her Captain," said Banks moving alongside Sterling and leaning on the railings. "She's like her mom in that respect," Banks added, winking at Sterling.

"I can't be seen to show favoritism, Commander," Sterling replied, continuing the pretense that the dog was a member of his crew.

Banks tutted at him then bent down to pet the dog. Contented, Jinx walked around in a circle a few times and curled up at Sterling's feet.

"These were clean on this morning," moaned Sterling, looking at the dog-hair that had already clung to the fabric around his ankle. The dog then scratched her ear with her augmented metal foot, flicking more hair onto Sterling's boots.

"At least we have some spare parts in case she gets injured again," said Banks, gesturing to the robot warriors below them.

"I'm already wondering whether to just have Razor tear them all down for scrap," replied Sterling. He wasn't joking; the idea had crossed his mind.

"Think of it this way, these things will either make life easier for us or they'll murder us in our sleep," Banks said, with a fatalistic nonchalance that Sterling found unsettling.

"I hadn't considered that they might murder me in my sleep," Sterling admitted. "I thought they might tear me apart while I was fully conscious, but being murdered by them in my sleep is a new thing for me to fret about, so thanks for that."

"Don't mention it, Captain," Banks replied, nudging Sterling with her shoulder. As usual, his first-officer had forgotten her own strength and almost toppled Sterling over.

"How are the repairs coming along?" Sterling then said, once he'd regained his balance. Jinx adjusted her position so that she was once again resting against Sterling's boot. Sterling didn't mind this time – he was just eager to move the conversation away from rampaging murder bots.

"Razor is in her element, as you might expect," Banks replied. "I swear she likes it when the ship gets beat up, just so she can fix it and correct all the mistake she says Fleet engineers have made."

"Don't knock it, we need her," Sterling hit back. "We're a long way from any repair dock, so without her mechanical wizardry we could be stranded out here forever."

"There's a cheery thought," said Banks.

"You mean like robots murdering me in my sleep?" Sterling countered.

"Touché…"

The captain and first officer continued to peer down at the Obsidian Solders for a while longer. Neither felt the need to speak. They were comfortable enough in each other's presence that these silences were not awkward. On the contrary, Sterling found them peaceful and he enjoyed sharing the calm with his first officer. His mind wandered and suddenly Captain Blake's comment about Sterling having no friends entered his thoughts. In truth, it had been playing on his mind for some time. The comment hadn't hurt his feelings; Sterling had never felt the need for close acquaintances. Even so, Ariel Gunn had been the closest person to a friend he'd ever had. That was until Mercedes Banks had come along. Whether what they had was friendship or mere camaraderie he didn't know. He didn't even know if there was a difference between these two relationship states. What he did know was that he liked it more when Banks was around than when she was not. And that – at least for Lucas Sterling – was a unique feeling.

"So, if we do get stuck out here forever, what, or who, would you miss?" Sterling asked.

It was a roundabout and fairly clunky way of trying to get to know his first officer a little better. Sterling realized that beyond her service record and Omega Directive test, he knew barely anything about her.

"No-one," replied Banks, with a brusque shrug of her shoulders.

"There has to be something, surely?" said Sterling, surprised by her curt response.

"You've read my file so you already know my story," Banks replied. She then cocked her head to the side and shot Sterling a quizzical look. "Why are you asking?"

"I don't read the personal stuff in the files," Sterling admitted. "I've never really considered any of it relevant."

"So why is it relevant now?" said Banks, still regarding him with an inquiring eye.

"I don't know," Sterling replied. In essence, that was the truth. He didn't really know why he was asking. "Just humor me, okay?"

Banks shrugged. "Okay," she said, pressing her lips into a pout and suddenly appearing deep in thought. "I was born on Shepherd Colony in G-Sector," she began, now staring into space at nothing in particular. "There's not much to do on a farming colony so I got into trouble a lot."

"That figures," Sterling replied, receiving another nudge for his trouble, though this time it was a little gentler.

"My father left when I was still in single digits, I don't really remember when," Banks went on. "My mother took it hard. She stuck it out for a few more years until she took too much Warp and fried her brain."

Sterling scowled. "That's some kind of drug, right?" he asked. He vaguely remembering reading about the narcotic, but knew little about it.

Banks nodded. "It grew like wildfire on Shepherd Colony. Almost everyone was into it, but not me."

"I'm proud of you, Commander," Sterling said, sarcastically. He realized he should probably have given a more sincere reaction, but personal conversations made him feel awkward. He remembered that was why he never had them.

"So, I ended up in the system, moving between foster homes and juvenile detention centers until I was old enough to join," Banks went on, either not hearing or ignoring Sterling's earlier comment. "Understandably, Fleet recruiters were more than a little wary of me until I aced the entrance tests. Then they discovered my unique abilities and I got bumped to officer candidate school. The rest, as they say, is history."

"Sounds like a lonely upbringing," commented Sterling.

Banks shrugged again. "People never wanted to be

around me because of my strength and my temper," she went on. "On an inner colony world, I'd have been in a jail somewhere by the time I was fourteen. On the outer colonies, if you can't fight you don't survive."

Sterling nodded, though in truth he didn't really understand. His own childhood had been completely different in most respects.

"The captain's console was always in my blood," Sterling said, after another period of quiet reflection. "I grew up on Mars. Both my folks were career fleet, like their folks before them. All of them died on the bridges of their ships before they were thirty-five."

Banks glanced over at Sterling. "How old are you again?" she asked, with a twinkle in her eye.

"Not quite old enough to break that particular curse," replied Sterling. He managed to see the funny side, though Banks' comment only reminded him that, traditionally, the Sterling family had not been built to last. "And the way things are going, I doubt I'll be setting any records for the longest surviving 'Captain Sterling' in my family," he added.

"The other Captain Sterlings didn't have a Mercedes Banks at their side," Banks said, nudging Sterling for a third time. Jinx stirred momentarily then went back to sleep on his boot.

"Then that makes me the luckiest Captain Sterling that ever lived," Sterling replied, shooting a smile at his first officer. Banks smiled back and for a few seconds they held each other's gaze, until it quickly became awkward and both had to turn away.

"Captain, Commander, am I disturbing you?"

Sterling looked around to see Lieutenant Razor on the walkway behind them. She was holding James Colicos' PDA and had activated her own computer on her left wrist.

"Not at all, Lieutenant, what is it?" Sterling said.

"I've been studying Colicos' initial research from Far Deep Nine," Razor began. The engineer appeared to be practically fizzing with energy. "The man was brilliant, truly. Even his initial observations and ideas were insightful and..."

"Yes, he was a very smart man," Sterling interrupted. The last thing he wanted to hear was a eulogy about how great James Colicos was. "But for a bona-fide genius he was also an idiot," Sterling went on. "What have you found, Lieutenant?"

"Colicos took my neural firewall design, the one I used to hack into the mind of the Sa'Nerran commander without being turned," Razor went on. Then she stopped and reconsidered her words. "Well, at least not turned yet, anyway."

"Lieutenant, if you don't get to the point soon, I may just press the nuke button on your brain and be done with it," Sterling commented. Banks smiled, though Razor appeared neither amused not offended.

"He took my design and within a couple of hours had made it orders of magnitude more efficient and effective," Razor continued. "He also figured out a way to program the firewall into our neural implants. It's a simple procedure that would take me no more than a few minutes per crew member."

Sterling pushed himself off the railings. Razor had just got his attention. "What sort of protection will it offer, Lieutenant?" Sterling said. He noticed that Jinx was still asleep on his boot. The act of him springing off the railings had not woken the dog.

"At this stage, I can't be certain, sir, and honestly the only way to know for sure is to test it," Razor replied.

"Test it?" Banks cut in. "You mean someone has to get turned to know how effective it is?"

"Basically, yes, Commander," Razor replied, bluntly. "But based on how my initial firewall worked and the many improvements Colicos has made, it's a fair guess to say the firewall could protect someone from the effects of the control weapon indefinitely."

Sterling clapped a hand over his fist. "Good work, Lieutenant!" he said, feeling like things were finally going their way. "Refine the procedure then when you're ready to test it, inform me directly."

"Aye, sir," Razor replied.

Razor was about to leave when Sterling had a thought. "Lieutenant, wait," he called out to her. The tall, white-haired engineer stopped and turned, standing to attention. "This firewall, will it have any additional benefit to your condition?" he asked.

"Negative, Captain, it will not help to undo the neural damage I've already suffered," Razor answered. There was no sadness or regret in her voice. She was merely answering a direct question with direct, factual response.

"I asked that asshole scientist to study your condition too,"

Sterling went on, hopeful that there was something more they could do for her. From a purely selfish point of view, this was because he needed his chief engineer. However, he also liked Razor. He liked her directness and her efficiency. "Is there anything on that pad that can help you too?"

This time Razor seemed less certain in her response. "Perhaps, Captain, though I have not yet had time to examine that data."

"Make sure you find the time, Lieutenant, that's an order," Sterling hit back. "Enlist Commander Graves to help. I'll make sure he understands it's a priority."

"I will sir," Razor replied. "Thank you."

"Thank me when this is all over and we have a dozen medals hanging from our chests, Lieutenant," Sterling replied.

"Being discharged from the service and having enough time left to enjoy life outside Fleet is all I ask, Captain," Razor replied.

Sterling nodded, remembering his engineer's unique motivation for excelling. "If there's anywhere left for us to go when this war is over, I'll see to it that you get the freedom to choose. Until then, I need you in engineering, doing what you do best."

Razor was about to leave when Banks stopped her. "Hold up, assuming we retake the Vanguard, don't Fleet regulations require an officer with a minimum rank of Lieutenant Commander to run the engineering section of a dreadnaught?"

Banks was smiling, which suggested she had made the

comment in jest. However, Sterling realized his first-officer had a point.

"That's actually true," Sterling said, straightening his tunic in readiness to give a field promotion to his engineer on the spot. "But that's a problem I'm happy to rectify right now."

"I appreciate that, sir, but no thank you," Razor replied, politely. "All I want it to be discharged, not promoted."

Sterling smiled. "As you wish," he replied, returning a respectful nod to his engineer. "You're dismissed."

Lieutenant Razor departed, again leaving Sterling, Banks and a sleeping Acting-Ensign Jinx alone on the balcony overlooking the horde of robot warriors.

"Well, that was surprising," said Banks. She cocked her head toward Sterling and shot him another of her mischievous smiles. "You can promote me, if you like?" she added. "I'll be captain, and you can be a commodore."

"I don't think that's how it works, Mercedes," Sterling hit back. "I can't just promote myself."

Banks shrugged. "Technically, we've been disowned by Fleet, anyway, so perhaps it's time we started making our own rules and ranks?"

"In all honesty, I think we've been doing that since the very beginning," replied Sterling. He then slapped his first-officer on the shoulder. "Come on, there's a number twenty-seven in the wardroom with my name on it. Care to join me?"

"It's a date," said Banks. "As long as I get to eat your crusts."

Sterling laughed. "It's not like I can stop you."

He invited Banks to lead the way and followed at her side. However, they'd barely made it to the door leading off the cargo bay when Sterling felt a neural link forming in his mind. And from the look on his first officer's face, Banks had received the connection too.

"Go ahead, Lieutenant," said Sterling, accepting the link from his weapons officer.

"We've picked up the Vanguard, Captain," Shade said. If she had been pleased by this fact, Sterling could not detect it in her voice or emotions. "It's right where Griffin projected it to be, though it's a few weeks out at our current best speed."

"That's closer than I expected," Sterling admitted. After Razor's warning that their rebound-surge could send them way off course, he was half-expecting to be months away from the Vanguard. However, he sensed that something was bothering his weapons officer. Shade was an expert at hiding her emotions, but the link between their minds also cut a hole through her armor. "Is there something else, Lieutenant?"

"Yes, Captain," Shade replied. Sterling felt a darkness fill his mind. "There is another ship on long-range scanners, sir. It's too far away for us to get a clear reading, but we can tell where it's headed."

Sterling cursed. "Let me guess, it's heading toward the Vanguard too?"

"Yes, Captain, I believe so," replied Shade.

"So, here's the sixty-four-thousand-dollar question, Lieutenant," Sterling went on, glancing at Banks. "Who is going to get there first?"

There was a moment of pause before Shade answered. "At the moment, sir, they will."

Sterling cursed again. "Thank you, Lieutenant, log that ship and monitor it closely," he replied. "If it changes course or pings a scan in our direction, I want to know about it."

"Aye, sir. Shade out," the weapons officer replied. Then the link went dead.

"Looks like boosting our engines is another job to add to Lieutenant Razor's growing list of chores," said Commander Banks, folding her powerful arms across her chest.

"I'll get her right on it, along with the dozen other things she's already doing to keep us alive," Sterling replied. "First, though, let's eat."

"Now you're speaking my language," said Banks, hitting the door controls.

The door swished open and Banks was about to step outside when she stopped and looked around her feet. Glancing back toward the balcony, Sterling spotted that Jinx was still asleep by the railings. Banks let out a sharp, shrill whistle and the dog pricked up her ears and came bounding over to them.

"There's a good little doggy!" said Banks, bending down and rubbing the Beagle's ears. "Grumpy Captain Sterling has some nice grilled ham and cheese for you. Would you like that? Yes, you would!"

Sterling shook his head at his first officer in dismay. "I don't know what it is about that dog that turns you into a gibbering fool," he said, as the three of them set off along the corridor.

"Come on, admit it, Captain. Jinx has been our lucky mascot," Banks hit back. "We'd have been stabbed to death, incinerated, blown up or had our heads blasted off a dozen times by now if it wasn't for Ensign Jinx's influence."

Sterling was far from convinced that the Beagle had provided any material benefits, other than improving the mood of his first officer. However, that achievement was worthy enough in itself, he realized.

"Fine, but it's still not getting any of my grilled ham and cheese," Sterling said, glancing down at the dog, which was merrily trotting along at their side.

"Aye, Captain, whatever you say," said Banks, raising an eyebrow at him.

This time Sterling took the lead, moving through the ship toward the wardroom, nodding and saluting at the crew members he passed by in the corridors. He knew their faces, if still not all of their names. More importantly, he knew that they had served their ship and its captain with distinction. This was despite the heavy price their mission had exacted – a price that was only set to get steeper. He knew not all of them would survive. He knew he would likely have to send some of them to their deaths. He would not do it lightly, or with casual disregard for their lives. He was cold, but not reckless. Whatever sacrifices they still had to make would be necessary, no matter how hard the decisions were and no matter the personal cost. In truth, Sterling had already considered himself lost, yet right at that moment he felt more purpose than he'd ever felt in his life before.

Out in the darkness lay the Fleet Dreadnaught Vanguard; a weapon capable of destruction on an apocalyptic scale. However, another ship was aiming to beat them to this prize. Sterling would not allow that to happen. The stakes were simply too high.

The Sa'Nerra meant to destroy Earth, and with the fall of F-sector they had come one step closer. Fleet had been on the run for years. For years the aliens had pushed back their lines, destroyed human colonies and turned human against human.

Now, it was payback time.

The end (to be continued).

CONTINUE THE JOURNEY

Continue the journey with book five: Dreadnaught. Available to buy from Amazon.

ABOUT THE AUTHOR

At school, I was asked to write down the jobs I wanted to do as a "grown up". Number one was astronaut and number two was a PC games journalist. I only managed to achieve one of those goals (I'll let you guess which), but these two very different career options still neatly sum up my lifelong interests in science, space, and the unknown.

School also steered me in the direction of a science-focused education over literature and writing, which influenced my decision to study physics at Manchester University. What this degree taught me is that I didn't like studying physics and instead enjoyed writing, which is why you're reading this book! The lesson? School can't tell you who you are.

When not writing, I enjoy spending time with my family, walking in the British countryside, and indulging in as much Sci-Fi as possible.

Subscribe to my newsletter:
http://subscribe.ogdenmedia.net

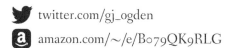

twitter.com/gj_ogden

amazon.com/~/e/B079QK9RLG

If you like Omega Taskforce then why not check out some of G J Ogden's other books? Click the series titles below to learn more about each of them.

Darkspace Renegade Series (6-books)

If you like your action fueled by power armor, big guns and the occasional sword, you'll love this fast-moving military sci-fi adventure.

Star Scavenger Series (5-book series)

Firefly blended with the mystery and adventure of Indiana Jones. Book 1 is 99c / 99p.

The Contingency War Series (4-book series)

A space-fleet, military sci-fi adventure with a unique twist that you won't see coming...

The Planetsider Trilogy (3-book series)

An edge-of-your-seat blend of military sci-fi action & classic apocalyptic fiction. Perfect for fans of Maze Runner and I am Legend.

Audiobook Series

Star Scavenger Series (29-hrs)

The Contingency War Series (24-hrs)

The Planetsider Trilogy (32-hrs)

Made in the USA
Monee, IL
21 March 2022